# THE
# NICOTINE
# CHRONICLES

### EDITED BY **LEE CHILD**

AKASHIC
BOOKS

BROOKLYN, NEW YORK

Published by Akashic Books
©2020 Akashic Books

Hardcover ISBN: 978-1-61775-858-4
Paperback ISBN: 978-1-61775-859-1
Library of Congress Control Number: 2020935754

The story "Smoking Jesus" by Eric Bogosian first appeared in the show *This Is Now!* (with Elliott Sharp) and was published in an earlier form as "Smoking" in *100 (monologues)* (Theatre Communications Group, New York, 2014).

Akashic Books
Brooklyn, New York
Ballydehob, Co. Cork, Ireland
Twitter: @AkashicBooks
Facebook: AkashicBooks
E-mail: info@akashicbooks.com
Website: www.akashicbooks.com

# TABLE OF CONTENTS

## PART III: HUNGRY FOR FLAVOR?

## PART IV: INHALE TO YOUR HEART'S CONTENT

# INTRODUCTION
## A FAULTY DELIVERY SYSTEM

F ood scientists have discovered a complex compound naturally present in, among other things, potatoes, tomatoes,
peppers, and eggplants. The compound offers us a number
of benefits: it improves our fine motor skills; it increases our attention spans; it improves our cognitive abilities; it improves our
long- and short-term memories; it lessens depression; it delays
and possibly even prevents Alzheimer's; and it decreases the risk
of Parkinson's. In and of itself, it has no real downside. It's called
nicotine. We should all get some.

The problem is the delivery system. To get a detectable benefit, you would have to eat enormous quantities of vegetables—
and who wants to do that? The most efficient way is to burn dried
tobacco leaves and inhale the smoke. Ten seconds later, the compound is in your brain, doing good in all its various ways. Un-
fortunately, the rest of the smoke doesn't do good. And therein
lies a great mystery of human behavior. To get the good, we risk
the bad. Or we prohibit ourselves the good, for fear of the bad.
Which approach makes more sense?

The stories in this book explore the issues around that di-
lemma. They come at it from every angle, and illuminate it in
every way. I'm deeply grateful to all of the contributors, and I'll
be deeply grateful to every reader. And to Akashic Books, our
publisher. I have contributed to several of Akashic's anthologies
(although never before as editor), including *The Cocaine Chronicles* and *The Marijuana Chronicles*. For those, I expected and re-

ceived no negative reaction at all. I suspect *The Nicotine Chronicles* might be different. Another mystery of human behavior.

*Lee Child*
*New York City*

# PART I

## THANK YOU FOR NOT SMOKING

HANNAH TINTI is the author of *The Good Thief, Animal Crackers,* and *The Twelve Lives of Samuel Hawley.* She teaches creative writing at New York University's MFA program and cofounded the Sirenland Writers Conference. Tinti is also the cofounder and executive editor of *One Story.* You can find her @hannahtinti.

# PARK & PLAY
BY **HANNAH TINTI**

Т he rooms at the Park & Play Motel are labeled nonsmoking but the guests smoke in them anyway. My boss Shirley fought this for a while but eventually gave up and put an old cigarette machine outside the office. The customer puts in the money, yanks a glass knob below the brand they want, and a cellophane-wrapped box drops down into the collection tray, along with a tiny book of matches. I bought a pack once but it wasn't for me. There's enough smoke in my life already. Sometimes people use the ashtrays we put in the rooms and sometimes they use the plastic cups from the bathroom or crush the ends of their filters into the side tables or flick their embers onto the carpet. It's my job to patch the holes.

Knock, knock, open the door, wipe the sink, scrub the tub, replace the linens, spray some air freshener, run the vacuum, lock the door, move on to the next. When I find burns in the sheets or towels I cut them into rags; burns in the wall-to-wall carpet I fix with glue and some fibers snipped from the corners; furniture burns I paint over with a nail polish color called Espresso that I keep in the pocket of my apron.

The woman in room 207 has a black eye and bruises on her neck and checks out of the motel early. She says she is an airline stewardess and that she's driving to Phoenix to see her sister, but she doesn't have any luggage in her trunk. Later, when I clean her room, I find where she's pressed her menthol cigarette into the wood over and over, until the burns become an etching of the

Leaning Tower of Pisa, a series of connected circles angling up the side of the window frame. There are eight floors, including the bell chamber. I recognize the image from my father's postcard collection. I wonder if she's seen the building in person or just in pictures like me. Most people don't tip at the Park & Play but the woman in 207 leaves five dollars on the windowsill beneath the drawing, as if she is apologizing for the mess.

After the nail polish dries I can still feel the bumps of the Tower of Pisa with my fingers. It makes me think of something my father said once, about how we leave a bit of ourselves every place we go. Skin cells. Traces. Human dust. That's why famous buildings are famous, he said. So many people pass through over the years, shedding parts of themselves, that the buildings start to breathe on their own. It makes the memories there more powerful. Because the buildings are remembering too.

The Park & Play Motel is two miles from the Chickasaw Indian reservation and three miles from their casino. There are twenty-eight rooms. Shirley is half-Chickasaw and has owned the Park & Play for ten years, supporting her husband, who lost both of his legs in Iraq. I started cleaning on the weekends during high school and then went full-time after my father got sick. The motel is nearly always full of gamblers looking for a cheaper place to stay than the casino, which is a high-end establishment with a theater and a hotel. My high school had their senior prom in the hotel ballroom. I didn't go because my father was in the hospital by then and we couldn't afford the tickets. Pastor Billy offered to pay but my father wouldn't let him. Pastor Billy brought me a corsage anyway, white roses in a clear plastic box, and I wore it on my wrist as I held my father's hand and all of the machines stopped blinking.

In the mornings I make coffee and put out the Park & Play continental breakfast, which is a bowl of apples and a box of blueberry muffins. Then I get my rolling cart and start pushing. I fill up on sheets and towels and follow the concrete path from room to room. I knock on doors. *Housekeeping.* I knock again. *Housekeeping.* Always twice before I put the key in the lock. You never know what you might walk in on.

I see sleepers sleeping in all kinds of ways. I see families sharing fast-food dinners. I see sex workers entertaining customers. I see kids left alone all night. I see mattresses overturned. I see old men weeping. I see bathtubs full of clothes. I see strangers hiding things under covers. I see tinfoil and pipes and spoons and bags of powder. I see people lying in pools of their own making. I see folks so sick they should go to the hospital. I see carpets turned into dark, fetid, squishy lakes. I see every kind of naked person doing every kind of naked thing. I see truckers burned red down one whole side of their arms and face from driving with the window open across the country and I want to ask them, *Where are you going?* And sometimes I do. Sometimes, when I'm tired, I lean back on the pillows of someone else's bed and close my eyes and think of Pastor Billy's hand on my forehead, the sweat of his palm making its way into my hair. His skin smells like Marlboro Lights, the same brand my father smoked. Pastor Billy is busy trying to expand his church but he stays after service on Sundays to talk. I tell him I feel empty inside and he tells me, *The Lord will send you comfort.*

I am still waiting for it to come.

When I talk about Pastor Billy my boss Shirley rolls her eyes. She doesn't go to church anymore. She says she doesn't trust white men. I tell her that I pray for her and she tells me that's my choice and like her I'll regret many of them in this life. After my father died she let me move into one of the rooms at the motel. She says it's temporary and she'll take the rent out of my salary but I've been here for a year and my paycheck hasn't changed.

Before he got cancer my father was a janitor at a strip mall. I'd go with him after hours and sit at one of the tables by the Chinese food place and eat scallion pancakes and do my homework while he worked. The owners of the Golden Dragon had a little shrine just inside the entryway, where they'd burn incense and put out oranges. It was the closest thing our town had to something foreign. But next door was a travel agency and when my father took out their trash he'd comb through for maps and pictures of faraway places. Then he'd bring the outdated brochures and travel guides home and cut them out and paste them into a scrapbook and together we'd make up stories of our vacations there. *Remember when we went to Rome?* he'd say. *All that pasta we ate? And how hot it was at the Colosseum?* He tracked down menus of restaurants by the Spanish Steps. He chose hotels. He even went down to the bank one day and got some Italian currency. Five dollars was the same as fifteen thousand lire. It made us feel rich, the colorful paper like magic in our hands. When he was in the hospital my father gave me the lire folded up in a handkerchief. He said, *See if you can exchange that for some ghost money.*

So far I haven't made it out of Oklahoma. The closest is my birthday when Shirley takes me to the casino to see a Russian circus act. There are trapeze artists and dancing bears and jugglers that stand on each other's shoulders, performing in front of a giant image of Red Square, the brightly painted domes of St. Basil's Cathedral rising to points like soft-serve ice cream. As I watch the silver rings being tossed in the air, I remember my father saying that Ivan the Terrible blinded St. Basil's architects when the cathedral was completed, so they wouldn't be able to make anything more beautiful. And it is beautiful. My eyes keep drifting from the performers to the backdrop, imagining that cluster of domes burned into the walls of the Park & Play. Shirley laughs at the Russian clowns and hugs me when the show is over. Then we have a steak dinner and drink virgin margaritas.

*I needed that,* she says as we drive off the reservation. *You did too, Rita.* She pinches my cheek. *Happy birthday.*

I tell her it was a real treat and try to keep my voice bright so she won't know that I'm lying. I watch the lights of the Park & Play in the distance getting closer and think about the human dust inside of St. Basil's. Over 450 years' worth of people on their knees praying. Good people and bad people and everyone in between. I bet some bits of Ivan the Terrible too.

The people in room 103 are having an affair. I know this because the woman is a blackjack dealer at the casino, and the man is Shirley's husband. The blackjack dealer rents the room on Saturday mornings, when Shirley has her AA meeting. She pulls her yellow Camaro into the parking lot after her all-night shift. She's one of the only folks left on the rez who speaks Chickasaw and she's always trying to get Shirley to speak it too. She says *Chokma?* and Shirley says *Chin-Chokma?* and then they both say *Sho-taha* and laugh. Shirley hands her a key and the dealer goes to her room and Shirley gets in her car and drives to the community center. Then Shirley's husband rolls out of the manager's office in his wheelchair and slips me fifty dollars to turn a blind eye. It's nearly as much as I make in a day, so I keep my mouth shut. I take the money. And afterward, I clean the room.

Shirley's husband smokes Camel Wides. He always carries a pack folded in the sleeve of his T-shirt, as if he's still in the army. Wides are nearly twice as thick as a normal cigarette. They are supposed to deliver more flavor and they are supposed to burn more efficiently too, especially when they are crushed into the wood of a headboard, leaving a deep white curve in the varnish. I try to fix the first mark with my Espresso nail polish, but the following week it's burned through again, along with two more arches, and when the third appears I recognize the outline of the Sydney Opera House. My father kept a promotional brochure of those white arches taped to the wall above our kitchen table. He said it took thirteen years for the opera house to be built and that it cost $102 million. He said the first person to perform there was Paul Robeson, who climbed the scaffolding when it was under construction and sang to the workers. My father got a record of Robeson from the library and we played it on the stereo. The deep, vibrating tones of his voice rolled over us like thunder. There are five different performance spaces at the Sydney Opera House. I count the cigarette burns on the headboard to make sure they got it right, the arches lifting like sails in different directions. I strip the soiled sheets and make the bed and imagine my father inside one of those white shells, surrounded by water.

I leave the nail polish in my apron.

The bills from Shirley's husband go into my travel fund, which I keep in an old peanut butter jar. When new bills go in I spread the money across the mattress and kneel down next to the bed for a fresh count. When I was a little girl my father and I would kneel like this and make a list of things to be thankful for—ice cream and waterslides and coloring books. Bedtime prayers that filled my mind with sparks before I fell asleep. After he was diagnosed I tried praying in a new way—asking for things and making promises. Then he died and the prayers stopped working. So now I look for the buildings. I check each room as I clean, touching the wood for cigarette burns, thinking, *This is a sign, and this and this*, and slip another dollar into the travel fund.

The more I put inside the jar the closer I feel to my father. But when I start to imagine getting on a bus or a train without him my mind freezes and I screw the lid shut tight.

An hour after the dealer leaves, I hear the tires of Shirley's car pulling into her parking spot. I watch her step into the sun, flushed and tender from AA. She puts her keys into her purse and walks over to her husband, who is outside the office in his wheelchair, reading the paper. As I lock the door to room 103 Shirley waves. The sheets from the bed are in my cleaning cart as I roll over and ask how her meeting went. She tells me it's the closest thing she's found to being all right. And then she bends down and kisses her husband on the cheek.

Pastor Billy has a wife. Her name is Constance. Before she was married she worked as a call girl and smoked Virginia Slims. She's one of the first naked people I walked in on when I started working at the motel and she's the only one who didn't cover up. Her breasts are smaller than mine and the back of her spine is twisted. She saw me staring and took a drag from her cigarette and said, *Scoliosis*. She said her customers didn't mind. She pressed ten dollars into my hand and told me to come back in an hour. When I checked the room later she was gone and an outline of the Eiffel Tower was burned into the lampshade. Turns out Virginia Slims are perfect for latticework, from the wide parabola at the tower base to the observation deck on top. I switched the burned lampshade with the one from my own room and before I went to sleep I would look at the Eiffel Tower and think about Constance's naked back, and the way her shoulder blade presses sideways beneath the skin, like half an angel's wing folded over. She wears a body brace now and long-sleeved dresses that button up past her neck. She still smokes, though. I've seen her in the parking lot at church, lighting up. She stands between the cars and stares at her reflection in the windows. She's not going anywhere now.

It was cheaper to burn the body. That's what Pastor Billy said and so I agreed. My father got delivered in a cardboard box. The cremains weren't like the stale ashes left behind at the Park & Play; they were gritty like sand, with small pieces of bone mixed in. The smell was different too. It reminded me of the incense from the Golden Dragon, the sticks burning ribbons of smoke in front of the shrine, the heavy scent like eucalyptus on a campfire. I can smell it even when the box of my father's ashes is closed. It sits on a shelf in my closet, waiting. Just like the jarful of money.

The blackjack dealer is sitting up in bed with a sheet wrapped around her, leaning against the headboard and smoking. She says, *Chokkowa*, so I come in. She is smoking a pink cigarette. I've never seen one before so I ask the brand and she holds out a box of Nat Sherman Fantasias, multicolored like a box of crayons. They aren't sold in our vending machine. She offers me one and I choose blue but I don't light it. Instead I point to the Sydney Opera House burned into the wood beside her. I say, *Did you draw that building?* She turns and stares at the mark like she's noticing it for the first time and shakes her head, and when I ask her if it was Shirley's husband she shakes her head again. Then she leans forward, takes a closer look, and says, *It looks more like a flower than a building.*

Right away I can see the petals, and the opera house transforms like a cloud changing shape. The floor starts sliding away beneath my feet. I crush the blue cigarette in my hand and lean against my rolling cart as I head toward the door. She says I'm a good girl, *Chipotatiik chokma chiya.* And I tell her I don't think either one of us is good.

Back in my room I turn on the lamp and the Eiffel Tower isn't the Eiffel Tower anymore either. The letter A flickers at me through the lampshade, a monogram made of Virginia Slim–sized holes. I saw what I wanted to see and now I can't see what I want. My father isn't sending me messages or telling me to travel the world. He's dead. And I'm at the Park & Play.

I open the peanut butter jar and pour the money I've collected onto the blanket. I do the math and realize that over the past six months I've lied to Shirley nineteen times. In my pocket is payment for the twentieth. I jam the new bills into the jar with all the others. I hear the office door slam. From the window I watch her husband roll down the cement walkway toward the blackjack dealer's room. Then I pick up the phone and call Shirley. I tell her the toilet in 103 just exploded, and she needs to get back to the motel as fast as she can.

After church on Sunday, I tell Pastor Billy about the money. How I earned it and how I was supposed to use it and how it doesn't feel right anymore. He listens and then he suggests that we pray. I close my eyes. I lean toward him and smell tobacco. I imagine tiny bits of leaf under his nails, grains of scent embedded in the whorls of his fingerprints. His own human dust. My throat goes so tight I can barely swallow.

He calls on the spirit of my father to listen. He asks him to guide me toward the right path. He squeezes my fingers and I feel the spirit lift me up and carry me out of Oklahoma, past the border of America, and across the sea. And all the buildings I've conjured from cigarette burns aren't made of smoke and ash anymore but iron and steel and stone. They are as real as the Park & Play Motel. As real as Pastor Billy's hands as he touches my head for a blessing.

And then his fingertips slide onto my back, to the place

where his wife's twisted wing folds into her spine. And he says that I should give the money to the church. He says this act will wash it clean. *It will wash you clean too*, he says, and something shifts inside of me, and I begin to feel dirty, even though I spent the whole morning scrubbing bathroom tiles with bleach.

I find Shirley outside the office, refilling the cigarette machine. The front door of the case swings open like a refrigerator, and she is stacking different-colored brands on top of each other. There are Lucky Strikes and Virginia Slims. Marlboros mixed with Camels. She doesn't say anything as I roll up with my cart, but there is a cloud of smoke around her head. I watch her lips suck and pull. The tip of the paper glows.

*I've never seen you smoke before*, I say.

*It only happens when I've been drinking*, she says.

I can smell it now. The air is stale and sweet and sticky around her, like she's been rolling through old cotton candy.

*I have something for you*, I say.

*I don't want anything from you*, she says.

And there it is again, the dirty feeling.

I stayed in my room after calling Shirley about room 103. Watched her turn into the driveway, then cross the parking lot with a plunger in her hand. A few minutes later Shirley came out of 103 pushing her husband's wheelchair, but her husband wasn't in it. She rolled the empty chair all the way to the street and then sent it barreling down the hill.

Now she jams all the wrong cigarette boxes into the wrong slots. She won't look at me. The cellophane is crinkling in her palms.

I reach inside my cleaning cart and take out the travel jar. I hand it over to her. She has to put down a carton of Merits so she can unscrew the top.

*How much is in here?*

*Enough for a vacation,* I say. *A long one.*

Shirley puts the lid back on. *He told me that he paid you off.* She sets the jar on the ground. She says, *How many times?*

The truth is too high so I say, *Nine.*

She bends in half like the number has kicked her in the stomach. She breathes out hard. She says she'll never forgive him and I'm not sure if she'll forgive me either.

The Italian lire are in my pocket, still folded in my father's handkerchief. I slide the cloth out and open the corners and the colors are bright. The bills so small they feel like play money in my hands. *Monopoly* or *Life.* I try to hand them to Shirley but she won't touch them.

I say, *These came from my father.*

She looks closer. *Italians haven't used lire for over a decade,* she says. *I don't think you can even exchange them anymore.*

There are faces on each of the notes. I read the names underneath: Guglielmo Marconi, Vincenzo Bellini, and Maria Montessori. I need this money to matter, so I tell Shirley the different ways my father and I used the lire on our make-believe trip. How we threw coins into the Trevi Fountain, how we bought blue gelato outside the Vatican that melted down our fingers, and how we tipped a gondolier in Venice so he'd stop singing because he had a voice that cracked so badly it hurt our ears.

Shirley takes a drag from her cigarette and leans against the machine. *I'm still not taking it,* she says.

The neon sign for the Park & Play flickers over our heads. We stand there until the tip of her cigarette turns gray and white and dangles loose, the shape just holding. With a flick of her wrist, the ash will fall. But she lets it grow and grow until it's nearly at the filter.

*Pretend money isn't always worthless,* Shirley says. *In China*

*they burn it after someone dies. So their spirit can travel to wher-
ever it is they're going, and buy anything they might need.*

I think about the shrine at the Golden Dragon. I rub the bills
between my fingers.

*Ghost money,* I say.

*That's right,* says Shirley.

I reach for her cigarette and take it into my fingers. The
shape of the ash breaks and it drops to the concrete between us.
I put the filter in my own mouth. It tastes like Shirley's lipstick.
I inhale and cough and inhale again until the tip is a burning red
ember. Then I press it into the face of Maria Montessori. The paper catches quickly. I suck on the cigarette again and then press
the tip into the next lira and the next, until they are all in flames.
Then I drop the money to the ground and watch the colored paper bend and curl.

Shirley picks up the travel jar and opens it. She takes out one
of the fifties that her husband gave me and adds it to the pile of
burning money. It takes longer to catch, but when it does it glows
around the edges. She sighs. She says, *That feels all right.*

I pull a twenty from the jar. I light it from the rest of the bills
and it ignites with a burst, as if it has been soaked in lighter fluid.
It doesn't feel all right but it feels like something. Something I
can't name yet. So I keep burning, we both do, until the travel
fund is nothing but layers upon layers of white dust, like flower
petals that have been peeled apart and cast into the wind. And
when it's done the jar is empty but I'm not anymore. I'm filled up
inside with sparks.

*Your dad can go anywhere he wants to now,* Shirley says.

And I say, *So can we.*

Our faces shine in the glass of the cigarette machine. Shirley
closes the door and latches it shut. I put out the last ember of our
bonfire with my sneaker, smearing the ashes into the hard con-

crete. And that's when the ashes blow back at me, as if the Park & Play has taken its first breath. Gray specks spatter my ankles. I can smell eucalyptus in the air. I think of where else I might want to leave traces. And behind me Shirley strikes a match.

**ARIEL GORE** is the award-winning author of a dozen books of fiction and nonfiction, including *We Were Witches*, *Hexing the Patriarchy*, and *F\*ck Happiness*. Her short stories have been included in *Portland Noir*, *Santa Cruz Noir*, and *Santa Fe Noir*, which she also edited.

# MY SIMPLE PLAN
## BY ARIEL GORE

This was during the strike of '92.

The tobacconist had run out of the real thing on day one.

The pharmacy sold out of patches and gum on day two.

The town filled Marco's café, trying to mask their true desires with caffeine and Campari. They ran their fingers through their hair. Their hands trembled like hummingbirds. They were quick to anger.

It's incredible, when you think about it, how fast an entire people can be brought to their knees. I mean, I got nothing against Italians, but these particular Italians had gotten on my last gay nerve since I'd washed up in their very picturesque hill town a few months earlier. So, yeah, maybe I *liked* imagining their torment now.

None of them knew about my stockpile.

*Non ancora.*

I intended to make my capitalist debut on the fourth day of the strike. I figured they'd be desperate by then, but still trying to wait it out without making drastic trips to Switzerland or Greece. My plan: I'd offer single cigarettes for two thousand Italian lire apiece. I'd sell them all fast—make enough to get out of this godforsaken town, catch a bus and then the train all the way up to Berlin, find the squat I'd heard about with central heating. I'd hunker down for the winter.

I wouldn't even have to sell to everyone who asked. I could make those provincial gossips *beg* me for their relief.

But my capitalist revenge dreams turned to shit on the cold morning of that fourth day.

The shot rang out before dawn.

The sound jolted me out of bed. I sat straight up, and for a split second I thought I was back home in America. *It was a gunshot, not a Fiat backfiring.*

From my mattress on the stone floor, I couldn't make sense of it. I took in the dirty white walls of the wine cellar I'd half disguised as an apartment. In my precoffee haze, I tried to reconcile the impossible: A gunshot. In Middle-of-Nowhere, Tuscany.

*What in the actual fuck?*

I stood up to look out the basement window, but darkness still pressed down on the stone street. I could hear faraway shouting, then the sirens.

I craved a cigarette right then like I was missing not some foreign chemical but a part of my own soul, and from each cell of my throat and my lungs, I thanked the universe that I had one. Yes, I had a cigarette. *Who's the homosexual slut now?* I snapped at no one.

The buy had seemed extravagant but oddly rational at the tail end of summer—spent my last two hundred US on two backpacks crammed full of stolen cartons of Nazionales and MS cigarettes from a desperate punk in Rome. I already had a ride to this town I'd seen in watercolors, and I had no reason to foresee that I wouldn't find work here or that I'd get caught up right away with the winemaker's daughter. I figured I'd just be traveling broke to a pretty town—no big deal, right? You can always make a few bucks doing this or that wherever you end up, right? *Well, not so in the watercolor town.*

You ever live in a world of crumbling castles where no more than three people will even say hello to you? And I spoke decent Italian then. Not even hello. They called me *l'Americano* when they talked about me; they rarely addressed me directly. And you can forget about hitchhiking out of here if you don't expect to get raped.

It puts you in a spot.

The only reason I survived at all was that Antonia, that shrill gossip with bright-yellow hair, let me stay in her wine cellar—I later realized it's so she can talk shit about me with more authority, but what was I gonna do? A wine cellar is practically an apartment. That and Marco, the old man who owned the café and let me clean it after hours in exchange for coffee and caprese sandwiches.

Well, survive I did.

No thanks to most of the locals.

So when news of the strike trickled in, I couldn't help the smile that crept across my face. I couldn't wait to start hissing, *Where were you in my hour of need?*

I stripped off the sweats and T-shirt I'd slept in and pushed open the arched wooden door that led deeper into the wine cellar. I grabbed one of my designated smoking blankets from the top of a small barrel and wrapped it around my body. The cold flagstones felt like ice on the soles of my bare feet.

I'd rigged a fan in the depths of that place, and the fan blew the smoke out a small window that opened only onto a deep ravine at the edge of town. I'd set up a bucket of water next to that window too, and after every smoke I brushed my teeth hard enough to make my gums bleed.

In the first days I hadn't wanted anyone to know I had the cigarettes for strategic business reasons, and even now, as I sucked hard on an MS filter, the hot smoke radiating like relief across my chest, I had only begun to understand all the ways the stakes had just changed.

I crushed the cigarette into the stone wall, flicked the butt out into the ravine below, and lit a stick of Nag Champa incense.

As the church bells clanged, I crept back into my living space, pulled on my army-surplus pants and black sweatshirt, and laced up my Dr. Martens.

The café would just be opening. Someone would know what had happened.

I took a deep breath, and didn't smell smoke. I climbed the steps from my place to the street level, sidled into the already-full café to listen.

Marco's café was that watercolor town's local news channel: street journalism with espresso. The sense they would try to make of it.

It seemed the victim had been old man Martelli, gunned down in the dark of dawn just a few steps from his car at the edge of the piazza. It was the first murder anyone could remember in that town since 1974. The first gun murder maybe ever.

"I heard he'd just come back from Napoli!" Antonia called out, hands on her hips and eyebrows raised.

Even I knew what that meant.

In those days, in that place, *Napoli* meant one thing: the black market. And since the state workers from the Italian tobacco monopoly had decided to strike, black market meant cigarettes.

Obviously Martelli had gone down to Napoli to buy a few cartons—at the very least.

Antonia raised both hands dramatically. "I looked in his car," she said. "No cigarettes."

Everybody nodded, like it made perfect sense.

Martelli had brought cigarettes to town, and somebody had killed him for them. Who would kill a man over cigs? Everyone moaned, because right then, on day four of the strike, probably most of them would have done it in a heartbeat.

I slunk back into my wine cellar, bolted the door shut behind me, and took off my clothes to go smoke.

I watched from my basement window as the woman known as Giovanna paced up and down the cobblestone street in her black stilettos, a familiar sight for my sore eyes. I marveled at the way the tips of the heels never got stuck in the cracks between the stones. I'd been holed up all morning and into the afternoon.

Lying on my bed, looking up, all I could see were those shoes, her thin ankles draped in sheer nylons, the hem of a black skirt. I always knew who that was. She kept pacing, like she needed a smoke badly. The rhythm of her tapping steps lulled me into a relaxed state. If anyone in this fucking town could help me, maybe it was Giovanna.

Now, Giovanna—like all the rest of the locals—had never given me the time of day, but I knew they hardly talked to her either. Town slut, she was the subject of at least half the gossip that poured through the café in any given week. I figured there was at least half a chance that her arrogance toward me was just the old pariah-saved-by-a-bigger-pariah kind of a thing.

Either way, *click click*.

I stood up fast and rushed to the widow. "Giovanna!"

She looked down at me. "*Pervertita*," she spat toward the cobblestones. "Pervert" tumbled and landed on my windowsill.

*Like, did she think I was trying to look up her skirt from here? How embarrassing.* "No," I hissed. "I—" I hesitated. "I have something."

Giovanna shook her head and clucked her tongue, but she click-clicked around the edge of the building anyway and next thing I knew I was scrambling up the steps and next thing I knew I was opening the door and next thing I knew Giovanna stood in front of me and next thing I knew I swallowed awkwardly.

*She was beautiful.*

"Come inside." I gestured fast and Giovanna walked into my actual apartment and I shut the door behind her.

"What do you want?" Her English was just fine.

I felt like such a tongue-tied loser. I touched my fingers to my forehead. "Giovanna, I have cigarettes."

Her eyes sparkled wild and I saw rainbow crystals. She took my arm like we were friends. The streaming energy of her sudden love for me burst into butterflies. "You have cigarettes?" She winked at me. *Did Giovanna wink at me?* "You bad girl," she growled, but then she froze suddenly, and she leaned away from me. "Did you kill Martelli?"

I stared at her. She had faint acne scars on her face, like a lacy white tattoo.

She lowered her voice. "A couple people have already mentioned you, actually. You know, Italians don't do guns."

"I'm from the West Coast. We don't do guns either." And I met her gaze and I wanted very badly for her to believe me as I pulled her deeper into the wine cellar.

When we rounded the corner to my stash, illuminated like a golden pyramid in the thin stream of afternoon light, Giovanna grabbed my shoulders and kissed me hard. I felt surprised and electric with painted heart confetti bursting from the stone walls and I said, "Wait! We have to take off our clothes."

Giovanna shook her head.

"Oh, no. I meant, you know. To smoke. We can't. We don't want our clothes smelling of smoke." I thought I might die of embarrassment. Like my beating heart might stop.

"Aha," she said. I could tell she still thought I was trying to get in her nylons.

"I mean, you don't have to," I said. "It's just what I've been doing. So people won't be able to smell it on my clothes."

Giovanna smiled, and took off her sweater slowly, like a stripper, and then pulled her dress over her head and grinned at me. Her breasts swelled, and I imagined Botticelli himself had never beheld skin so delicate.

"Holy shit." I stared down.

Her belly arched toward me.

I whispered-stuttered, "I had not heard that you were expecting," and I held a blanket out to her.

Giovanna winked at me as she took my blanket, letting the edge of her hand touch mine. "No one knows," she said. "Or even *you* would know. Now, can I have a cigarette?"

What did she mean, *even I would know*?

I handed her a pink lighter. "Help yourself." And I carried her clothes farther away from the smoking spot under the window and I took off my own clothes too. My skin was pale and red where my army pants rubbed my waist the wrong way. By the time I sat down next to Giovanna, and lit my own cigarette, the revelation had started taking over my brain: I mean, maybe this was the reason I'd ended up in this backward watercolor wash-out town to begin with. To meet Giovanna. To help her get out. I said, "It doesn't seem like single motherhood is really a thing here. I mean, what are you gonna do?" They already called her a whore, and worse.

Giovanna just smiled wide. Her teeth were stunningly crooked. She rested her head on my shoulder. "I know," she whispered. "The only kind of single motherhood allowed here is widowhood." She took my hand in hers, and brought it to her tight belly.

I felt turned on with a savior fantasy like in a fairy tale; my whole chest went warm even though I wondered if it wasn't kind of creepy on my part.

But then Giovanna took my face in her hands and leaned

in to kiss me again. When she pressed her lips into mine I tasted tobacco and vanilla and she dug her fingernails into my back and scratched me hard and our sparkling nakedness and all these sought-after and dangerous cigarettes made me feel powerful and vulnerable, like a giant mango about to explode, but I didn't tell Giovanna that because I didn't want her to think I was so weird that I compared myself to fruits we couldn't even get in this town. The soft of her breast against my palm made me shiver.

I said, "Giovanna, I know a squat in Berlin. With central heating. All we have to do is sell these cigarettes, then buy our tickets. There's work in Berlin, I'm sure of it. And all kinds of families without men. I've made money painting in the streets. Tourists—they all want their picture. I can show you how to do murals!"

Giovanna nodded slowly. I could tell she was mulling the idea, warming up to it even. "Street muralists," she hummed, and she rubbed her sweet belly. She was fixed on the cracks in the stone floor, and bit her lip.

Yes, I would take Giovanna away from all this.

She looked back up. Just the slightest hint of lipstick clung to the edges of her lips. "We can't sell the cigarettes here. They find out we have the cigarettes and they're going to think we killed Martelli. But . . . I might have a way." She took another cigarette from the pack and lit it. And in that golden, dusky light through that tiny little window, Giovanna, naked and pregnant, blowing smoke rings toward the fan, was a picture I wanted to paint.

In the dark of morning, I stood in the archway of a ruined castle at the edge of the piazza, my two backpacks still quite full of cigarettes. I'd shoved a single change of clothes into a side pouch. I fingered the wad of lire in the pocket of my army-surplus pants. Marco, from the café, would hardly notice the missing money.

Giovanna had wanted me to take all of it—she said if he left his cash register full of money every night he deserved to learn a lesson—but I still had some morals then.

"Good morning, *bella*," Giovanna whispered from behind. *Bella*. I could get used to that. I could imagine it all: we'd paint the walls of our squat blue, make a cradle for the baby from a milk crate.

She wore black gloves, and dangled a key in front of me, bringing one finger to her lips. "*Shhhh*. No one can see us leave town together." She glanced over her shoulder. "You take the car. I've got a ticket for the first bus. I'll meet you at the railway station in Grosseto in time for the 6:15 train."

I nodded.

But when Giovanna pointed to the car she had in mind, my skull felt heavy. I wanted a cigarette. "How do you have a key to Martelli's car?"

She pouted, just a little. "We were engaged." She smiled and winked at me. He must have loved that wink.

*What was it about Giovanna that made me see everything in flush pinks and reds?* I closed my eyes against all those colors and frowned. Sternly I said, "We can't take Martelli's car."

But Giovanna laughed her easy laugh and replied, "Don't worry, *bella*, we'll have it abandoned at the station by dawn." She pulled me in, and when she pressed her full breasts against mine I knew all things were possible.

Yes, in Berlin we would have central heating. We would march through the streets holding hands and that song about the ninety-nine red balloons would play from a boom box somewhere out of sight. We would be artists, and have the baby in summertime. I wondered if Giovanna wanted a boy or a girl or a herm—if she'd want another child after this one. Yes, in Berlin we would get femi-fists tattooed on our biceps and we would probably meet Nina Hagen.

"Let me take one carton," Giovanna said, and she reached over my shoulder and unzipped my backpack and slid out a carton of MS. A light, cold rain started to fall and the dark sky began to blue and Giovanna kissed me once more and let her tongue graze my teeth. "Drive safely, *bella*." I felt the imperative of my mission: yes, I would be the one to get Giovanna out of this place. She didn't need this parched Catholic morality any more than I did.

She said, "Oh!" like it was an afterthought, almost forgotten, and pushed a brown paper bag toward me. "I packed a surprise for you—for later." It smelled like cloves and old libraries. Everything she touched smelled good.

I liked the way she said *for later*. I imagined something soft and heavy, a sensual token of her gratitude—something worth waiting for. Just then the church bells started to clang the early-morning hour and I rushed to Martelli's car. I threw my things onto the passenger's seat and I shifted that car into neutral and eased out of the piazza, then started the engine, and took a sharp right over the bridge that crossed the ravine and led out of town. At the bottom of the hill, I followed the arrow that pointed toward Grosseto. The sunlit freedom of it all. I shifted into high gear, reached into the brown paper bag without looking. The hard thing inside felt like a dildo and a shiver of excitement ran from my fingers and down my arm. As I began to caress it, the thing seemed a little cold. I peered inside the bag.

*What in the motherfuck?*

And right then is when I heard the sirens. My heart contracted as everything came into focus: I was driving a murdered man's car, the passenger seat piled with cigarettes that might as well have been his haul from Napoli, my fingerprints on the gun. I fumbled for a pack and opened it. My hand shook as I held the Nazionale between my fingers, but I managed to light the thing. I looked up into the orange of the sunrise and felt a tightening and a fluttering at the same time, like a bird was trapped in my chest. I inhaled, knowing this would probably be my last cigarette for a long time, but just then, as the nicotine flooded my veins, the trapped bird opened her wings with something like grace.

I rolled down the driver's-side window and blew the smoke into the air, took another hard drag. I reached over and grabbed a half-empty pack and threw it out onto the street, watched it tumble and bounce behind me. I grabbed a whole carton then and opened it. The sound of the cop's brakes screeching behind me was the sound of my opportunity. I pushed all my weight onto the gas pedal, and glanced into the rearview mirror as that watercolor town melted into a blur, and there in the chipped corner of my mirror that constable scrambled to pick up all the packs. Yes, I would abandon Martelli's car at the Grosseto station, jump on the train and change my clothes in the tiny bathroom, pay for my ticket once we were already speeding north and away from that crumbling hill town where no one had so much as asked my name.

I lit another cigarette off my last, and tossed the butt out the window. I thought of beautiful Giovanna, all rainbow crystals and black stockings, her little wink. And I couldn't help but smile again: *I was your one chance out, Giovanna. And now you can really go fuck yourself.*

Minna Proctor

**CHRISTOPHER SORRENTINO** is the author of five books including, most recently, *The Fugitives*.

# THE RENOVATION OF THE JUST
## BY CHRISTOPHER SORRENTINO

They were smoking when Dormer opened the door, two unexpected strangers standing expectantly on the step where
they'd just rung the bell, both with cigarettes fuming in their
hands. It was odd. It was, in fact, rude. The first words out of
Dormer's mouth addressed that rudeness—politely but deci-
sively, he thought.

"I'm sorry," he said, "but this is a smoke-free home."

"Well," said the man standing on the right, "we're not in your
home yet."

Both men wore suits that fitted them poorly. The one who had
spoken wore one that was too small. The one who had remained
silent wore one that was too large. They were about the same
height and easily could have switched suits. For a moment Dormer
thought about how they might effect that, and whether it would
make a difference. Perhaps they lived together. He spoke again.

"I'll have to ask you to put those out."

Too Large glanced at Too Small and backed up a step, raising the cigarette to his lips for one last drag. Then he threw it on
the broad, well-tended lawn. Too Small snapped his away from
between his thumb and forefinger, following the arc of its flight
with visible satisfaction. It had traveled farther than Too Large's.

"There," he said. "Now can we come in and speak to you?"

"I don't know you."

"Okay, Mr. Dormer," said Too Large, speaking for the first
time. "We can stand out here and talk if you like."

"How do you know my name?"

"All the mail in the box is addressed to you."

"He's kidding," said Too Small. "Don't kid him. Mr. Dormer is a serious man."

"Well," said Too Large, "it is."

"You just moved in here, what, about two months ago?" said Too Small.

"Closed on the place on the twelfth of February," said Too Large.

"How would you know that?" said Dormer.

"A matter of public record," said Too Large.

"I'm afraid we haven't explained ourselves very well," said Too Small. He reached into his jacket and produced a card. Dormer looked at it.

"They didn't mention anything about the place before you offered on it, did they?"

"They never do," said Too Large.

"It's a shame. Personally, I don't think it would make a difference to an educated buyer." Too Small took an appreciative look at the house's tidy exterior.

"But not to say anything just kind of leaves a bad taste in your mouth. Totally unnecessary," said Too Large. "But, then again, why take the chance?"

"You know what you are? You're a cynic. You're at work all day, aren't you, Mr. Dormer? You know what it's like to spend all day with these cynical types. It gets old fast." He turned to Too Large. "You're totally predictable," he said.

"Reliable," said Too Large.

"Reliably a pain in the nougat." Too Small tapped the side of his head. He then reached into his shirt pocket and removed another cigarette. Automatically, Too Large reached for one as well.

"Really, I have to insist on your not smoking."

"Sorry," said Too Small. "Reflex." He flipped the unlit cigarette after the first one. Too Large simply put his back in his pocket.

"Asthma, is it? Allergies?"

"It's probably just distaste. Mr. Dormer is an educated man with good sense," said Too Small.

Too Large nodded and smiled.

"I used to smoke," said Dormer. "I stopped a long time ago. Terrible habit."

"Tell me, did you find it hard to quit?"

"Sure it was hard. But I knew what was at stake. I knew what was really important. Now, please, tell me what I can do for you."

"Well, I'm glad you asked. It saves me the trouble of telling you."

"It doesn't really," said Too Large.

"No, I suppose it doesn't. I don't know what I was thinking. Of course I still have to tell you. It's merely that I don't have to figure out how to introduce the subject. Although I suppose standing on your doorstep might beg the question."

Dormer took another look at the card. He opened the door all the way and stood aside.

"No matter what you people do to the place, it always looks the same to me, somehow," said Too Small.

"Not that you haven't done a nice job," added Too Large, quickly, placing a lightly restraining hand on Too Small's forearm. "You've really refreshed this room. Bold color here, texture there, rich and varied materials to add interest, statement pieces to announce yourself."

"What the heck is that?" Too Small was pointing at what looked like a large knife hanging on the wall over the mantel.

"It's a fauchard. Or just the blade, actually. Sixteenth-century weapon. My wife gave it to me. I'm of French descent."

"Beautiful," said Too Small.

"Thank you."

"Not at all. Seeing what you've done to the place is one of the pleasures of the job."

"Everyone must be very happy here," said Too Small.

"We're enjoying our new home, yes."

"Can be a tense time, moving in. No tension?"

"Of course not."

"You and your wife are getting along okay?"

"That's really none of your business."

"Is she at home?" asked Too Large.

"Yes, is the family here?"

"She'll tell you the same thing," said Dormer.

"I wouldn't dream of asking. I'm perfectly satisfied with your answer. But they are here?"

"Why, yes."

"Excellent. If you'd collect everyone, we'll meet and briefly explain here in the living room," said Too Small.

Dormer found his wife in their bedroom. She was fresh from the yoga mat and flushed with health.

"Who was at the door?"

"It was some men. They're downstairs."

"What kind of men?"

"Some kind. They seem to be here on official business." He handed her the card.

"I've never heard of them," she said.

"But here they are. They want to talk to all of us."

Dormer left his wife to change her clothes and found his son in his room, sitting in the shadows behind curtains closed against the day, watching a video featuring a continuous zoom into the depths of a Mandelbrot set. The repetitive music that accompanied the video was unsettlingly reminiscent of the soundtrack from a pornographic film that Dormer thought of now and then, occasionally, from time to time. The boy, Charlie, was snacking at his desk against all instructions. Dormer told the wayward youth to meet him downstairs. He thought he may have heard a response.

"Here's where we need to focus," said Too Small. He was standing in a small passageway that led from the living room to the dining room. There was a framed poster on the wall behind him. Dormer couldn't quite make it out, although he'd hung it there himself only a week beforehand. He closed his eyes to try to recall the poster.

"Who wants to be the body?"

"Body?" said Dormer's wife.

"You said you were going to explain," said Dormer.

"We are explaining," said Too Large. "How about you, young man? You look like you can handle anything you put your mind to."

Charlie got up from the couch and shuffled wearily over to the passageway.

"Now lie down," said Too Large.

"Don't jump the gun," said Too Small, "let's get everyone involved. Mom, you come through here into the dining room. Do you have any oven mitts? Go ahead and put one on. Your right hand will do fine."

"Sit down, everyone!" Dormer yelled. He hadn't expected to yell, but he was suddenly very upset. This was getting out of control. "You said you'd explain what you were doing here and you haven't."

"I'm so sorry," said Too Small. "You're absolutely right. Everybody, gather round. Here's the deal. This young man will be the body. Or object, if you prefer. Heavy, still, motionless, inert. A stone in an overgrown field. You're a natural! Mom will assume the posture of everyday life. An oven mitt, as if you've just come from putting a pie on the windowsill to cool. And you—"

"I don't really bake," said Mrs. Dormer.

"Oh, I wouldn't worry about that. For example, this little ray of sunshine clearly is more than just an object on the floor. It's in the spirit of things. And you—"

"I don't bake," she said again.

Too Small drew Too Large aside and the two conferred for a moment. "We don't ordinarily like to skip steps, but perhaps you should simply emerge from the kitchen holding the cigarette."

"Cigarette?" she asked.

Too Small and Too Large immediately produced cigarettes.

"Please!" said Dormer.

"I'm sorry," said Too Small. He muttered, "Thought she was inviting us to smoke."

Too Large crumpled his in his hand and let the shreds of tobacco and torn paper sift through his fingers onto the floor.

"What would make you think such a thing?" said Mrs. Dormer. "None of us smoke here."

"*Smokes*," said Too Large. "None of us *smokes*."

"Of course you don't," said Too Small. "Let's try it a different way. Ordinarily we'd prefer not to regress to these earlier reconstructive steps, but I think it may help to illustrate the necessity of our requests. So, Mr. Dormer, you will slip into your home. You'll pass through the hallway, to the left of the staircase, enter the first doorway straight ahead, proceed to the left of the staircase, go through the doorway you'll see ahead of you, and then there'll be a corridor running parallel to the staircase on its left-hand side, at the end of which you'll enter through the doorway. Then you'll pause."

It didn't sound very much like Dormer's house, but before he had a chance to mention this, Too Small had gestured at Too Large, who stepped forward to take Dormer by the elbow and lead him back through the hallway to the front door. He opened it and gently pushed Dormer onto the step.

"When do I come in?" asked Dormer.

"Oh, immediately." Too Large shut the door.

Dormer stood on the step for a moment, uncertain. Then he tried the door. It opened. He passed through the hallway to the left of the staircase and entered the doorway at its end. There was a second staircase, with a passageway running along the left. He crossed it and then entered through the doorway at the end. There was a third staircase. He heard music—tinny, repetitive, electronic music that seemed to stir unseemly memories. He continued along this hallway more slowly and paused at the doorway before crossing the threshold into the space beyond it, where he found himself in the passageway between the kitchen and the dining room. The poster was of a field of crops, large ovate leaves flowering with pale-green five-pointed blossoms, extending toward the horizon and the setting sun. He saw his son kneeling on the sofa, kneeling with his back to him, wearing a pair of headphones. Despite the headphones, Dormer could clearly hear the music and, over it, someone moving around in the kitchen. In one hand he found that he was holding a large and heavy stone.

All four others were looking at him.

"That was good," said Too Small.

"We're not quite there yet," said Too Large.

"Who's out in the kitchen?" said Dormer.

"Nobody *yet*," said Too Large.

"Is that your cigarette, Mr. Dormer?" asked Too Small, suddenly unsure. He pointed at the crushed cigarette on the floor.

"I don't know," said Dormer, now unsure as well.

"You'd better take another," said Too Small. He withdrew one from his pocket and handed it to him. "Light?"

Dormer leaned forward to accept the light.

"You'll notice that you gained entry quite easily," said Too Large.

"As you get used to the house, these things won't seem quite so strange," said Too Small.

"It feels like home already," said Mrs. Dormer. She looked at Charlie. "Doesn't it?"

The boy nodded, remembering to put a noncommittal smile on his face. Dormer looked at him with a sensation of surprise. For an instant, he appeared preternaturally mature, almost a man. Then the sensation faded.

"You'd never know you'd just moved in," said Too Small. "Most people, even if they unpack quickly, they still have boxes here and there, pictures they haven't hung. But it looks like you've been here for years."

"It feels like we've been here for years," said Dormer.

"It feels like we've been here forever," said Mrs. Dormer.

Too Large and Too Small simultaneously broke out into a short burst of laughter, then stopped. "It doesn't take long at all, if it's the right place for you."

"Where's that music coming from?" Dormer asked.

"I don't hear any music, honey," said Mrs. Dormer.

"Me either, Dad," said Charlie. But his face was mocking.

"Is it your music?" Dormer asked the two men. "Are you playing music somehow?"

"I *think* I hear something," said Too Small, solicitously. "Is it a sort of soft, rhythmic clicking?"

"No, it is not a soft, rhythmic clicking. It's right there, plain as day. You can't hear that?"

Dormer felt a kind of sharp, needling irritability. He drew on the cigarette, then took it out of his mouth and stared at it furiously. "There's something wrong with this cigarette," he said. "It won't draw properly."

"Well, what do you care?" asked Too Large. "You don't smoke."

"There's something wrong with it," Dormer said again,

"That isn't it," said Too Small. "The cigarette is fine."

"No," said Dormer, holding the cigarette up. "It isn't."

"Well, have another," said Too Small. He reached into his pocket, fumbled a little, then withdrew the pack. "Uh-oh," he said. He crumpled the pack in his hand. Dormer felt a sinking sensation. "I'm out."

"Me too," said Too Large.

"I saw you put one away," said Dormer.

"I'm sorry?"

"A little while ago, on the doorstep. You took one out and then put it away."

"That may be, but I must have smoked it since then."

"You didn't. You haven't."

"Well, you did leave us for a while."

"Oh, stop holding out on him, will you?" said Too Small.

"Well, what do you know?" said Too Large. "It was in my other shirt pocket."

Dormer hadn't noticed, but Too Large's short-sleeve dress shirt unusually had two pockets, one on either side of his chest. Both seemed to be monogrammed. Dormer took the proffered cigarette and a light.

"Well, if we're *all* going to smoke . . ." said Too Small. He took a full pack of cigarettes from his shirt pocket and opened it. He passed cigarettes to Too Large, Mrs. Dormer, and Charlie, who expertly tapped the end of his cigarette on his knuckle and inserted it into his mouth. Too Large provided lights.

"Ah," said Mrs. Dormer. "That's heavenly." She raised her chin and exhaled a conical jet of smoke toward the ceiling.

"Isn't it? How about you, young fella?" Too Small balled his hand into a fist and gave Charlie a friendly sock on the shoulder.

"Yeah, great."

Again, Dormer noticed that his son seemed to have matured—he looked like a grown man, a strange man. The music grew louder.

"I think," said Too Small, "that when we're done with our cigarettes, we should proceed. Young man, are you clear on what we're doing?"

"I think so," said Charlie. He needed a shave.

"You should shave once in a while," Dormer said pedantically. "You look like a bum."

"*So* uptight," said the boy. He turned to Mrs. Dormer. "See, this is what I've been telling you. What are you doing with this guy?"

"Please," said Mrs. Dormer nervously, "not now."

"This guy?" said Dormer.

"It's a phase they go through," said Too Small. "Disrespect, insolence. They grow out of it, but before they do . . ." He shook his head and whistled. "Well, all I can say is, my own parents were saints. Saints!"

"Let's move on," said Too Large.

"Naturally," said Too Small. "Big guy, are you ready to perform your role?"

"I guess," said Charlie.

"Excellent."

"I'm still not entirely comfortable with this," said Mrs. Dormer. "Why does he have to be . . . be a body?"

"It's really no more than a role," said Too Small.

"Fundamentally meaningless," said Too Large.

"This cigarette is defective too," said Dormer, suddenly.

"What are the odds?" said Too Small.

"You can have another one in a bit, but I think we may have to do some more backtracking," said Too Large.

Too Small took a furtive look at his wristwatch. Dormer also noticed that someone could be heard moving around in the kitchen again, and that the music had stopped. He dropped the useless cigarette and ground it under his shoe.

"Now," Too Small was saying, "Mr. Dormer, please go upstairs and descend by the back staircase into the kitchen."

"Back staircase?" said Dormer.

"Please," said Too Small. "The sooner we get this done, the sooner we'll get this done."

Dormer turned to go back the way he'd come.

"I'm afraid you can't go that way now," said Too Large.

Dormer returned to the first staircase and climbed the stairs to the second floor. He passed his own bedroom, the bathroom, and Charlie's bedroom, pausing for a moment to peer inside. In the dimness, he couldn't quite make out the room's contents, but they didn't look familiar. He moved down the hallway and opened the door to what he had always understood to be a large linen closet. There he found a steep, narrow, ninety-degree, winding staircase. It creaked when he stepped onto it. The painted handrail had been worn smooth and bare. He descended to the first floor and pushed open the door. There was his wife, bustling from the range to the countertop. She wore an apron.

"They have you in here now?"

"Who, the powers that be?" She laughed and came over to kiss him skillfully on the cheek. "If anyone's expecting to eat, where else would I be?"

"I don't think I have time to eat," said Dormer.

"Always rushing. Sure you don't have the time?" She presented him with a plate of donuts: powdered sugar, cinnamon, and glazed.

"Donuts?" he said. He reached for one.

"Well, just this once. I know how *snacky* you've been since you quit." She patted his belly. "Besides, Chuck's going to be here working on the staircase this morning."

With his mouth full, Dormer asked, "Since when have we started calling him Chuck?"

The kitchen door opened behind him and Charlie entered from outside, carrying a toolbox. He had a full beard, had broadened in the shoulders. The sinews in his arms rippled as he set the toolbox on the counter. "I've always been Chuck," he said. "Ever since I was a little boy."

"Well, you're not a little boy anymore," said Mrs. Dormer. There was something about her tone Dormer didn't like. She extended the plate toward Chuck.

"Oh, no thanks. Maybe later." He took out a pack of cigarettes and shook one out. "Care for one?" He held out the pack to Mr. and Mrs. Dormer. Mrs. Dormer took one.

"Mr. Dormer gave it up," she said, leaning toward Chuck as he lit her cigarette.

"For Lent?" asked Chuck. They laughed unpleasantly for a moment.

"Oh," said Dormer, "what the hell. I'll have one."

"No, you will not," said Mrs. Dormer. "Doctor's orders." She plucked the cigarette from between Chuck's lips and brought it over to the sink, where she ran it and her own under cold tap water. "We'll wait until he's gone. Now," she said to Dormer, "go forth. Hunt! Gather! Bring home the bacon!" She kissed him again on the cheek and then turned him around, her hands on his shoulders, and gave him a little push.

Dormer left through the kitchen door. He walked up the

driveway toward the front of the house. That was very peculiar, he thought. He rounded the corner of the house and mounted the front steps. One of the steps was loose. He was sure he'd fixed it shortly after moving in. Too Small and Too Large were waiting for him.

"That was superb," said Too Small.

"I have some questions," said Dormer.

"We're at your disposal," said Too Large.

"Got a cigarette?"

"That's not much of a question." Too Small withdrew a cigarette from the pack in his pocket and handed it to Dormer. Too Large supplied the light.

"That was very strange," said Dormer.

"Look," said Too Large. "We hear that all the time, asking people like you to do things like this."

"Some people do a terrible job," said Too Small.

"And you're not one of them. None of you is."

"*Are*. None of you *are*," said Too Small.

"I'm pretty certain it's singular," said Too Large.

"We won't argue."

"I'm pretty certain Mr. Dormer gets my drift," said Too Large.

"Something's happened to Chuck," said Dormer.

"Chuck's fine. Chuck's normal," said Too Small.

"Just regular Chuck," said Too Large.

"What's the matter with my son?" insisted Dormer.

"Son?" said Too Large.

Dormer felt . . . a tightness. Tension. Frustration. Irritability. Tremendous fatigue. An inability to focus. A sense of anxiety. A headache. An enormous desire for another donut. And something was wrong with his cigarette, again. He threw it down. Too Large began to whistle "I Don't Want to Set the World on Fire."

"Do you hear music?" asked Dormer.

"Well," said Too Small, "he is whistling."

"Not that music. Real music."

"Thanks a lot," said Too Large.

"Is it," said Too Small, "a kind of resonant clanging, like a small gong gently and repeatedly being struck?"

"No," said Dormer. "It isn't like that. Do you have another cigarette?"

"All out."

"Me too."

"But I saw you open a pack."

"But then you left us for a while."

"I need a cigarette."

"I've got an idea," said Too Small. "Go inside and get one from your wife."

"Good idea," said Dormer. He moved to the door and tried the knob. It was locked. "She never locks the door during the daytime," he said.

"Apparently she does," said Too Large.

"Kitchen door," said Too Small. He jerked his thumb toward the rear of the house.

Dormer trudged down the driveway. A pickup truck he hadn't noticed before was parked at its end. A sign painted on the door said, simply, *CHUCK'S*. He tried the kitchen door and discovered that it, too, was locked. He rattled the door, then pounded on it. "Let me in," he called. The music was booming; he was surprised none of the neighbors had appeared to complain. Possibly she couldn't hear him over it. He hadn't realized that his wife liked to listen to this kind of music. It aroused odd, licentious feelings. It was embarrassing. He went back up the driveway and rounded the corner of the house. Too Small and Too Large were gone. He climbed the steps again—the step he'd fixed was still broken, and another was missing its tread, the dirt and weeds beneath visible behind the riser. The front door was still locked.

He came back down the steps slowly, hearing his heart pounding in his ears. He really needed a cigarette. Here and there, amid the weeds and overgrown patches of grass in the unkempt yard fronting the unpainted house, were rocks. Bending over, he weighed a few in his hand before he found one, a large and heavy stone that he could grip firmly. He carried it down the driveway. Without hesitating, he used it to smash one of the glass panes of the kitchen door. He reached in to unlock it and let himself in.

Inside, the music was deafening. He didn't bother calling out. Was he just coming home from work? He couldn't remember, but the light didn't seem right. He scanned the kitchen surfaces for cigarettes. He reached on top of the refrigerator and felt around—he knew that she kept a pack up there, for when she was cooking. Nothing. All there was were two butts in an ashtray, one with lipstick and one without. Why had he ever agreed to quit? At the very least, she should have quit when he did. But then, what did she do with him anymore? Bitch. It wasn't fair. He could smell the smoke. Still holding the stone in his hand, he left the kitchen, passed through the dining room, and entered the short passageway that led to the living room, where the music seemed to be coming from. He entered the living room and saw his son kneeling on the sofa, his back to Dormer, wearing a pair of headphones.

But they were not headphones. They were his wife's hands, clamped to either side of Chuck's head, which was buried between her thighs. She opened her eyes and, suddenly aware of him, snapped her head forward. Without taking her eyes from him, she pushed Chuck's head away. Dormer could see her mouth calmly form the word *Stop*. She was naked, and she was oiled, and they had very deliberately spread one of the new bath towels across the cushions of the sofa. It reminded Dormer of a pornographic film that he thought of now and then. Chuck lazily turned to face him, placing one foot on the floor and wiping his beard, obscenely. He smiled noncommittally, and said something that Dormer couldn't hear over the music. Dormer stepped forward, raising the stone as Chuck pushed himself up and bringing it down on Chuck's head before he was fully upright. He then looked at his wife, registered that she had seized the fauchard from where it hung over the mantel and was holding it in both hands. Dormer walked, stumbled, backward into the short passageway, unable to recall why he'd been in the living room. He straightened the framed poster, his hands disturbingly leaving some sort of dark stain on the wall; unable to make it out, he thought, not for the first time, that they really needed some light in the passageway.

Then, smiling with satisfaction, fresh from a recent phone conversation with the woman from the local newspaper, who so admired what they'd done with the house since acquiring it that she'd called to ask if they'd be averse to her and a photographer coming out to take some pictures and do a brief interview for her monthly column, "New Neighbors." Whistling, he was headed toward the stairs to go and tell his wife the good news when the doorbell rang. So soon? He reached for the doorknob. They were smoking when Dormer opened the door, two unexpected strangers standing expectantly on the step, both with cigarettes fuming in their hands.

JONATHAN AMES is the author of ten books of fiction and nonfiction, including *Wake Up, Sir!* and *What's Not to Love?* He is also the creator of two televisions shows: *Bored to Death* (HBO) and *Blunt Talk* (Starz). His novels *The Extra Man* and *You Were Never Really Here* have been adapted into films. His latest novel is *A Man Named Doll*.

# DEATHBED VIGIL
## BY JONATHAN AMES

### I.

The nursing home called at seven a.m., waking him. They said she had a few hours. It had happened fast, during the night. A stroke. She was going quick.

He told them, "Tell her Sol's coming. Whisper it in her ear."

He was assured this would be done, and he hung up and put his cell phone back down on the bedside table. He sat up in bed and looked around the room. Sunlight seeped in around the edges of the brown curtains, and he didn't know where he was. It looked like a shabby motel room. And smelled like one. Dead cigarette smoke. Which he hated. Which disgusted him.

A panic began to well in his chest. He saw his large suitcase against the wall. *Where the hell am I?* Then it came to him all at once: *Los Angeles*.

Then he got out of bed. All he knew was that he had to get across the country before she died. What he didn't know then, of course, was that three others would die. Two by his hand.

### 2.

He used the motel room phone and called the front desk. He told them to order a taxi to take him to the airport, to LAX. Then he showered quickly, had a motel-room coffee, and went out to the cab.

He didn't bring his bag. It was too big, and he felt the need for speed, to be able to move quickly and lightly, to just get to her, and anyway, he'd paid for the motel room for two weeks, in advance. And he needed to come back. And he wouldn't be gone long. Maybe a day. They said she only had a few hours.

So he left his bag in the room and just took his wallet and his phone, but forgot his charger.

The traffic was thick. The motel was in North Hollywood; LAX was twenty miles away. Rush hour starts early in Los Angeles.

He was wearing his work clothes—a blazer, white button-down shirt, gray slacks, and thick-soled black shoes. It was late September. His blazer would be warm enough in New Jersey.

The taxi got him to LAX by eight thirty. Sol wasn't good with phones and online things, and so he had the cabbie drop him off at the first terminal, went to the first airline counter he saw, American, and was able to get a ticket—a window seat—on a noon flight, which would have him to Newark by nine p.m.

He killed a few hours in an airport restaurant, drinking bad coffee and reading the paper, but not really reading it, and then he got on the plane, and the whole flight he prayed that his Great-Aunt Lina, his only family, would hold on until he got there. He simply couldn't bear the idea of her dying alone. She had made it to almost 102. This couldn't be her reward, her end—to die alone in a nursing home bed.

So he had to make it there in time and she had to hold on. He had to say goodbye. He had to tell her one last time that he loved her.

When he was born, Lina, who was fifty-two and a great red-headed beauty, took one look at Sol and made him her favorite in the world. She was a manicurist at Saks Fifth Avenue in the city and twice divorced, and everyone in the family, in Brooklyn where he grew up, thought her love for Sol was because she never had children of her own. An illegal abortion in the early forties, at the start of the war, had sterilized her.

But Sol didn't care about the family's theories. Lina had made him feel more loved than anyone ever had, including his own mother. *Sol and Lina.* Theirs was a love affair between an older relative and a little boy—who had become a middle-aged man—that had lasted fifty years.

And Sol knew that he had killed her. That she was dying because of him.

Three days ago he had told her he was taking a job in LA, but would be back once a month to see her. Which had been a lie. He'd be lucky if he'd make it back every two months on the money he was going to make, but he knew it didn't really matter what he told her. Her memory was completely gone. She'd forget what he had said ten minutes after he left. She'd forget that he had even been there.

Still, he had hated to leave her. Hated that he had to move to LA. But he didn't have a choice, didn't know what else to do. He was a washed-up cop. Fifty years old. Had worn a uniform for the NYPD his whole career; never became a detective. Retired at forty-eight and started working security, but couldn't hold a job.

He'd boxed—Golden Gloves, Police Athletic League, smokers—since he was a teenager and it had scrambled his brains. He didn't process things right anymore, and it seemed to kick in after he left the force. He didn't know what exactly was wrong—he was afraid to go to a doctor—but words and the names of friends that should be easy to access were increasingly gone. He'd reach for them in his mind but there'd be nothing there. The files were empty.

And if somebody pissed him off, there seemed to be no ability to pause, to assess: he would just lash out. And he'd always had a good right hand. Which still worked. Too well.

So he was hitting people—hurting people—he shouldn't. And when he hit them, they felt it for a long time. He was a solid six one, 190. A light heavy. And he looked like an ex-pugilist—thick, immobile neck; rugged skull, covered in buzzed-down black-gray grizzle; square jaw; thin white scars in black eyebrows.

He was ugly and handsome and his mind was going. He felt like he could hardly remember his own life. He knew he had done things—grown up in Bay Ridge, been a cop, got married, went on trips—but it was like a book he had read a long time ago: the details had faded and the story had happened to someone else.

But not Lina—she was etched deep in his mind. She'd been there from the start, always loving him, always caring for him, and she had outlived everyone—his mother, his father, all of them.

But then he went to LA and he cursed himself for abandoning her, and all because he was broke. He'd burned a few bridges—his outbursts weren't well-suited to security work—and he'd gone six months without a job and was running out of money; his pension wasn't enough to live on.

Not knowing what else to do, he'd called an old friend, an ex-cop who'd moved to LA years ago and ran a bodyguard service. Sol told him things had dried up in New York—without going into much detail—and the friend offered Sol a job. It helped that he hadn't seen Sol in a decade. He didn't know that Sol wasn't quite right anymore. That something was broken in his head.

And Sol didn't let on, and within a week of their call, Sol had emptied out his apartment near Fordham, in the Bronx, and was ready to go. He'd been divorced since his midthirties and lived simply. It was easy to erase himself, to remove any trace of his life in New York.

And no one would really notice that he was gone. He was an

only child, and as his mind betrayed him, he pulled away from the few friends he did have.

So all packed up and ready to go to LA—he had reduced everything he owned to his one large suitcase—he told Lina about the job that Thursday. She'd hardly spoken the last six months and she didn't say anything when he told her. She just nodded and seemed to smile, and then turned the palm of her right hand upward on her wheelchair arm. That was how she communicated of late, small gestures, mostly of resignation and acceptance.

But he wasn't sure she had understood what he'd said, and if she had, he was certain that she would soon forget it. He parted from her that day as he always did, kissing her on the top of her head and saying, "I love you, Aunt Lina," and then walking off, unable to look back, not wanting to see her alone in her chair, forsaken.

He flew to LA the next day, Friday, and was supposed to start work on Monday. He got that cheap motel room on the edge of North Hollywood, and on Sunday morning the nursing home called. As soon as they told him she was dying, he realized that she *had* retained what he said and it had broken her will. Had killed her. Forty-eight hours after he had left, she was dying.

### 3.

When he landed in Newark, he called the nursing home, which was in Leonia, and they said she was still alive. He got in a taxi and hoped that she would hold on for another forty-five minutes.

He had put her in the nursing home, which was called Maple Ridge, ten years ago. Before that, she had been living in a small apartment in Queens since the early eighties, and Sol had visited her there every Sunday, unless he had to work, for years.

As Lina aged, she lived quietly, had very few friends, and spent a lot of time knitting Sol beautiful sweaters and scarves, which she would present to him on their Sundays, when they'd have lunch and play cards. They did this for almost two decades, but then after she turned ninety, she kept having falls, and he was constantly going to the ER in Forest Hills to retrieve her.

Luckily, she never broke a hip, but after a while it was clear she couldn't take care of herself anymore, and so he looked at a bunch of places and Maple Ridge was the nicest, nicer than the ones in New York, and without fail, since he put her there, Sol had kept up the tradition of visiting her every Sunday, as well as every holiday.

Getting to Leonia from the Bronx hadn't always been easy— he had to cross the George Washington Bridge and something was often going on there, even on Sundays—but he didn't care about the drive. It was worth it to him to sit in traffic: he loved being with Lina. She was the one person all his life that he felt comfortable with, that he could just be at ease around, not have to prove anything.

And they'd always had good conversations. They would talk boxing—she was the one who introduced him to the sport, watching it with him on Saturdays when he was a kid; and they also covered city politics and baseball and his problems with women. She was from another time, a more glamorous time, a real lady, and she was his best friend. Just about his only true friend.

The first few years at the nursing home, they could still play cards—gin rummy was their game—and he'd take her out to eat. But eventually she became wheelchair bound, her dementia was in full bloom or full decay, and for the last year, they would just sit together without talking. Sometimes he'd read the paper or a book. It seemed to make her happy just to look at him.

### 4.

The traffic was light on a Sunday night, coming from Newark

Airport, and he got to Maple Ridge by ten p.m., gave the driver a big tip for luck, and rushed into the facility, which had a hushed feeling, the quiet of sleep.

He signed in at the front desk and inhaled the nursing home's familiar smell, urine, which they could never erase, no matter how hard they tried. Then after scribbling his name and the time on the ledger, he walked quickly down the long, quiet hallway to Lina's unit. When he got to the nurse's station he couldn't remember the name of the nurse who was sitting, mostly hidden, behind the raised counter.

She was staring intently at her computer screen and didn't sense that he was there—she hadn't heard him approach, the floor was covered in a thin carpeting, good for wheelchairs—and he didn't know what to do. He couldn't say *Excuse me* to someone he knew so well—he had spoken to her hundreds of times over the years. He should say her name, make her look up at him that way. But he couldn't find her name, it was missing, and he just stood there in the hallway, frustrated, almost wanting to cry. *What is wrong with me?* he asked in his mind, though he knew the answer.

Then he put his hand on the counter and that caught the eye of the nurse, and she looked up from the glow of her desktop. She was a middle-aged Filipina, tiny and round and kind, and her eyes, behind her gold-rimmed glasses, filled with tenderness when she saw it was Sol. Her name was Angelie, but Sol couldn't bring it up. Where her name should be, automatically, was empty space.

"Is she still alive?" he asked.

"Yes," Angelie said, and she came around the counter to hug him. They all knew at Maple Ridge how much he loved Lina.

Then she took him down the hall and into Lina's room, which was in shadows, and they went past her roommate, whose blankets were up to her chin. She was a heavyset woman in her eighties and the light from the hallway shone on her face, and she looked at Sol with scared eyes. The roommate loved Lina, and just on the other side of the curtain that separated them, she knew that Lina was dying. Sol nodded at her, trying to convey reassurance, while also scratching in his mind for her name. He had known her for a year, which was a longer tenure than most of Lina's roommates; there had been a lot of death in that room.

Then he and Angelie were on the other side of the curtain, and there was a nurse sitting in a chair by Lina's bed. Lina's little bedside lamp was on and the nurse had put a pillowcase over the lampshade to dim it, and it cast a faint glow on Lina, who lay curled on her side, facing the thin light.

She was breathing raspingly, and her white hospital blanket was pulled over her bony shoulders, and her red hair, which had turned a beautiful orangish-white with age, was damp on her skull. Her cheekbones were protruding and her skin looked yellow and waxy. She was radically different from how she had been just a few days before.

Angelie whispered to the bedside nurse, "This is the nephew. He'll sit with her now." And the nurse, whom Sol didn't recognize, stood up and walked past them, without saying anything, just nodded at Sol with sympathy and left the room.

"She's with hospice," said Angelie, and then she went to Lina, bent over her, stroked her head gently, and said, "Sol is here."

But Lina didn't wake, and Angelie adjusted her covers, and then turned to Sol and said, "I think she's been waiting for you. We told her you were coming. The doctor didn't expect her to make it this long."

"I never should have gone to LA," Sol said. "I did this to her."

"No," said Angelie. "You can't think like that. It's Miss Lina's time. She's ready to go. And you know—she always does what she wants and this is what she wants." She had a nurse's take on death—its inevitability and its beauty.

Then Angelie left the room, and Sol sat down in the chair vacated by the hospice nurse. Lina's hand, like a child's, was up near her chin, poking out from the covers, and he took hold of it and it was tiny and cold in his large fist, but her fingers still looked beautiful and elegant. Her nails, which she had always been proud of, were painted red.

He then squeezed her hand ever so slightly and she opened her eyes and knew that her Sol was there, that he had come for her.

## 5.

The first four nights, he stayed by her side. They brought him a reclining chair, but he hardly rested; it was too uncomfortable and he couldn't sleep. *And* he was afraid to sleep. What if she went while his eyes were closed?

They let him use a shower and brought meals to him from the dining room. The nurses charged his phone and he called his friend in LA—his new boss—and told him what was happening. The friend told him to take as much time as he needed.

Because of her stroke, he couldn't give Lina water—she would drown—and so what was going to kill her in the end, slowly, would be thirst, dehydration. They had thought that Sunday morning, when they called him in LA, that she was going quickly, but with Sol by her side, she suddenly wasn't in a rush.

She slept most of the time, but every now and then she would open her eyes and he wasn't sure if she saw him or not. That first night she definitely seemed to acknowledge him, but after that it was unclear.

He held her hand for hours at a time and like some kind of mantra, he kept on saying, "I love you. I love you. I love you." He wanted those to be the last words she heard.

He only left her side to go to the bathroom or bathe. He was becoming wildly sleep-deprived but was obsessed with the idea of being there the exact moment she went. He was determined she shouldn't be alone and, secretly, not that there was anyone to tell, he'd come to have a selfish desire to witness that last moment, like it was something exotic or forbidden. As a cop, he'd seen several people die, but this was a vigil. A deathbed vigil. And he was waiting for it: that moment, that divide, when she would be here and then no longer here.

On Wednesday night, the fourth night of the vigil, something beautiful happened. It was around two a.m. and she became radiant. Her eyes were suddenly open and clear—she definitely knew he was there—and she looked beautiful. It was like eighty years had been shed, and she was a twenty-year-old woman, full of health and life, and something akin to joy seemed to inhabit her face. And her eyes seemed to be talking to him, telling him that she loved him. He almost felt like some kind of miracle was occurring, that the stroke was reversing itself, and he squeezed her hand and whispered, over and over, "I love you. I love you. I love you."

And this time of radiance lasted about two hours and then passed. She fell back asleep and hardly woke the whole next day. From that point forward, she seemed to worsen even more. Death was imminent.

On the fifth night, Thursday, he couldn't take it anymore— the reclining chair, the sleep deprivation—and he broke down, got a taxi, and went to a cheap motel, not far from the nursing home. He told Angelie—who had the night shift again and whose name he had come to remember when he heard someone use it—to call him at any sign that Lina was close. To not worry about waking him and that he would come back right away. Angelie promised she would call.

So he left the nursing home at one a.m. and was back by seven a.m., and Lina was still alive. He stayed with her that day till two a.m. and then went back to the motel room, which was a twin to the one in LA—shabby and reeking of dead smoke, which Sol hated.

He'd always hated the smell of smoke, had since he was a child. He associated it with his father, a cruel man, an unhappy man, who sometimes took his belt to Sol. Nicotine always seemed to be coming out of his father's pores, which disgusted Sol, and their house always smelled of smoke, like the remnants of his father's anger.

Then his father died from smoking: a heart attack, like an ax blade, took him down when he was sixty. He was sitting at the breakfast table, fell out of his chair, and was dead. The doctor said it was because of cigarettes.

Then Sol's mother—whom Sol loved very much, she was Lina's niece and also had beautiful red hair—died six months later of lung cancer. She had inhaled secondhand smoke for thirty-five years of marriage, and Sol wasn't with her when she went. She died on the operating room table when they tried to remove a tumor from her lung, and he didn't get to say goodbye.

## 6.

On the seventh day of the vigil, which was Saturday, a massive storm hit the East Coast in the afternoon. It was a modern nor'easter—vicious and cataclysmic and a month early in the season.

The rain beat against Lina's window, and it was dark by three p.m. She was lying on her side, facing Sol and the window, and at five p.m. her hands grew icy cold and her breathing became intermittent and labored. He stood up and pulled back the blanket at the end of the bed—her feet had turned purple. It was coming now. These were all the signs, and like the time of radiance, it lasted about two hours. The intervals between her ragged breaths grew longer and longer, each breath seemed like it might be her last, and then she would fight to take one more. Sol thought of her as a boxer who is losing but wants to go the distance, and he thought, too, how people always tell their loved ones in these moments, *It's all right, you can go, just let go.*

But he didn't want to do that. He wanted her to make it through the last round, and it seemed to be what *she* wanted. She was fighting so hard with each breath to hold on, and so he started saying, "Take one more breath, Aunt Lina . . . Take one more breath . . . I love you . . . I love you . . . I love you . . . One more breath . . . One more breath . . . I love you . . . I love you."

And all the while he held her hand and then her jaw did something strange and grotesque and violent, it seemed to unhinge and then reset, and then she took one more breath and this time it was her last. No more breaths came.

An hour later, Angelie came around the curtain to check on them, and Sol was still holding Lina's hand. He was quietly crying and said, "She's gone."

## 7.

He returned to the motel around nine thirty. He'd watched them pack her body in ice—she had willed herself to a medical school—and then one of the nurses gave him a ride. No taxis were running in the storm.

The streets were like rivers, and when they got to the motel, the parking lot was practically flooded. It was an old-fashioned, single-story motel—the walkway outside his room was exposed and right on the parking lot—and he got out of the car, thanked the nurse for the ride, dashed into his room, and still got soaking wet.

He went to turn on the lights and realized that the power was out. The room was dark and he opened the curtains to the large window that faced the lot, but no light came in. When they had pulled into the lot, he hadn't noticed how dark it was—the rain was beating down so hard on the windshield and the lights from the nurse's car had lit a path to his room.

But now he realized there were no lights on in the lot and no light coming from anywhere. Sol didn't know it but a quarter-million people in New Jersey and New York were without power. He took out his cell phone to use as a flashlight, but it was dead: he'd forgotten to ask the nurses to charge it for him.

He fumbled his way to the bed and picked up the motel phone: also dead. So there was nothing to do but strip down, get into bed, and hope to sleep. He got under the covers in the darkness, with the rain lashing the window to his right, and he was very tired and closed his eyes, and as soon he did, he saw in his mind that moment when Lina's jaw had unhinged and her face had been crucified in pain.

He figured it was one last electric pulse from her body, a big one, the final charge, and then his mind wouldn't stop, despite his exhaustion, and he kept seeing it—the jaw unlatching, shifting to the right like an old typewriter; her face torqued and ugly and horrific; a mask of terror.

And he couldn't stop seeing it in his mind, that moment, it was on a loop, a terrible loop that wouldn't stop, and he desperately wanted to sleep, it went on and on, but then something, finally, distracted him: the smell of cigarette smoke. He held the blanket to his nose—there were traces of old smoke in the fabric, but the smell in his room was stronger than that, and he realized it had been there since he came into the room. It wasn't the stale smell he had become somewhat accustomed to: it was fresh smoke. But where the hell was it coming from?

He sat up in the bed. It was almost like someone was in the room, smoking, and he wondered if he was hallucinating. Was his dead father in the room, mocking him?

He got out of the bed—the room was pitch-black, dark as a cave—and he felt his way around, touching the bureau that held the television, and then he made his way, by instinct, into the bathroom and shouted, "Anyone fucking in here?" And he waved his hands around in the darkness, but there was no one in the bathroom as far as he could tell, and the smell of smoke wasn't as strong in there.

He then ran his hands along the wall to make it back to his bed and he touched something that felt like a door—it was metal, not like the cheap stucco walls. He reached down and found a knob and turned it. It was locked, and he realized it was the connecting door to the adjoining room. He remembered noticing it when he first checked in, but hadn't paid it any attention. Every motel room seemed to have one.

He then got down on his hands and knees by the sill of the door and inhaled deeply, and there the smell of smoke was strong. Very strong.

*Bastard*, he thought.

Some asshole on the other side was smoking, and Sol became enraged and lost control of himself—that early symptom of his growing dementia—and he stood up and pounded on the door to the adjoining room and shouted, "You gotta quit smoking over there! It's making me sick!"

But he didn't hear anything back. He put his ear to the door. Nothing. And so he blundered out of the room, out of the darkness, and into the storm.

He was going to tell this asshole to quit smoking, to show some consideration, he needed to grieve, and he went to the outside door of the adjoining room and the rain, whipped by the wind, was soaking him—he was in boxer shorts and T-shirt and bare feet—and there was a little bit of diffuse moonlight from the storm clouds above, and he pounded on the door. "Fucking open up!"

And the door swung open halfway, and a big, angry man, at least six four, was standing in the shadows; some light source inside the room was partially illuminating him. He had a shaved head and a huge distended belly, covered in tattoos, and the only thing on him was a towel around his waist. He looked at Sol standing there, soaking wet, and said, "What the fuck you want?"

And in the opening of the door, Sol's eye was drawn to the light source inside the room and he saw that it was a two-foot Maglite—the kind that cops used as weapons—and it was standing straight up on the bedside table, shining its powerful light upward, like a torch, and next to the bedside table he thought he saw the arm of a woman tied to the corner of the bed.

"What are you doing in there?" Sol said, almost whisper-like.

"Fuck you," said the man, and he slammed the door, and Sol stood there in the rain and then he banged his fist hard against the door. He was a cop again.

And the door swung back open and this time a gun stuck out at Sol and Sol kicked at the door and it flew into the man and the gun jerked to the ceiling and Sol charged, tackling the man into the room, and the gun fell from his hand, and they went down hard onto the carpet next to the bed, and Sol caught a glimpse of the naked woman tied there, she looked young, and Sol scrambled up the big man's body, he was squirming to get away from Sol, but Sol was strong, very strong, and he stayed on top of the big man and brought down his fist like a mallet once, twice, and then Sol sensed something behind him and he turned and there was another man there, equally large, and he held a second big Maglite in his hand, poised like a steel baton, and Sol knew that because his mind wasn't so good anymore he had made a terrible mistake, a rookie mistake: there wasn't one bastard in there smoking, there were *two*.

And the big Maglite scythed down toward Sol's head—he saw it coming—and then it exploded into his left eye socket and there was a sheet of flame in his mind and then there was nothing.

## 8.

An hour later, Sol regained consciousness. He was lying on his belly, and they had rolled him over by the wall.

His head was facing the bed, and he saw that one Maglite was on the bedside table shooting its light up, and one was on the bureau on the other side of the room, also facing upward like a torch, and it was next to the gun and an overflowing ashtray.

The two flashlights provided illumination, mood lighting, and the large man with the belly and the tattoos was on the bed, his big body between the girl's legs. He was thrusting, like an animal, assaulting her, and the other one was on the other side of the bed, smoking a crack pipe and assaulting her mouth.

Sol's head was in a pool of sticky blood and he lifted his hand up slowly and felt the left side of his head—where his brow and eye socket and eye should be there was a hideous swelling as large as a cantaloupe.

But Sol somehow felt very calm and very clear. From all his years of training in the ring, he had a reserve of strength and a tolerance for pain that was not normal, and he rose up quietly and smoothly, he felt a sort of perfection in everything, and very adroitly he stepped over to the bedside table, picked up the Maglite, and brained the one between the girl's legs, killing him instantly.

The other man stepped back in fear and shock, trapping himself in the corner, and Sol quickly came around the bed and the man threw up his arm to protect himself, and Sol broke his forearm with the Maglite, and then smashed him on the side of his head when the arm dropped, and the man crumpled at Sol's feet, almost in a kneeling position, and with two more blows, Sol caved in the back of his head.

Sol stared down at the bloody heap and then looked up, like a cyclops with his one working eye, and the girl was trying to say something, but she could barely talk with the first man dead on top of her. So Sol hauled the large body off the girl, pushing it to the floor. There were now dead men on both sides of the bed.

"Untie me," the girl rasped.

Sol started with the knot by her left hand, but his fingers were suddenly very thick, he could hardly use them at all, and then he felt incredibly weak, the weakest he'd ever felt in his life.

"I have to sit down," he said, and he sat facing away from the naked girl, and he bowed his head and touched the enormous swelling protruding from his brow, and then he looked up and Lina was there, wearing the nightgown she had died in.

"Sol," she said.

"I'm so glad you're here," he said, and he felt so happy to see her. She hadn't died after all, which pleased him to no end; it had all been a mistake.

But she looked troubled. "Are you all right?" he asked.

"I'm cold," she said.

"It's the ice for the medical school," he said. "That's what's making you cold." It seemed so obvious to him.

"Oh, you're right, Sol," she said. "You're always right. I love you."

Then something was nudging him, and he turned and the girl was poking him in the back with her foot. "Please," she said, "untie me."

She was young, early twenties, a slender brunette, a girl's figure really, and he saw that there were purple finger marks on her neck, and he turned to tell Aunt Lina that he needed to help the girl, but she wasn't there now, and he tried to stand to look for her, to find her, but he couldn't stand and he thought, *I never should have looked away*, and he felt his heart break, he could feel it snap, he was sure of it, and then he fell to his side, at the girl's feet, and he was dead.

## 9.

It took the girl a few hours but she managed to untie herself. The two dead men were johns who had gotten too rough, but she didn't think they would kill her, until the other guy showed up and they killed *him*. So then they were going to have to kill her, she figured, she was a witness. But they told her she was fine, that they wouldn't hurt her and that in a little while they would dump the body in the Passaic River, but first they wanted to stick to their plan: party out the storm. Then the other guy wasn't dead after all—he rose up, his face was a mask of blood, and he had just one eye—and then he killed the two johns with the big flashlight.

And then the man, some stranger, died again. This time for good.

Her wrists were rubbed raw by the wet sheets they had used as bonds, but as the sheets dried, it had become easier to escape. She was shaky as hell and close to losing it, but she managed to get her clothes on and she peeked out the door.

The storm had let up a little, enough so that she could drive away. Her car, a Honda, was still there. No one but her and the two dead men—and the dead stranger—knew she'd come to this place. She hadn't told any friends and she didn't have a pimp. She worked solo. One of the johns had texted the address of the motel to her on her burner phone, which she would throw away immediately. She didn't want anything to do with the cops and she didn't think they would ever find her. If they even looked.

She pulled out slowly from the dark motel parking lot and drove out into the storm. No one saw her go.

When the cops came to the motel later in the day, in the afternoon, when power had been restored, they didn't know what to make of the crime scene. Three middle-aged men, all with their heads bashed in. Two of the men were truckers from Illinois, their cabs were in the lot. The storm had held them up and they were both listed as sex offenders in Illinois. Rape convictions; one of them with a minor.

And the other man was an ex-cop from New York, who at some point had joined the party.

The Leonia detectives in charge of the case didn't put much effort into it—it was decided after a few weeks that no official report would be made—and a month after Sol died, the NYPD collected his body, which was no longer needed as evidence, and had it cremated and buried.

Two months after that, the motel in North Hollywood tossed Sol's bag into their dumpster in the alleyway, where a small homeless man found it.

All of Sol's clothes were too big for the man, so he sold what he could, but he did keep the bag itself and one thick blue sweater, which Lina had made for Sol years ago. The sweater kept the man warm at night for the next few months, until he forgot it one day in some bushes by the side of a road.

# PART II

## SMOKING MAY BE HAZARDOUS TO YOUR HEALTH

Gordon Trice

**LEE CHILD** was fired and out of work when he hatched a harebrained scheme to write a best-selling novel, thus saving his family from ruin. *Killing Floor* went on to launch the *New York Times* #1 best-selling Jack Reacher series with over 100 million books sold in forty-nine languages. *Forbes* calls it "the strongest brand in publishing." The series has spawned two feature films and an Amazon Prime Video series.

# DYING FOR A CIGARETTE
## BY **LEE CHILD**

The producer's notes came in. The screenwriter saw the e-mail on his phone. The subject line said *Notes*. The phone was set to preview the first several words of the message, which were *Thanks again for making time for lunch today*. The screenwriter looked away. He didn't open the e-mail. Didn't read more. Instead he backed up and sat down on the sofa, stiff and upright, straight like a poker, palms cupped on the cushions either side of his knees.

His wife sat down on his lap. She was an hour back from the beauty parlor, still in her afternoon attire, which was a cream silk blouse tucked into a navy linen skirt, which when standing fell just above the knee, and when sitting, especially on a lap, crept a little higher. She was wearing nothing underneath either item. She wondered if he could tell. Probably not, she thought. Not yet. He was preoccupied. She lit a cigarette and placed it between his lips.

He said, "Thank you."

She said, "Tell me about lunch."

"It was him and three of his execs. I think at least one of them was financial."

"How did it go?"

"Exactly like I was afraid it would."

"Exactly?"

"More or less," he said. "Possibly even worse."

She said, "Did you make the speech?"

"What speech?"

"About dying."

"It's only a line. In the first paragraph. Not really a speech."

"Did you say it?"

He nodded tightly, still a little defiant. "I told him for years I had been a good little hack, and I had always done what he wanted, as fast as he needed it, overnight sometimes, even sometimes on the fly while the camera was rolling. I told him I had never let him down, and I had made him millions of dollars. So I told him overall I figured I had earned the right to be left alone on this one. Because finally I had the one great idea a guy might ever get in his life. I told him I would rather die than see it compromised."

"That's the speech I was talking about."

"It's only a word."

"With a lot of preamble."

"It's a strong first paragraph, I agree."

"How did he take it?"

"I don't really know. I went out for a cigarette. He was okay when I got back. He said at first he thought I was nuts for not seeing his point, but now I had gotten him thinking maybe I was right and he was wrong."

"What was his issue?"

"This has always been about the British Army in World War I. Am I right? Hasn't it? Since the very first moment I got the idea. You were the very first person I ever talked to about it."

"Actually, I think that must have been a previous wife. Or several ago. The idea was already well established when I came on the scene."

"Was it ever anything but the British Army in World War I?"

"Don't they like that?"

"He said the studio asked if it was an English-country-house movie."

"What was his answer?"

"He said maybe English-country-house people, but not in the house. Obviously. In the trenches, in France or Belgium, or wherever else they had trenches."

"So is it a problem?"

"He said the studio thinks the audience would relate better if it was the Civil War. With actual Americans involved."

"I see."

"I reminded him there was an essential story strand involving an airplane pilot. The infancy of the technology. A huge metaphor. It could not be dropped or altered in any way. I reminded him that airplanes weren't invented yet, during the Civil War."

"I think they had hot-air balloons."

"Not the same thing at all. A hot-air balloon is automatically a slow-motion scene. We need speed, and fury, and noise, and anger. We need to feel we're on the cusp of something new and dangerous."

"What did he say to all that?"

"He agreed with me that the studio's idea was bullshit. He said he only passed it on because it came from the top. He said he never took it seriously. Not for one minute. He was on my side totally. Not just because of the airplanes. Because of the ideas. They're too modern. This is all fifty years after the Civil War. The characters know things people didn't know fifty years before."

"He's right, you know. The ideas are modern. You got it through, even to him. That's great writing, babe."

"He said the same thing. Not babe. He said it was my best writing ever. He said I could say things in four words other writers would need a paragraph for. He said I could get things through, even to a cynical old moneybags like him, about how the thoughts my characters were having were building the postwar world right in front of our eyes."

"Flattering."

"Very."

"He's right, you know," she said again. "It stands to reason. Obviously the postwar world was built from new ideas, and inevitably they were forged during the war itself. But to see history happen in front of our eyes is fantastic. It's going to be a classic. It's a shoo-in for Best Picture."

"Except that the postwar world he was talking about was post–World War II. The 1950s, in fact. He thinks the story should be set during the Korean War. With actual Americans. And foxholes, not trenches. He thinks foxholes are better. Necessarily more intimate. An automatic reason to shoot a scene with just one or two actors. No extras. No background hoo-ha. Saves a fortune. He said one or two guys alone in a trench would look weird. As in, who are they? Are they malingerers? Did they pull the lucky straw and get to stay behind on sentry duty? Or what? Either way, he figures we would need to burn lines explaining. At the very least we would need to have them say, no, we're not malingerers. It would be an uphill task to get anyone to like them. But guys in a foxhole don't need explaining. They're taking refuge. Maybe there are two of them. They tumbled in together. Maybe it's a shell hole. Maybe it's a little small, so they're resentful of each other right from the start. They have to figure out how to get along. He said the modernity and the futurism in the ideas made no sense in World War I. It had to be the 1950s. He said we could still keep the airplanes. Jet-fighter technology was in its infancy. There were the same kinds of stresses. All we would need to do was give the guy a more modern kind of helmet. The actual lines could stay the same. He said some things never change. Some truths are eternal."

"How did you react?"

"I let him know I was very angry, and then I went out for another cigarette."

"How long were you gone?"

"I don't know. Ten minutes? Maybe more. It's a big restaurant. It's a long walk from his table even to the lobby."

"You shouldn't do that. Obviously they talk about you, at the table, while you're gone. Him and his people."

"Actually, I think they mostly make calls on their phones. Like multitasking. Probably trashing other writers' dreams. I saw them finishing up when I came back in, every time. They were looking kind of guilty about it."

"You should watch your back."

"It doesn't matter if they talk about me anyway. They can't make me agree. This is my project. I could take it somewhere else."

"Where?"

The screenwriter didn't answer.

His wife snuggled tighter. She pressed her chest against his. No bra. She wondered if he could tell yet. She felt like he should. Certainly she could. Just a thin layer of silk.

She said, "He might be right about the foxholes."

"The point is the whole structure of English society was reproduced in the trenches. The officers had servants and separate quarters. It was a microcosm. We need it as a baseline assumption. Like a framework for the story."

"But a foxhole could reproduce American society just the same. Kind of quick and dirty, kind of temporary. Two recent arrivals, required to somehow get along with each other. Like a metaphor of its own. Maybe one of them could have been drafted out of Harvard or Princeton or somewhere, and the other is a street kid from Boston or the Bronx. At first they have nothing in common."

"Cliché."

"So is a country-house drama with mud. You were a good enough writer to make that work. You could make anything work."

He said, "That's not the worst of it."

"What more?"

"He said the hero can't be a loner. He said there has to be a buddy, from the first scene onward."

"Really?"

"He said he realized all along in the back of his mind he had been seeing it as a buddy movie set in Korea. He said my draft was the right heart in the wrong body. He said it wasn't a story about one Englishman. It was a story about two Americans. He said sometimes writers don't truly understand what they've written."

"What did you say?"

"Nothing. I was speechless. I went out for another cigarette."

"How long this time?"

"The same. Ten minutes. Maybe more. But don't worry. What was there to talk about? Suddenly I realized I had gotten it ass-backward. I thought I was owed one particular thing, because I had been a good worker. They thought I was owed a different thing. Which was not to laugh in my face and turn the picture down flat. They were looking for a polite exit strategy. Ideally they wanted me to withdraw the proposal. That would save everyone's face. Artistic differences. So they were nibbling it to death. Trying to make me break."

"Did you?"

"Turned out I was wrong. They were serious. I got back in and started to say something about how we had all agreed at the get-go that the artistic vision would not be compromised, ever, in any way, and now here we were with two best buds in Korea. But he cut me off early and said, sure, don't worry, he understood. He said I had to remember every single idea in the history of the motion picture industry had gotten a little scuffed up when it came out of the writer's head and collided with reality. Even the famous screenplays that get studied in film school. The lady who brought the coffee added some of the lines. It was about what worked on the day."

"What did you say?"

"Nothing."

"You didn't go out again, did you?"

"I wanted to. I wanted to register some kind of protest. But I didn't need to go out. Not even me. So I stayed at the table. He took it as an invitation to keep on talking. He said I could reclaim the movie by writing a great death scene."

"Reclaim it?"

"He said I could own it again."

"Whose death?"

"The buddy's. Obviously the hero has to be alone for the final stage of his journey. So the buddy has to go, page ninety or thereabouts. He said he was sure I would knock it out of the park. Not just the final flutter. But the reasons for it. What was driving that guy to his doom?"

"What did you say?"

"Nothing. My head was spinning. First a completely unnecessary secondary character was being forced into my movie, thereby making it actually no longer my movie, but then I'm being told it can be my movie again if I yank the intruder out again. Seemed staggeringly Freudian to me. He had such faith I could do it. He said it will be my finest work. Which would be ironic. Maybe the Writers' Guild would give me a special award. Best Death of a Producer-Imposed Trope."

"What happened next?"

"I left. I skipped dessert. I came home."

"I'm glad," she said.

She snuggled closer.

She said, "But I'm sorry the world will never see that scene. He was right about that, at least. You would have knocked it out of the park. Some kind of noble sacrifice. One for the ages."

"No," he said. "Not noble. I think I would make it small. The big things have already been done. The friendship has been forged. I suppose the final scene has to be in a foxhole. The two of them. They've gotten that far by being strong. Now the buddy is about to exit the picture by being weak. That's the dynamic. I think that's the way battle movies have got to work. Personality is revealed by the big things first and the little things last."

"Weak how?"

"This is the 1950s, don't forget. Even the studio doesn't want to drag it into the present day. So people smoked. Including the buddy. Now he's in the foxhole and he's out of cigarettes. He's getting antsy. People smoking means it's already an R-rated movie anyway, so twenty yards away we can have the mangled corpse of one of their squad mates, who the buddy knows is an occasional smoker, which almost certainly means he's got a nearly full pack in his pocket."

"Twenty yards beyond the rim of the foxhole?"

"And there's an enemy sniper in the area."

"Does he stay, or does he go?"

"He goes," the screenwriter said. "Twenty yards there, twenty yards back. The sniper gets him. It's both tiny and monumental. He wanted a cigarette. That was all. A small human weakness. But it was also a determination to live the way he wanted to, or not live at all. Which then explains and informs his earlier actions. We know him fully only at the moment of his death."

His wife said, "That's lovely."

She snuggled even tighter, and scooched her butt even closer.

She said, "So really it's a fairly small decision. Isn't it? It's English accents in 1916, or American accents in 1952. Does it matter?"

He didn't answer. He had noticed.

\* \* \*

Two years and seven months later the movie came out. It was not about the British Army in World War I. It was compromised in every possible way. The screenwriter did not throw himself under a train. Instead he moved house, higher up the canyon. Then eight months later the buddy won the Oscar. Best Actor in a Supporting Role. The guy's speech was all about how fabulous the writing was. Then an hour later the screenwriter won an Oscar of his own. Best Original Screenplay. His speech thanked his wife and his producer, the rocks in his life. Coming off the stage he pumped the statuette like a heavy dumbbell and figured some compromises were easy to live with. They got easier and easier through the after-parties and the interviews and the calls from his agent, which for the first time in his life gave him a choice of what to do and when and how much for. The years passed and he became a name, then a senior figure, then a guru. He and his wife stayed married. They lived a great life. He was honestly happy.

He never twigged exactly how his ancient compromises had been engineered. What had killed his artistic vision had been his cigarette breaks. They were ten-minute voids, ripe for exploitation. It was the producer's idea. He had done it before with difficult writers. As soon as the guy stalked out, he would call the guy's wife, to report the latest impasse, to get advice on what to say in the short term, to talk him down off the ledge, and then to build an agenda for the wife to discuss with the guy that night, strictly in his own best interests, of course, for his own good, because there was a lot of money and prestige on the line here, and in the producer's experience a little grumpiness would be quickly forgotten when there was a gold statuette to polish. In this case the wife thought, *He's right, you know*, and he was.

Megan Bayles

**ACHY OBEJAS** is the author of the
short story collection *The Tower of
the Antilles* and the novel *Ruins*, and
the editor of *Havana Noir*.

# THE SMOKE-FREE ROOM
## BY ACHY OBEJAS

Alina walked around the small apartment, sniffing the air. She had been very specific about it needing to be a smoke-free space and now here was the owner's preteen son swearing it was when she could practically feel the nicotine sinking into her skin.

You don't have to believe me, the boy said in perfect English, insolent and bored as he leaned shirtlessly against the door. You can find another apartment—and good luck with that.

She was sure he knew he had her cornered. Though she wasn't in Havana for the art biennial, everyone else seemed to be—moneyed collectors and curators who had swooped in and laid stacks of hard cash for every decent room in the casas particulares and for the few available in-law units. The hotels were booked solid.

Alina walked in a figure eight from one room to the other, trying to scout out the worst of the stink. There was a perfectly made bed with two flat pillows and a giant egg-like curve in the middle where she imagined she'd roll at night; a polished mahogany dresser that'd be worth a pretty penny back in Berkeley; a rocking chair; a bookshelf with faded hardcovers she'd explore later. In the room with the hot plate (meaning the kitchen), there was a table with a glass top, a toaster, a microwave, and a ceramic ashtray on the counter.

This is what I mean, she said, outraged as she picked up the ashtray. It was blue and shaped like a dolphin. I told your mother

I needed a smoke-free room and she said she had one, but clearly you let others smoke here.

Do you see anyone smoking here now? asked the boy.

I want another room, please—a *real* smoke-free room.

This is a *real* smoke-free room. And it is also the only room we have. Believe me, if you don't want it, my mother will be happy to give you your deposit back. She can get more from someone else. See this?

He held up his buzzing cell phone.

There are other people ready to take this room right now if you don't want it. He was smirking.

I want to talk to your mother.

The boy shook his head. It's not going to make any difference.

She stared at him until he shrugged and turned. Fine, he said, leading her down the narrow hall to a set of uneven wooden stairs painted different shades of brown. She followed him up, her face at his waist level, just inches from his bare skin, until she was hit by a blast of white light that almost knocked her off the stairs.

They emerged onto the roof, where the boy disappeared behind a series of snapping white sheets on a line. The building was on a rough-hewn and crowded colonial street, but here she could see the ocean all around them. Alina pushed a sheet aside only to be smacked by another that wrapped around her head and shoulders for a moment and forced her to pause to extricate herself. She spied the boy talking to a woman in a triangle between the spiteful linen. He was moving his hands excitedly and she was standing impassively, one hand anchoring a loose colorless housedress on her hip, the other pressing a cigarette to her mouth. Alina could see the initial slope of her breasts through the armholes as the dress floated around her. The Gulf of Mexico glittered in the background.

As Alina struggled to get around the sheets, mother and son turned in her direction. He slouched. Her grayish-brown curls bounced in the high currents. Finally, the mother stepped forward and held the sheets back like curtains.

You have a problem with the room? she asked, but Alina could barely hear her. They were in a whirlwind, the laundry clapping around them. The woman—her name was Margaret, Alina knew from their correspondence—repeated herself in sharply accented English, and Alina followed her mouth this time. It was plump and swollen and showed large, slightly crooked teeth. The cigarette stuck out from between her lips, improbably lit, and suddenly Alina was submerged in a haze of nicotine. How was it possible for the wind to be blowing that hard and smoke to still cling to her?

Margaret (pronounced Mahr-gah-reh, as it turned out) took her arm and drew her back to the narrow stairs. The noise disappeared the instant they ducked their heads inside.

We agreed on a smoke-free room, Alina said in English, breathless, her hair now tangled and stiff. She tried to run her hand through it but it got ensnared in a knotty mess.

Yes, that is our smoke-free room, Margaret responded in Spanish, but you're right, it is not really smoke-free.

They were standing on the stairs, inches from each other, when the boy came up behind his mother and tried to squeeze through. Alina stepped back, flattening against the wall as he pushed past them both. For a fleeting second, she could smell Margaret's breath, a mix of mint and tobacco. The boy clattered down all three stories and landed out of sight with a loud thud.

I can give you your money back, Margaret said, shrugging as she pulled away from the wall. Or you can stay. Up to you. I can give you discount.

Well, I appreciate that but it really won't take care of the smell. Alina wondered if Margaret's mouth was bruised. Her lips were red, almost purplish.

It's all I can do, Margaret said, sitting down on one of the top steps, sucking on the cigarette and exhaling a blurry serpent. You decide. Then she pulled her cell from her housedress and took a call, jabbering and laughing as if Alina was no longer there.

The next morning, Alina awoke in a ball in the center of the bed to the simultaneous beeping of the alarm on her cell and an impatient knocking on her door. She scrambled up and caught the bath towel she'd draped to dry on a chair the night before and wrapped herself in it. Just a moment, she said in Spanish, though it didn't come naturally to her.

That, said Margaret, pointing with a red-tipped cigarette at the loud beeping cell on the bed, has got to stop. Her English sounded smoother this morning.

A flustered Alina scurried back across the room and turned off the alarm. Then she pushed a strand of hair out of her face. A whiff of nicotine caught her nostrils and she felt her stomach quiver.

Breakfast is served, Margaret said with a flourish, bowing and pointing to the stairs, again with the cigarette.

Uh, thank you, okay, Alina muttered.

She watched Margaret come up from the bow like a ballerina emerging from a penché, her back perfectly straight, which caused the housedress—was it the same housedress, or did Margaret just have a closet full of those colorless things?—to sag and reveal her breasts completely. They were heavy and free.

You know, don't you—of course you know—that smoking is bad for you, right? I mean, you know that.

Margaret laughed. Oh yes, she said. Very bad. So is sugar. And rum. And a starch-heavy diet. And walking on concrete without arch support. Sun without sunscreen. All very, very bad. But at least I won't get Parkinson's or dementia. Are you coming for breakfast, yes or no?

No, no, Alina said, flustered. She closed the door on Margaret's indulgent smile and turned around. The window across the room, she hadn't noticed the day before, was covered in a tarry grime.

After a full day at the National Library, Alina met up for dinner with a professor from the University of Havana's literature department. To her surprise, the professor—whom she knew only via e-mail—had brought both her husband and her brother. The husband turned out to be a bureaucrat of some sort and the brother a cab driver angling to hook up with a foreigner—meaning her, even though she'd been born in Havana. All three were Olympic smokers; the husband—stern, his nose wide and ruddy—silently puffed on a cigar and stared at her throughout the meal. The fumes came thick and white from his nose, like a long horseshoe mustache. The brother told bad jokes and touched her arm with a familiarity that unsettled her. He smoked hand-rolled cigarettes, one after the other, until they were nubs. By the time dessert rolled around, she had crossed her arms over her chest and was holding her breath.

When she got back to the house, not a single light was on in the vestibule or living room, and she had to use her phone to make her way to the stairs. As she passed the kitchen, she heard laughter and banging and leaned slightly against the door, only to catch a glimpse of Margaret, now sitting on the counter and rolling her hips, cigarette in her right hand, while another woman pumped her arm under her housedress. Alina jerked back, a hive of blue-green smoke buzzing around her head, and stumbled to the stairs as stealthily as she could. She was sure Margaret hadn't seen her but completely unsure if she would have cared if she had.

In her room, the sounds from the kitchen drifted up louder and clearer. Alina dug in her travel bag for the earplugs she used on the plane and lit a lavender candle with the hope of dispelling the stench. The women downstairs were giggling, screaming. Alina could swear someone was beating a pot like a drum; chairs fell, furniture scraped the floor. The plugs were useless and she pulled them back out.

She threw herself facedown on the bed, put a pillow in the hollow center to keep from caving in, and grabbed the second one to cover her head. Now all she could hear was breathing: steady breathing, hard but controlled. No more laughter, just gasping and panting, like a train taking a curve ever so slowly, her body leaning with it, machinery squealing beneath her. There were flashes of orange, blue, and a flood of vapor. Alina pulled herself up to her elbows, bringing her right hand back from between her legs, and coughed.

Everything okay in here? It was Margaret at her open door, her face hidden behind a gauzy veil.

What? Yes. Did you just walk in my room without knocking? Alina pulled on the bedsheet to cover herself even though she was still fully dressed from the day.

Yes—I mean, no, I knocked, you didn't answer, said Margaret. I could hear you breathing—not regular breathing, but very hard. I wanted to make sure you were okay.

She dragged on the cigarette as if she was powering up.

Don't come in my room.

Your breathing was very ragged. I can't have a sick woman in my house.

You don't.

I don't know, said Margaret, and tilted her head as if looking for symptoms of some kind.

Alina shot up and closed the door, pushing the woman out into the hallway. She bolted it, then positioned the back of a chair under the doorknob. Later, Alina realized she couldn't remember if they spoke in English or Spanish.

Every day, a feverish Alina would uncoil from the nest in the bed, take a cold shower, and flee to the National Library or the university or wherever her appointments took her: a private apartment at the Focsa building, a house made of cardboard in Marianao. Everyone around her smoked; even in the Special Collections room at the library, students would sneak a vape or two. Everything was dank, the heat an anvil on her head. She drank more than a gallon of water a day, but seemed to have the hiccups nonstop. Every time she thought someone had invited her to drinks or a meal for a professional reason, they'd bring an unattached (or perhaps attached—who knew?) brother or cousin or friend along without notice. They also fully expected her to pay.

You know what helps with hiccups? a librarian asked her one afternoon, looking at her meaningfully. Did she also have a brother who wanted to meet foreigners who weren't really foreigners?

What? Alina replied. She was so very tired.

A good cigar.

A good cigar? You've got to be joking, she said, and gathered her books and notes into her satchel and swept out of there.

Out on the streets men blew kisses at her and, tasting her own sticky brown tongue, she started blowing them back, which only made them laugh. Her mouth was tingling, her nose was tingling, her throat was tingling too. She was so lightheaded.

Are you okay? asked one of the valets at the Hotel Inglaterra in English as she walked by.

Yes, yes, of course, she said in Spanish—but wait, is the biennial over? Do you guys have any rooms available?

You're looking for a room? The hotel doesn't, no, but I know someone . . .

Is it a smoke-free room? A *real* smoke-free room?

He pulled her close to him by the wrist. He smelled like a spray of violet water and a sweet, sugary cigar. She didn't mean to but she burped in his face and he laughed, obviously repulsed but also somewhat amused. Alina knew he was going to tell someone about this later, over a shot of rum and a cigarette no doubt. Never mind, she said, embarrassed. Never mind! And she shook him off, waved her hand at a bici-taxi, and gave the driver Margaret's address.

As soon as she settled in, the driver began to pedal, his calf muscles expanding and contracting like billows. She realized immediately they were racing—there was another bici beside them, and the drivers were egging each other on, speeding over potholes and rocks and barely dodging pedestrians. Trying to stay upright, Alina kept falling over to one side or the other in the passenger seat. She could feel her muscles working, knotting. The passenger in the other bici-taxi was screaming bloody murder, but she couldn't open her mouth except to breathe in the brume. Every second, it seemed they were on the verge of flight.

It's free, don't worry about it, the driver said when he dropped her off. He'd bumped fists with the other driver as he rushed by and was now laughing up a sweaty storm. Alina stumbled out from the passenger seat. She was so dizzy, so nauseated, she had to wait for the desire to vomit to pass before she dared enter the house.

She found a vase full of sunflowers in the vestibule and an envelope from the university addressed to her. The lamp was on but she figured she'd open the note upstairs. She began to tiptoe across the room to the stairs when she heard thin music playing from behind Margaret's shut bedroom door: "*Porque el sentimiento es humo / Y ceniza la palabra . . .*"

She was surprised to realize she understood every word. She stopped and tried to place the song . . . She walked over to Margaret's door and pressed her ear against it. The music played on but there was also a vague rustling, a shuffling, and she imagined Margaret dancing, swaying to the sad melody, maybe holding an invisible partner, maybe not. Alina's hand turned on the doorknob but it refused to move.

Suddenly her eyes were watery, her nose running; she felt on the verge of sneezing.

Alina? Margaret asked tentatively from inside the bedroom.

She dropped the doorknob, which rattled on being freed from her grip, and sprinted across the room to the stairs, scrambling as if she were being chased by a cloud of bats.

That night, Alina felt a weight along her body, like a leg between her legs. She tried to roll to one side and then the other but she was pinned. When she pushed up, her clitoris would rub against a cyclonic force, and when she dropped down, a heft would fall on her stomach and make her grunt. At some point just before daybreak, she prevailed. Whatever had held her lifted; a fresh breeze blew improbably through the room.

When she opened her eyes, she found Margaret sitting cross-legged in her room, on the chair that had been propped under her doorknob, in the same housedress, her bare feet black on the bottoms. She was playing with a lighter and an unlit cigarette. Alina just shook her head as she got up. She felt a strange tingling in her left hip when she made her way to the bathroom, where she washed with the door open, first her face, then her armpits, and, finally, between her legs. She brushed her teeth and decided against combing her hair. Her sniffling was gone; her eyes were dry. Her cheeks bloomed.

When Alina stepped back in the room, Margaret—who'd

watched her every move—stood up and positioned the cigarette between her lips. She raised the lighter and looked over at her.

Must you? Alina asked.

Margaret nodded. I don't know if you can stay here anymore.

Oh, I can, said Alina.

Margaret blinked. She lowered the lighter. I smoke a lot, you know. The nicotine will stick to your skin. It'll get in your bloodstream.

Alina imagined pulling Margaret to her, her hand going to the woman's waist and feeling the elastic band of her underwear beneath her housedress, the way her breasts would press against her.

It would all happen in a blue fog, and without a word.

**CARA BLACK** is the *New York Times* and *USA Today* best-selling author of nineteen books in the Private Investigator Aimée Leduc series, which is set in Paris. Black has received multiple nominations for Anthony and Macavity awards, a *Washington Post Book World* Book of the Year citation, and the Médaille de la Ville de Paris—which is awarded in recognition of contribution to international culture. Her latest novel is *Three Hours in Paris,* a World War II thriller.

# SPÉCIAL TREATMENT
BY **CARA BLACK**

*Dawn, September 1944,*
*near the Ardennes Forest, France*

I n dawn's blood-orange blush Mila laid the last explosive on
the track. Deep-green forest and birdsong her only companions. Her deft fingers pinched tobacco from her pouch, rolled
it between the cigarette paper, licked the edge, and sealed it.

Putting her ear to the metal rail, she listened for the vibration
of the milk train. Nothing yet.

Mila struck a match and lit her cigarette. Glanced at her
watch. Time.

She crushed the thin copper tube containing the cupric chlo-
ride of the pencil detonator under her heel. Wedged it carefully
inside the *plastique* and checked her watch again.

Perfect.

She clambered down the rail embankment to her bike and
rode twenty kilometers back. At the train station, she parked her
bike. Catching her breath, she shook the dust off her bare legs
and wiped the sweat off her upper lip.

Once inside the station café, she wondered who her contact
was; the gaunt man in overalls, who looked like a POW in hiding
or a mechanic? Or the man in a rumpled linen suit with gray eyes
who dabbed perspiration from his brow with a handkerchief? If
German soldiers decided to pay a visit, she'd melt out the door.

Mila ordered what passed for coffee these days—a chicory

mixture—eyeing the young woman at the sticky café counter next to her. Instead of holding the cup handle with three fingers the young woman cupped the demi-demitasse as if warming her hand. The signal.

She was Mila's contact. Code name, Azores. The café ceiling fan whirred listlessly, stirring hot fetid September air.

She caught Azores's gaze in the smudged mirror behind the counter. Dark eyes, hollow cheeks. Figured her for a fellow partisan based in the next forest. The Allies were advancing and needed the German supply trains destroyed. Sabotage was their business.

Mila removed her compact, prepared with loose powder, spilling it in a dusty pink patch on the counter. With her finger quickly wrote, 20 k.

Azores's hand wiped it away a second later.

Message understood.

Doing so, Azores's palm revealed red-brown scarred circles. Unmistakable marks of cigarette burns. Reflexively, Mila cringed imagining the pain. Had the SS tortured her?

Azores slid something into Mila's jacket pocket. Her movement invisible to anyone in the café. As planned.

Immediately, Mila bought a phone token from the middle-aged man behind the counter. Then descended the stairs to the humid tiled downstairs that held the WC. Mila slotted the token in the telephone and pretended to make a call. In her pocket she found a slim packet of German cigarettes, Nordland, nonfilters. Took a cigarette, careful to look around, scratched a match that sparked, flamed, and lit the tip of a cigarette. She inhaled the harsh metallic-tasting tobacco. Awful, these German cigarettes. She preferred rolling her own.

She read the message written on a cigarette paper inside: *Inform engineer to uncouple at Ville Comblay.*

The engineer would uncouple the first passenger cars, leaving the German supply sections to explode, and the partisans would handle the rest.

*According to plan.*

She replaced the cigarette paper back into the packet.

Looked around again.

In the WC, she threw the disgusting half-burned cigarette in the hole of the Turkish toilet. Pulled the chain.

At the mirror, Mila fixed her hair into one thick braid down her back. Took rouge and smudged her lips. Shimmied out of her reversible skirt, turned it inside out, pulled it back on, and belted it. Satisfied she had a different look, she smoothed down the skirt before mounting the steps. Guttural voices in German reached her ears. A raid? Stifling her fear, she waited, her heart pounding.

After a minute came the creak of the café door, conversations resuming.

Upstairs, she saw an empty space at the counter. Patrons murmuring. Azores had gone.

If Azores had been a plant, this message could be compromised. Or Azores could have left to relay info to her partisans. Mila tried to steady her nerves. Focus. Either way, she'd activated the time pencil on the delay fuse.

*Too late.*

Seconds later, she put francs on the zinc counter for her coffee, shouldered her bag, and gave a quick *"Merci"* to the waiter behind the counter.

Then out the door into the early-morning heat on the station platform. Mila kept walking. Kept her pace even. Her heart racing.

Would she be arrested?

Halfway up the train platform she took out her compact and checked in the mirror to see if anyone had followed her. German troops patrolled in the rail yard.

Perspiration beaded her forehead. The arrival announcement echoed over the loudspeakers. She stayed at the front of the platform watching for the Neufchateau train.

It appeared on time, steam billowing from the locomotive accompanied by the reek of oil and hot metal. A clanging bell heralded the short snaking line of railcars baking in the sun. Numbers chalked on their sides. The sun beat down, perspiration stung her eyes, her leg muscles ached.

*Concentrate.*

There came cranking, the shifting of metal, as men in blue work coats loaded wooden crates onto open railcars. Now German soldiers in *feldgrau* uniforms patrolled the rear by the train, their boots crunching on the gravel embankment.

After a small contingent of soldiers mounted the open railcars, she climbed into the first one with her ticket. The conductor blew the whistle. Mila felt a lurch and grabbed the car rail. Heard the grinding as the flatbed coupled to the cars down the track. The military supply cars.

Mila gripped the rail until the train chugged ahead, finally leaving the platform and gaining speed.

*Not out of the woods yet.*

Mila made her way to the engine car, knocked twice, and the door opened. The engineer's blue cap pitched low over his sweating forehead. His thick arms and grease-encrusted hands worked levers in the sweltering heat.

"Felicité," she gave her code name.

"Max," he replied with his.

Mila handed him the Nordland packet of cigarettes.

Max tapped out a cigarette, lifted it to his thick lips, and lit a match. He fished the cigarette paper out. Read it, then tossed it in the stoked furnace.

"We're carrying two extra passenger cars," he said.

A complication. The mission was to cut off the munitions supply to Bastogne.

"We weren't informed," she said. "The explosive goes off at 9:00."

He shrugged. Blistering heat came from the coal-fed engine. "*Pas de problème*. The passenger train only goes to the next station." He put the cigarettes in his pocket.

"You know what to do?"

He nodded. "Everything ready?"

She nodded.

She returned to the first passenger car. Tired, so tired. No sleep last night and she struggled to stay alert. She fingered the *carte d'identité* in her pocket. Worried since the name on this one was already known by the Gestapo.

A group of ten or so young boys in short pants sat in the car, their bare legs dangling from the seats. A young woman, Mila figured their teacher or chaperone, passed out *langues de chats*—butter biscuits shaped like cats' tongues. Name tags were clipped to the boys' short-sleeved shirts; children sent to safety in the countryside.

"*Bonjour, mademoiselle*." Mila smiled at the young woman wearing a blue scarf with butterflies knotted around her neck. "How far are you going?"

"Just the next stop."

Relieved, Mila took out her small chipped-enamel alarm clock, calculated the time, and set the alarm. She organized her bag, her pistol inside, wrapping the handle around her wrist.

It seemed only a few seconds, but it must have been much later when loud ringing from the alarm clock jolted Mila awake. The railcar shuddered keeping time to the wheels clacking rhythmically over the rails. The train would reach the point soon and she needed to prepare.

The train rounded a bend and the passenger cars glinted in the morning heat. Laughter carried on the wind from the open windows.

As they hurtled past fields of yellow mustard seed bent in the wind, she saw a pointed church steeple in the distance. The bucolic countryside where one could almost forget the war.

She stood up, balancing on her espadrille-shod feet, reverberating from the clacking train wheels. A measured, hypnotic pounding in the gusting hot air. Mila wiped her hands, sooty from the windowsill, on her skirt. Her tongue was parched. She pinned up her braid in the heat. Apprehensive, she looked at the time.

Had the engineer miscalculated? The cars should have been uncoupled ten minutes ago.

Or were the cars already uncoupled? Something didn't seem right. He needed to explain.

She slid the railcar door open to the space between the carriages holding luggage racks and the WC.

Then came a crunch. A thundering shaking. The unmistakable sound of an explosion.

*On time.*

She felt for the gun in her bag.

Then a screeching whine and she was thrown across the floor. Rammed against the metal siding. Pain shot up her shoulder.

More thundering of an explosion.

Her body jerked. A whining of steel against steel as the train derailed. From the window, orange-red sparks painted the morning like fireworks.

The force shot her back against the door, pinned her down

under suitcases, the collapsing luggage racks. She heard cries and shouts from the children.

This wasn't supposed to be happening. They should have been past the explosive site. Why hadn't the engineer uncoupled the passenger cars?

Screams. The screaming she heard came from her throat. The train had shuddered onto its side, and she was pinned against the damaged half. The rest of the car crumpled, an accordion of mangled metal.

She pulled herself up, willing her body to cooperate—her arms strained, her nose filled with smoke billowing from the interior. Roast meat if she didn't get out. Or explode first. Frantic, she reached the twisted door handle, pulled with all her might. Flames licked the car ahead. Choking with the smoke, she somehow managed to pull herself out and fell onto the gravel embankment.

Where were the partisans?

Grass smells in her nose, dirt under her fingernails, a line of ants. Scraping her hands in the dirt to pull herself forward, her hand came back with a blue scarf.

The teacher sat slumped, her eyes open to the azure sky.

"Are you all right, *mademoiselle*?"

Then she saw the woman's severed arm in the grass. In the lilac bush was a little boy's torso. His legs in short pants dangled from a tree. The damn engineer hadn't uncoupled the right train cars. Horror coursed through her.

She pulled herself up by her fingers in the dirt. Her legs were on fire with pain. The thumping of boots came from the grass embankment.

In the smoke and flames, bodies were being pulled from the train.

"Saboteurs. *Ya wohl . . .*" Soldiers fanned over the embankment among the bodies thrown from the train, going through the pockets, the bags. Would they shoot her? Panicked, she pulled off the bag strap cutting into her wrist, now using her scraped raw elbows to crawl away. But her hands were sticky with blood. Her own blood. She threw her papers and documents into the licking flame. Kept crawling toward the bushes, her gun now in her pocket.

Cries of pain, the Germans shouting, the crack of gunshots.

The partisans should have surrounded the uncoupled supply train blown off the track. By now they should be recovering munitions, opening fire on the soldiers. But she saw only German troop trucks pulling up, heard gunshots but no returning gunfire.

Someone tipped off the Germans. Her mind went back to Azores . . . the train engineer. Both would identify her.

So terribly wrong: innocent children killed and her alone with a pistol to battle the arriving troops. She'd deal with them later. She had to get to the convent, recoup, and salvage this botched mission.

But her legs didn't work. Head down, she worked her way, straining to pull herself along on her elbows. Trying to half crawl through the crackling brush, grass, with dirt in her mouth. Angry tears streaked her face. Her scratched arms bled, her legs useless and trailing heavy behind her.

Shouts in German. Keep going, she had to keep going. Burning pain lanced up her legs. With her hands out she gripped a tree sapling as the forest appeared.

She pulled with all her might. Pull by pull, grabbing rocks and anything to move herself forward. Perspiring and panting, she kept at it. Finally she stuck a thick twig between her teeth and bit down. Otherwise she'd scream as her raw skin was scraped off her bleeding legs. Tree to bush through the green dappled forest for she didn't know how long. Then she passed out.

* * *

Mila came to struggling for breath. A hand covered her mouth. The hand belonged to a black bird towering over her. Cloying scents of antiseptic mingled with damp. Her legs throbbed in pain.

The bird leaned closer, removing her hand, whispering in French, "We found you at the gate." This black bird, Mila realized, was a nun, her pale face framed by a stiff black wimple. "You were on the train, *non?*"

She tried to sit up. Her elbows stung, her legs were bandaged. "Felicité," she said, gasping her code name.

"Valentine," the nun responded. The code for the convent contact.

She had to trust this nun. No other choice. "Where are the partisans?"

"Shh." The nun put a finger on Mila's lips. "No idea. The Abwehr's here investigating the sabotage."

Already. Azores had betrayed her. Or the engineer.

"What happened?"

Gray gothic arches loomed above her. Cots with moaning figures, blood-soaked blankets, ringed what she took for a cloister.

"You bombed a train with little children."

"Things went wrong." Mila pulled the nun close, winced at the pain, and whispered, "Someone betrayed our plan. Our target was the supply cars going to the front."

She saw horror in the nun's eyes.

"You have to believe me," said Mila. "This wasn't meant to happen." Her legs throbbed with pain. Around her came more groaning and moans.

"Give me your papers," the nun whispered.

Mila shook her head. "Gone."

Not only had she tossed her forged identity papers into the flames, she'd lost her gun somewhere on the embankment near the teacher's body. Not only had she failed her mission, she prayed to God the false papers with her photo had burned. The little boy's torso swam in front of her eyes.

"*Schwester? Kommen sie hier bitte,*" a German voice barked.

"*Oui, monsieur, un moment,*" the nun said, and leaned down. "The Germans threaten reprisals."

She had to trust the nun. What else could she do? "They're looking for me."

Alarm filled the nun's pale face.

"Hide me."

She felt the nun's arms behind her back, helping her sit up. Her legs hung from the cot. When she tried to stand up she tumbled back. She couldn't feel any strength in her legs. Only the lancing pain. She couldn't walk.

"Bandage my face," she whispered to the nun. "Please, now."

The nun bandaged her face, hung sheets around the makeshift cot. Put her finger to her lips and stole away.

Mila fought the pain tossing and turning. She heard the cries of the wounded punctuated by a pumping of a hand-operated oxygen tank. Behind the sheets lay the makeshift operating area under the arches.

Darkness fell. Kerosene lanterns lit the temporary clinic. Intermittent shots rang out in the night.

German reprisals?

She shuddered and felt herself reaching for something to shoot the bastards. But her legs were useless. Her arms ached and defeat seeped into her bones.

On and off she dozed, her dreams filled with the young woman's lifeless gaze. The nightmare of the German work camp she'd escaped from with the partisans' help.

The morning, cream-yellow slants of sun, penetrated the shadows through the break in the sheets. Birds twittered in the courtyard above the tramp of boots. Through the eye slits in the bandage she saw gray-green uniforms walking among the wounded.

Looking for her. The sheets parted.

"Name?" a voice demanded beside her bed. She could see the pistol glinting at his hip.

Ice filled her veins, she cleared her throat. Mumbled "Marie" in a hoarse voice.

"Your papers?" The soldier smelled of tobacco, sweat.

"Lost? I don't know."

"Remove your bandages."

Now she was caught. Her hands itched under the sheets to grab his pistol. She could just reach it . . . her fingers were touching the leather holster, sliding up to the metal . . .

"*Désolée, monsieur*," said the nun. "The doctor insists she stay bandaged to avoid infection of her burns."

The black flash of the nun's habit. Coarse wool brushed her knuckles. Seething inside, she pulled her fingertips back under the sheets.

"Show me her identification."

"We've got so many patients. I want to help but I'm not aware of her identification."

"We're ordered to look for saboteurs," he said.

A swish of the nun's habit, the fabric brushing the sheets. "Of course, please check with Mother Superior."

Finally, she heard his boots shuffle away.

"Never do that again," said the nun, her voice close to her ear.

The nun had seen her hand.

"My job's to take them out."

"And risk the life of every patient here? Cause our convent to be burned to the ground and more reprisals out in the village?"

*Why not?* died on Mila's lips.

"At least you didn't say you wanted to save his soul," said Mila. "None of these soldiers have one."

"Killing brings more killing."

Mila wanted revenge. She'd bide her time.

What good was she? Hiding, her legs useless. The Allies were coming and her partisans were supposed to damage the supply lines to Bastogne.

Behind the rigged sheets her eye caught on a sagging, half-broken wheelchair. Wincing, she pulled herself onto the old-fashioned cane seat, World War I vintage by the feel of it. Fighting the pain, she grabbed the worn wheels, concentrated on rolling them over the uneven stone pavers and cracks.

Two soldiers headed her way. Sweat dripped down her neck under the bandages, her useless toes dragged on the stone. As fast as she could, she turned the wheels to the right. The chair glided down a ramp into a refectory with long wooden tables, a stone fireplace filling one wall.

Keep going. She had to keep this chair moving. Summoning what strength she had, she rolled the wheels down a hall. Then into a vaulted storeroom lined with sacks of flour and barrels of sea salt. Wanting to rest, she forced herself to keep going, drawn by sweet yeasty smells of baking bread. Heaven.

A figure fed wood into the fire below a huge wall oven.

Baking bread at a time like this?

Candles sputtered, throwing shadows on the damp stone. In the corner her eyes made out the white coat of a doctor. As her eyes accustomed to the flickering light, she gasped. The doctor bent over a man in blood-soaked blue overalls lying on flour sacks. Max, the train engineer.

The traitor?

A wizened nun, older and thin, straightened up, wiped her brow, and ignored Mila. She took a set of surgical instruments glistening in the light from a blue-and-white-checked towel.

"All sterilized, *docteur*."

"Will he live?" Mila said. *Live long enough to get the truth out of him?*

"Ask me tonight if the Abwehr don't find him," the nun said. "Hand the doctor the instruments when he asks."

"But . . ."

"It's only your legs that don't work," she said.

In the following days, Mila made use of the order and convent routine: the baking, her anointed role as nurse to the wounded engineer. But she couldn't stomach the morning prayers, only pretending to avoid the Germans' notice.

She watched for the soldiers and crouched, hiding under the huge rough-hewn wood flour table when they made the rounds. Her plan was simple: hide here, recover enough to walk, and join the partisans.

An old woman from the village brought the nuns potatoes from her farm. Mila traded the old woman cigarettes for gathering yarrow, red clover, wood sorrel, and yellow dock from the forest. Mila ground these into a paste using the kitchen's mortar and pestle. During her childhood, Mila had helped her grandmother make medicinal salves to treat burns, cuts, skin lesions. She winced applying her herbal salve, smelling of plants and the forest, on the raw, singed flesh of her legs. Even applied her ointment to the engineer's wounds.

Each day, Valentine, the nun, joined her—wrapping bandages and sterilizing surgical instruments. Sister Valentine, as she called her, was around the same age as Mila.

"Your salve is healing your burns," said Sister Valentine. "You're good with patients. A natural healer."

"My mother was a nurse," she said. "But that's not my calling."

"Why not? Your mother taught you well, obviously. Wouldn't she be glad to know how you're helping?"

Mila looked at the birds in the courtyard, the green canopy of trees. Cast back into the past for a moment, she struggled to explain. "My mother treated fellow prisoners at a women's camp. One of the guards accused her of stealing. The Boche beat her to death. My father disappeared in a roundup. Me, I'm getting them back . . ." Mila stopped rolling a bandage. "But you wouldn't understand."

"Why's that?"

"What do you know of that hell? Your family gone. You just pray for everyone's souls."

"I took my vows last year. It released me to let the past go." A tranquility showed in Sister Valentine's eyes. "I'm guided by God's vision in how to help those who need help."

Mila took a pinch of tobacco, papers, and rolled a cigarette from her hidden stash. Lit it, trying to think of a comeback. But at that moment a soldier walked through the cloister ward. Mila put her head down before he could glimpse her now-unbandaged face. His heavy boots clomped on the stone coming toward them.

Had he recognized her? Matched her face to a *Wanted* poster? Her hand trembled, the cigarette smoke in a crazy spiral.

Her nerves rattled even after he'd passed by.

A day later the nuns brought in a bandaged young woman for Mila's help. The woman lay semiconscious. Mila removed her jacket and felt something heavy in the pocket.

A wallet with fifty francs, ration coupons, and her *carte*

*d'identité*. Sylvie Villon, age twenty-four, a teacher in Rouen. But the photo on the card startled her. This was the young woman from the train, the dead woman whose blue scarf with butterflies she'd found on the embankment by her severed arm. This injured young woman only had a vague resemblance to the dead teacher. The teacher whose death she'd caused.

By mistake the dead woman's papers had gone into this young woman's pocket. Mila thought quick. When no one looked she hid them.

Her burns itched less now. Her burned skin was shedding on her legs revealing spots of new pink skin. She chopped off her braid with the surgical scissors so her hair more resembled the teacher's photo on the ID. She forced herself to stand, put weight on her legs. Using a broom, she made herself take a step. Then another. Mila planned and envisioned her escape to the forest and to finding the partisans. At night by the oven, as the loaves baked, the engineer spoke rambling disconnected words. She understood little, not knowing if he expected replies. A monologue punctuated by *eh voilà, compris?* She'd nod.

She found Sister Valentine in the chapel. Praying on a kneeler. The smell of melting wax from the votive candles.

"You have to help me," she whispered to the nun.

"Of course, we will pray. Together."

"Prayer won't help this situation." Mila heard the wounded. Those moaning in pain outside in the cloister. "Help me fight back."

"This is fighting back."

"You don't understand."

"So tell me."

"My mother treated injured women in the camp. But that wasn't good enough. A guard accused her of theft. The commandant rewarded her with special treatment and beat her to death.

My train to a work camp derailed and I escaped thanks to the partisans."

"I'm sorry." Sister Valentine reached into her pocket and pressed something in her hand.

In the flickering light of the votive candle, Mila found a pack of Gitanes cigarettes. French ones. Inside a message on a cigarette paper. She unrolled it. *Evacuate the patients slowly to the post office within two weeks.*

"The Allies are coming." Mila pulled her closer. "Did the partisans give you this?"

"Days ago. Nothing more."

"You must get them a message. Tonight you have to help me."

"To do what?"

"Help me contact them so they know the Germans' movements. Tell them I'm here."

"I'll try but I won't help you take lives."

"What do you know of war? Losing your family?"

Sister Valentine took out her rosary. Made the sign of the cross. "My brother and father were hanged in the village," the nun said, her voice low. "Left to hang from the lampposts as a warning. They'd done nothing but the Germans demanded ten lives for every German killed. My mother and grandmother were in the fields harvesting the wheat when a plane strafed and killed them."

Mila had no idea. "That's why you're helping the partisans, I understand."

"Do you? I forgave those men. Left the heaviness of revenge to concentrate on good. Do you think killing will solve anything? I find peace in trying to heal people. To save lives. I think you do too."

"Never."

"You're afraid to let goodness in and you feel guilty for not taking revenge for your mother. Ask yourself what she'd say."

Mila didn't want to think what her mother would say. Or about the past. But the honeysuckle vines in the cloister brought her back to her family's kitchen, scents from something bubbling on the stove, reminded her of the honeysuckle draping the wall by her mother's laundry tub, simple things yet the warm feelings of home.

Mila woke up in the night racked by dreams of her mother. The last thing her mother had told her: *Don't let the demons win.*

As Mila washed the engineer's wounds she began to understand his rambling words. He spoke about his pigeons, his treasured roost on the rooftop of his mother's farmhouse, the gray-spotted pigeon who carried messages. The slow dawning of his meaning came clearer to her every night. He'd communicated with the partisans by carrier pigeon. Yet every time she tried to talk with him, his answers made no sense.

She battled impatience at her slow recovery, chafing to move on. Disappointed at the few steps she managed. Every day she forced herself to take more, until one day a week later she walked the perimeter of the vaulted cavern. Once, twice, and then she'd ventured to the courtyard entrance.

She longed to walk out past the old stone covered by flowering honeysuckle to the courtyard. It looked so peaceful, so calm now since most of the wounded had been sent to a hospital in Rouen or evacuated. Tempted for the millionth time to walk out the nunnery doors to the dirt road, find her way back to the partisans.

This morning she saw no French police, no German soldiers. Why not? she thought, breathing in the perfumed honeysuckle. But a prickling in her heart held her back. Nursing the wounded had begun to feel important, vital, and a tranquility seeped into her from the nuns.

What if she stayed?

Just then she heard the rumble of a car engine, slamming doors. She saw a parked black Mercedes with small swastika flags on either side of the hood and a Wehrmacht driver accompanying a man entering the nunnery gate.

Mila stepped back behind a stone arch.

Chills rippled her spine. Obviously familiar with the cloister, the man headed to the head sister's office in the convent rectory.

She couldn't make out the uniformed driver's features but the man with him looked innocuous—rumpled brown linen suit, round sunglasses, blond thinning hair, on the slight side, reminding her of an academic. A professor.

A French collaborator? But he was speaking German to the soldier. He looked familiar.

The wizened nun stepped out to greet him at the cloister's door.

"We know the saboteur's here. She's the last of the partisans," he said now in French.

*The last of the partisans.*

He took off his sunglasses to reveal a darting gaze. Those gray eyes . . . where had she seen them?

Then it came back to her. Her heart raced. The man in the café when Azores passed her the message.

Behind him was Azores. The traitor.

No wonder they'd found the partisans. As fast as she could, she hobbled back to the oven room.

"Trouble, you're just trouble," the old nun shook her finger at her. The wounded engineer was nowhere in sight. "He's conducting another search."

Mila saw the panic on the nun's face. "Who's he, that man in the brown suit with the soldier?"

"Sister Hilde understands German—according to her he's an investigator from Berlin."

Berlin. With her senses on alert now, she knew she'd put the convent in danger if she was discovered.

Sister Valentine rushed into the oven area.

"I need to wear a habit, sister."

"But rules forbid that."

"I'm sure the pope would grant an exception. Get me one from the laundry, please." Mila reached under the flour sack for the *carte d'identité* she'd hidden.

"This one's large enough for you." Sister Valentine thrust a nun's black wool habit at her, helped her put it on, and attached the starched wimple below her chin. "You'll go with Jacques and deliver the bread."

At the back of the cloister by the chicken pen, Sister Valentine handed her the basket with a bottle of unlabeled wine. A man with a red-veined nose sat on a horse cart. "He's going to the next village. *Bonne chance.*"

Before Mila could thank her, she was gone.

Jacques took the basket and the wine. In the heavy wool nun's habit, Mila's leg dragged as she struggled climbing up into the cart. Jacques clucked and the horse took off, tumbling Mila onto the seat.

For the first time in weeks Mila felt the sun, smelled the cut hay, heard cows mooing. Alive. Not hiding in the dank, vaulted cloister by the bread oven, the engineer's festering wounds, his ravings at night.

Gunshots came from the cloister.

Her heart sank. "Go back."

"You crazy?"

She grabbed the reins, turned the cart around.

"What are you doing?"

Outside the henhouse she got down. "Go get what partisans are left."

"Who?"

"You know, old man. Now." She slapped the horse's rump.

Perspiration dripped down Mila's back under the black wool. She took the pitchfork off the wall by the haystack. The driver, the soldier who'd accompanied the Berlin investigator, was coming toward her from the cloister.

"What's going on?" she said, pretending not to have heard.

He stepped close to her, gesturing with his machine gun. "Come along with me. Orders."

The sounds of prayers and women's screams came from the cloister. Gunshots.

They were murdering the nuns.

Mila stabbed the soldier with the pitchfork. Hard. As he crumpled in surprise, she pulled his machine gun off him. Took the keys in his pocket and the grenade attached to his belt.

The peace of the cloister was riven by gunshots and moans.

Sister Valentine was sprawled on the cloister's pavers. Blood trailed from her gunshot-ridden body. Her eyes open to heaven.

But what had God done for her?

She closed Sister Valentine's eyelids, kissed her still-warm brow. Pain lanced her heart. So senseless.

Seized by fury, she limped through the cloister, the machine gun hanging from her shoulder hidden in the folds of her habit. She reached the old oven. There were the engineer, the man in the rumpled linen suit, and Azores.

"Looking for me?"

"We've caught every partisan," said the man in the suit. His pistol pointed at her. "Except you."

She drilled him in the chest. Looked at the engineer and Azores who'd reached for a sharp bread knife. She shot Azores in the knees, sending her to the floor; next the engineer, who collapsed in pain.

"Now for you two, *spécial* treatment." She crouched beside Azores, pulled her head back, and took the knife. "Traitor." She slit her throat.

The engineer she'd nursed cried out, his hands on his bloody knees.

"You too." She sliced the knife across his thick throat.

That done, Mila took off the bloody habit and left it on the stone floor.

As she hobbled through the cloister, she took a pinch of tobacco, rolled it in the cigarette paper. Licked the tip. She paused and took the pin out of the grenade. Tossed it back. Mila slid into the driver's seat of the Mercedes.

As the grenade exploded, she slid the keys in the ignition, lit her cigarette, and shifted into first gear.

David Imperioli

**MICHAEL IMPERIOLI'S** first novel, *The Perfume Burned His Eyes,* was published in 2018 by Akashic Books and was translated into both Italian and French. The Rome International Literary Festival of 2018 commissioned his short story "New York City—33 AD," which he read at the Basilica Maxentius of the ancient Roman Forum. Imperioli was coscreenwriter of Spike Lee's *Summer of Sam* and writer/director of the film *The Hungry Ghosts.* He also wrote five episodes of *The Sopranos* for HBO, in addition to playing the Emmy Award–winning role of Christopher Moltisanti.

# YASIRI
## BY MICHAEL IMPERIOLI

*We found a man in a canoe . . . he had with him some dried
leaves which are in high value among them, for a quantity of it
was brought to me at San Salvador.*

—Christopher Columbus, *Journals*

*Domingo, 7 de Octubre*

Chu will come for me a little past eleven, which means we
will have to hurry in order to begin precisely at the stroke of
midnight. Chu has brought me many clients over the past
five years and for that I am grateful to him. Our relationship has
been beneficial for us both and for the many people who have
been in need of my services.

But tonight . . . tonight will be different.

Chu has asked me to lie. And I am very ashamed to admit
that I have agreed to lie. And though I have a very good reason,
a reason that is not based on greed or my own personal gain or
profit, it remains a lie and for that I will pay. Skillful means is not
an acceptable excuse in my line of work; the lie carries its own
weight of negativity.

I have always kept my *cuadro* clean. That is, I have always
used my gift with integrity. But tonight I have consented to
something that puts my gift in jeopardy. I have agreed to this, so
do not feel sorry for me. I will be judged; my sin will be measured
in terms of damage inflicted, nature of intent, and final result. I

will accept punishment and do penance. I go to be sentenced willingly.

I am what is called a *vidente*, a seer. I am not an *interventor*, "one who intervenes." Chu has told tonight's client (a very rich American who builds apartment buildings) that I am an *interventor* and will be able to affect and influence whatever fateful situation the client has found himself in. The truth is that I have no ability to intervene on anyone's behalf, no ability to change or manipulate the fabric of reality. As I said, I am a seer. Or more accurately, "He" is the seer, "The Leaf" is the seer and I am His voice. He (The Leaf) is the holder of power, my gift is the means to interpret what He sees.

"He has eyes. You are His mouth"—the words of my mother's mother, my Grandma Martita.

Yes, I am His mouth, but still they call me a seer.

In addition to being a seer, I am also a *torcedor*—a roller. And despite how the two skills may seem to go hand in hand, it is very rare that one person would be adept at both. I do want to state, for the record, that rolling (and cutting or shredding) is not something I pursued to enhance my craft of seeing. I am merely fortunate to be the heiress to two lineages: one of seers and one of rollers. My mother's father, my Grandpa José Ivan, was a roller who married a seer. In most cases, these two lines would exist far apart from each other. Seers tend to live in the cities and rollers can be found predominantly in the countryside or farmland. The rollers that you might see in the old city are usually not very skilled and just for the tourists who are killing a few hours buying trinkets before they go back to the cruise ships. They are the bottom of the barrel among *torcedores*.

Most rollers today work for big companies that export their products all over the world. There are some rollers who only roll for seers and *interventors*, usually these people have other sources of income. A very small percentage roll for both commercial and ritual purposes.

Grandpa José Ivan was one of the few who rolled for both the sellers and the sacred. I would watch him as a little girl (before I or anyone else knew about the gift of sight I possessed), sitting near his feet on the floor of his *cobertizo* as he worked. I would often play with a set of building blocks he made out of ceiba wood. They were painted with bright-colored letters and pictures of little animals.

One day when I was nine he had me sit at his table and poured me a cup of coffee. He was rubbing leaves of different sizes and colors in his hands. He would rub fast and soft at the same time, firm and delicate, with *respeto*. That was the word he used most often to describe the attitude a *torcedor* must have toward Him. Never The Leaf, always Him or He, as in:

*He does not tolerate disrespect.*
*He does not tolerate abuse.*
*He does not tolerate overindulgence.*
*To dishonor Him is to unleash grave vengeance.*

It is with this mind-set that he would rub the leaves between his stained and calloused brown hands. He rubbed like he was washing his child or caressing his lover. So deliberate, so kind. Then he put his hand in my face.

"Tell me what you smell."

My first reply to this was: "I smell the leaf."

"No, no, no . . . tell me what you smell."

I tried for an answer he would like: "I smell Him."

"No, no, my little love . . . like what? . . . Like what does it smell?"

"Like leaf?"

"Beyond the leaf . . . like what?"

I sat silent. I was angry at myself for not knowing the correct answer. He rubbed again and put his hands over his own face and inhaled deeply.

"I smell the eight-day storm and the Trujillo fires."

He rubbed again, took another deep inhale.

"I smell the funeral Mass of Valeria Oquendo's babies, the twins."

Rubbing again and breathing it in.

"I smell your mother's twenty-eighth birthday cake, the pink one."

Another rub, another sniff.

"I smell Raffi's rum, the eight barrels broken when the cart collapsed on itself and crushed poor old Locoburro."

He rubbed twice as long and put his hands over my nose. "Tell me what you smell."

I closed my eyes and breathed in as deep as I could. "I smell the brown dog from Polanco's hill. The one they shot after she ate her own puppies."

I had no prior knowledge of any brown dog or a hill called Polanco's. I had *seen* for the first time. My grandpa later told me that he had witnessed the aftermath of the mad bitch who devoured her young out of starvation. This had occurred on another island during a hunting trip my grandpa had made nine months prior.

He put me on his knee and hugged me. I think he cried a little bit though I am not certain. I never saw him cry but he may have that day. I have an image of tears in his eyes. Shortly after this incident, my grandpa began to teach me how to cut and roll. But even more importantly, my grandma began to allow me to sit with her when she was with clients; a privilege not granted to my sisters, who were both older than I, or even to my mother.

My sisters and my mother were not seers.

This would incite much jealousy in them, causing me to suffer greatly for many years.

*Lunes, 8 de Octubre*

Chu was late. We didn't arrive at the client's house until well after midnight. In the past I would have refused to go any further and would have demanded he take me back home. But in light of the fact that the night was a sham . . . a lie . . . well . . . the time we would begin had no importance at all.

Chu must have felt the same way. He smoked a Marlboro in the car as he drove me to the client's house near Miramar. Chu had never, never, ever smoked a cigarette in my presence. The overprocessed, pulverized, corrupted, and degraded leaf was an assault and an affront on everything that I held sacred.

But on this night, none of that mattered in the least.

The rich American lived in the penthouse apartment of a building that he'd built and owned. In the daylight he had glorious views of the ocean, the lagoon, and the bridge. But at this time of night, all that was visible from the floor-to-ceiling windows were the lights of the old city and the tourist hotel strip.

His housekeeper led us into the foyer which opened into a large living room, dining room, and kitchen; all one huge, open space. The housekeeper said nothing as she showed us to the table where I would be performing the charade. I asked her name, and without looking at me she replied, "Milagra," in a voice that was barely above a whisper.

After Chu and I sat at the table, Milagra began bringing over the items I had requested: a bowl of cooked (but cold) rice, a glass of milk, three uncooked eggs, a large loaf of bread with all the crust removed, a bottle of white rum, and a small dish of sugar. She arranged everything in a neat row in front of me then looked up and smiled, silently asking for my approval.

I nodded, opened my leather bag, and extracted three Gran Coronas, a box of wooden matches, and a white ceramic ashtray made especially for me by Grandma Martita. It was crafted in the shape of the Hand of Christ, the center of which was marked with stigmata: a small bloodred island surrounded by the smooth whiteness of His Holy Palm.

When the aroma of the Coronas reached my head, tears began to fall from my eyes. It was then that the American entered the room. My tears were ignored and the necessary introductions were made; his name was Fred (which I assumed was fake) and Chu told him my name—Yasiri—which may as well have been fake. The American sat across the table from me. Chu said his farewells and offered to drive Milagra home. She conveniently lived near the bar that never closed, which was where Chu would always wait out my sessions.

Before they departed Chu asked when I thought I would be finished. I stared at him and didn't answer. He had never asked me this question before. It had always been two and a half hours, invariably 150 minutes. Why should this night be different? Should we shorten the time spent since it was all phony anyway? Why waste a possible precious hour or two of sleep . . . or drink, or cocaine, or whatever it was that Chu would be doing? I wanted to tell him to come back in ten minutes to pick me up and put us all out of our misery.

But I said nothing.

Chu said he'd be back at three and then he and Milagra were gone. I was alone with Fred.

Fred was in his early forties. He was tall and large-boned, tanned and handsome. He had a thick head of dark-brown hair peppered with flattering gray. He hadn't shaved in a few days and his stubble was mostly white. His lips were thick and fleshy and turned down slightly at both corners of his mouth. His eyes were red and moist and revealed that he was exhausted, his vital energies drained to low levels. My first impression was that he liked to drink expensive red wine and eat lots of beef. This was just an assumption I made, mind you . . . I was not seeing yet. It was not a difficult deduction to make. Many rich Americans came here and bought houses and condominiums to indulge their gluttony and avoid paying income tax by establishing residency for six months and one day out of the year. His kind was more and more common on the island.

Fred asked if I had everything I needed. I told him I did.

"A man I was business partners with is trying to destroy me." He looked toward the kitchen as if he'd forgotten that Milagra had gone home. "Can I have a glass of wine? Is that okay? You're welcome to join me if you like."

"It's better if you don't." I don't know why I said that. It wasn't true in the least.

"All right," he said with annoyance. "Should I continue?"

"Please. And please refer to your business partner by name."

He began talking in a rapid, manic burst of words. "Alvaro. His name is Alvaro. Alvaro and I have been successful together in the past but now he is proving himself to be very unreliable as a partner and I am constantly being put in the position of having to pick up his slack. Alvaro is a man without discipline, a reckless man who carries on affairs with many women, some of whom are close friends of his wife's. He drinks too much, smokes marijuana, and snorts cocaine. On top of all that, he doesn't really know the development business. I brought him into it and taught him everything he knows. He can't function in this type of work without me. But I can't rely on him anymore so I requested that we dissolve our partnership."

Fred looked to the kitchen again. He shook his head and continued: "My request sent him into a rage and a panic. You see, I have a great opportunity to develop the abandoned naval base into a resort complex. He knows this and wants to be a part of it, of course. It's a project that will be very, very lucrative. But I can't carry him anymore. My reputation has suffered because his behavior is a reflection on me and it's put my relationships with investors in jeopardy."

He stopped talking and stared at me as if he wanted my approval, my agreement that he was in the right, that he was just. "Alvaro's cousin is in a very high position in the Ministry of Health and Human Services. He has the ears of the most powerful politicians and can make a lot of trouble for me if he wanted to. And not only does Alvaro want to be involved in the naval base project, but as revenge for my wish to be rid of him, he wants to become the majority partner, which is what I've been throughout the relationship. I tried to reason with him and presented my case and made a very generous offer to dissolve the partnership, but he refused and has threatened to ruin me by spreading poisonous lies and rumors among our associates."

He looked to the kitchen a third time. "Can I get myself a glass of water? Is that permitted?" His annoyance had turned to anger.

"Yes. Water is fine."

He did not offer me any and returned from the kitchen with a tall glass of ice water and sat back down across from me. "Can you help me?" It pained him to ask this of me. He was not a man used to asking for help. Especially from a young woman. A young native woman.

"Of course I can help. It's why I am here." It was the most blatant lie I've ever told. "What would you like me to do?"

"I want Alvaro out of my life. He's an evil man, he beats his wife and abuses his children. He abused his son so terribly he drove the poor boy to suicide. I'm also afraid he may do something to physically harm me. I want him out of my life. I'll pay whatever you ask."

I could easily tell he was lying too. But who was I to judge? I stared at my hands for a long time, then I picked up one of my Gran Coronas. I had already cut all three of them at home. I lit a match, let the sulfur burn off, and then toasted the end of the cigar. I did not pray or offer up the white substances as I normally would. There was no need. Tonight was a perversion. A blasphemy. I didn't want to desecrate it any more than I had to.

I lit my Corona and puffed. It drew tighter than I was prepared for. For a second I thought perhaps I had been mistaken and it was not rolled by my hands at all. But that assumption was ridiculous. It was mine of course and I had rolled it too tight. It was shoddy work. Like work I would have done when I was a child. I took this as a very bad sign.

On the second puff I heard my grandmother singing a very old song, probably a slave song, that told of a couple who ran from the farm and hid in the jungle. They want to be married but are all alone in the middle of the forest so they ask the trees themselves to be their witnesses as they make their vows before God.

On the third puff I could smell my grandfather's aftershave.

On the fourth puff I tasted my eldest sister's tears on my tongue.

And on the fifth puff . . . it was always the fifth puff . . . I began to *see*:

Alvaro was a simple and good-natured man who was too impressed by wealth, power, and all their trappings. He was a carpenter by trade and had a small business on the island that did repairs, renovations, and a bit of light construction. He was introduced to Fred over the telephone by a mutual friend who lived in Miami. Alvaro agreed to meet with Fred when he came to the island and would discuss ways he could help Fred initiate a luxury apartment project—the very building we were sitting in.

When Fred arrived from Miami on his rented forty-two-foot yacht *Superba*, Alvaro, his wife Demaris, their sixteen-year-old daughter Rosa, and eighteen-year-old son Quique were waiting on the pier with flowers, chocolates, and pastries. After Fred checked into the Astor-Morgan, the most expensive and luxurious hotel on the island, Alvaro and his wife hosted a dinner at their home in Fred's honor. Fifteen of their friends toasted Fred and wished him luck with his endeavors. The next day Alvaro and his family drove Fred to the old city and showed him the fort and the cathedral. Demaris prepared a picnic lunch and they ate in the park on a hill that overlooked the sea.

In the evening, Fred invited Alvaro to dine with him at the hotel. He explained in detail to Alvaro what his plans were and what he needed in order to accomplish them. Over after-dinner Scotch, Fred proposed they work together on the project. Alvaro was overjoyed. They shook hands and Fred made a toast to the success of Porta Liguria, the name Fred had already chosen for their building.

The next day they visited a potential site for the project and then had lunch at Fred's hotel. As they lingered over espressos, the manager of the hotel brought over a folder of documents and handed them to Fred. Fred explained to Alvaro that he had taken the liberty of having his attorney draw up a simple agreement that would create the new company they would use to build Porta Liguria. Fred explained in detail how this would work and what Alvaro's payments and responsibilities would be. Alvaro looked over the three-page document and was ready to sign immediately, but Fred insisted Alvaro have his own lawyer look it over first. Alvaro took his new friend's advice and two days later the agreement was signed and notarized.

This was the beginning of what promised to be a fruitful pairing. Fred had financial resources and investors in Florida, Arizona, and Texas, and had no problem funding the project. Alvaro was able to hire the necessary local crews and subcontractors and was also skilled at knowing the palms that needed to be greased in order to expedite their affairs. In the first year, Alvaro made more money then he had ever made in his life. This was before the building was even finished and its apartments sold off. Things were going so well that they began looking at sites for a second project. Fred said he could easily get the financing for another building and was having contracts drawn up by his lawyer in Miami.

Alvaro could not believe his luck. He and Demaris started looking for a new house in one of the city's best neighborhoods. When Fred delivered the contracts to Alvaro he asked him to have his lawyer review them as quickly as possible in order to secure a particular investor. Alvaro, distracted by his desire to surprise Demaris with a down payment on a house, forgot to bring the contracts to his lawyer. He was so happy and had grown to trust Fred so much that he read through the contracts himself. Feeling that all was in order, Alvaro signed the documents and returned them to Fred. Fred asked if his lawyer had any questions or comments but Alvaro lied and said no, everything was fine.

The next day Alvaro drove Demaris to a house she had fallen in love with and told her it now belonged to them.

Around this time, unknown to Alvaro and Demaris, Fred began picking up Rosa from school every day and taking her on long drives down the coast. He professed his love and said he had fallen for her the moment he first saw her on the pier. She was flattered by the attention and promised to keep their meetings secret. One day Fred bought her a gold bracelet and expressed his desire to marry her when she finished school. That afternoon he brought Rosa to his hotel and they drank champagne at the bar to celebrate their intentions. After their second glass he asked if she would like to see the view of the city from his suite. Rosa knew what this could mean but she was in love with Fred and trusted him. In the living room he began to kiss Rosa as the sun started to set over the bay. They sat on the couch and Fred began to remove her clothes. When she was in just her bra and panties, Fred pinned her arms down and spread a thick piece of duct tape over her mouth. Rosa struggled and cried as Fred taped her wrists together behind her back and ripped her underwear off. She was helpless.

Fred did things to Rosa that the worst john wouldn't do to the most unfortunate whore found in the filthiest alley. Things that before that day were unimaginable to Rosa. And throughout the entire ordeal Fred took pictures. When he was finished with her, he showed her the bathroom and handed her a bar of soap and a towel. After she washed and dressed he gave her money for a taxi and showed her to the door.

Shortly after his assault on Rosa, Fred hired a private detective to surveil Alvaro's son Quique. Quique was a slight and soft-spoken young man whose features were less than masculine in Fred's opinion. Fred had suspicions about him from the first time he'd dined at Alvaro's home and the detective found evidence that confirmed Fred's theory: Quique, who was now in his first year of college studying education, hung out in the gay bars downtown. Quique kept to a pretty consistent schedule of specific bars on specific nights and the detective gave his itinerary to Fred. It was a Friday night when Fred took a taxi from his hotel to La Maria for a cocktail. Quique was sitting alone at the end of the bar sipping a glass of white wine. The seat next to him was empty and it appeared he was waiting for someone. Fred walked directly over and asked if the empty seat was taken. Quique said no before he turned his head and a split-second later he was looking right at Fred. Quique went red with embarrassment and stuttered as he tired to explain why he was there. Fred smiled, rested his hand on the boy's shoulder, and said, "Your secret is safe with me . . . Can I buy you a drink?" Fred told him that he was pleasantly surprised to find Quique in the bar and that he'd always felt an attraction to the boy. He asked Quique if he liked "to party." They went into the men's room together and Fred gave Quique three large hits of cocaine. The pair stayed in the bar for two hours talking, drinking, and even briefly dancing together. Quique got very high and drunk and called his mother to say he would be staying at a friend's house.

In the taxi, Fred discreetly and tenderly rubbed Quique's thigh. But once they were in Fred's hotel room things changed, and the same debauchery endured by his sister was inflicted on Quique. And all of it documented with photographs. When Fred was finished, Quique was offered the soap, towel, shower, and taxi fare. Neither he nor his sister ever spoke of what happened in Fred's suite.

It was not long after this incident that Porta Liguria was completed. The apartments sold out in a matter of weeks and Fred, as per the contract, took ownership of and furnished the penthouse. Alvaro was paid his share and used it all to purchase a brand-new Cadillac.

The site of the next apartment project had already been secured and ground was finally broken. Two months later, Alvaro received a registered letter from a legal firm in Miami. Alvaro was confused about what the letter actually meant so he took it to his lawyer, who scolded Alvaro for signing a contract without his knowledge and called him a fool. The letter said that Fred was exercising his "option of dissolution," which meant that Alvaro was no longer part of the new construction project and had waived his right for any cash buyout settlement as long as the partnership was dissolved before the building's completion. There was nothing the lawyer could do, the contract was legitimate.

Alvaro called Fred who was now living in the penthouse at Porta Liguria, but Fred would not answer his phone. Alvaro drove like a demon to Fred's home but the housekeeper said that he had left for Miami a few days prior and she was not sure when he would return. Alvaro drove to the new construction site but the project manager Nestor, a longtime associate of Alvaro's, said that he was no longer allowed on the premises. Alvaro refused to go. A fight ensued, and the security guards dragged Alvaro out to the street, giving him a nasty beating along the way.

Alvaro went to a bar in the old city, drank half a bottle of rum, and pissed himself as he wept with his head lying on the bar. The bartender told him he had to leave but Alvaro shouted and took a swing at him. Two customers came to the bartender's aid and together they forced Alvaro out the door and shoved him into the gutter where they kicked him in his gut, ribs, and back. Alvaro vomited all over his shirt and pants.

He woke up in his own bed a day and a half later. Alvaro had no idea how he got home and he could not recall much of what had happened. Demaris brought him some coffee and the details started to become clear. As Alvaro recalled how he had been swindled by his partner, his phone rang. It was Fred, who said he was surprised that Alvaro would be so angry, since he himself signed the rider that allowed Fred the option to dissolve the partnership. Alvaro confessed that he didn't show the contract to his lawyer. Fred laughed but stood firm, saying his decision had been made and he didn't owe Alvaro a dime.

Alvaro got dressed and went to El Batay, a dive bar near

his house, and got as drunk as he could without pissing himself, weeping, or causing any ruckus. El Batay became his daily routine. After two months of this, Demaris changed the locks on their house and told Alvaro she couldn't live with him unless he stopped drinking. But her words had no effect. Alvaro drank even more, and after his friends at the bar got tired of letting him crash on their couches, Alvaro started sleeping in his car.

One morning the police woke him up, knocking on the window of his Cadillac. Alvaro lied and told the cops he had drunk too much the night before and had misplaced his house keys, but the officers told him they were there for a much more serious reason. Alvaro's son Quique was dead. He had been found by Demaris hanging by his neck in the attic of their home.

The news of Quique's death reached Fred the next day. Fred's only reaction was to delete all the photographs he had taken of the boy. Then he ordered a bottle of tequila to be delivered to his house and a large quantity of cocaine.

At three in the morning he thought he saw Alvaro in the street in front of Porta Liguria. He watched as the man he thought was Alvaro went into the backseat of a black car and sat there for a long time. Fred removed a loaded revolver from his safe. He went back to the window and watched the black car for what seemed like hours. Suddenly, the man got out of the car and Fred realized it was not Alvaro at all. His mind was playing tricks on him.

Fred became very paranoid and began carrying a gun. He also hired extra security at Porta Liguria. His cocaine use increased and he would stay up all night and only sleep for a few hours during the day. Even with the extra precautions, Fred knew it was only a matter of time before a slipup happened and someone got to him. He would pack his bags and move back to the US, even leave Miami and go to Houston. But he had to wait three more weeks or he'd lose a fortune. He needed twenty-two days to establish the six-month-and-one-day residency requirement that would exempt him from federal income tax and net him a gain of three million dollars.

One night he told Gallo, his coke dealer, that he was worried that someone was trying to harm him. Gallo told Fred that he had eliminated one of his main competitors through the work of an *interventor*: "No fuss, no muss, no blood, no cops." Fred was open to the idea but the old woman Gallo hired had passed away, so he introduced Fred to Chu.

The last thing I *saw* was myself in the elevator of Fred's building.

I looked at Fred and he was smoking a cigarette, his eyes wide and waiting for my solution to his problem.

"You have a home in the States, do you not?" I said.

"I do. Yes, in Miami. I'm going back soon. I'll be gone from this shithole of an island in three weeks but I'm worried something may happen in the meantime."

"Perhaps it's better if you leave now."

"I can't leave now. I won't. Can you help me or not?"

"Of course I can help. It's why I'm here," I lied through my teeth. "Do you have an object that belonged to the person?"

Fred thought for a few seconds then shook his head. "I . . . I don't . . . I don't have anything of his. How can I get anything of his? It's not possible."

"Do you have anything he might have given you? A gift?"

Fred was frozen for a moment and then came to life, springing to his feet: "Yes. The Scotch. The Johnnie Walker Blue!" He went to the kitchen and took a wooden gift box of Scotch from a cupboard. He brought it to me. "Take it! Get it out of my house!"

I stood up and told him I had what I needed. He handed me an envelope thick with cash. I called Chu to tell him we had finished early and waited in the lobby until he came to pick me up.

*Jueves, 11 de Octubre*

Chu called me at eleven p.m. and told me that Fred's fully clothed body had washed up on the beach of the Astor-Morgan Hotel. The police were investigating but there was no blood, no wounds, no obvious cause of death besides the water in his lungs.

Fred's money had been well spent; his wish had indeed come true. Yes, Alvaro was truly out of Fred's life . . . as was every other being in the world.

*Domingo, 30 de Diciembre*

Today I began my new job rolling cigars for the cruise-ship tourists who wander the narrow streets of the old city. I am happy to say that my mother's radiation treatments have been a success. Her cancer is in remission.

The last thing I *saw* was myself in the elevator of Fred's building.

# PART III
## HUNGRY FOR FLAVOR?

Susan Johann

**ERIC BOGOSIAN** wrote and starred in
the 1987 play *Talk Radio*, which was
nominated for a Pulitzer Prize and
a Tony Award. For the film adapta-
tion in which he starred, Bogosian
received the Berlin Film Festival's
Silver Bear prize. His stage work
off-Broadway has garnered three
Obie Awards and a Drama Desk
Award. In 2015, Little, Brown published his nonfiction book *Opera-
tion Nemesis*. In 2019, Bogosian was
featured in the Safdie brothers' film
*Uncut Gems*.

# SMOKING JESUS
## BY ERIC BOGOSIAN

I've tried to stop smoking.

I know it's important not to smoke. In fact, it's stupid to smoke. I smoke, but I try not to smoke. Every time I light a cigarette I think, *I should not be doing this*.

I want a better life. But it's an uphill battle, it is an uphill battle because I try to do the right thing, but I don't do the right thing. And . . . I smoke anyway.

Fuck it, I don't smoke that much. The chances that something really bad will happen to me as a consequence of my smoking habit are slim. In fact, the chances that something else might happen to me for other reasons are far greater. Something will happen to me, though.

Sooner or later. That's guaranteed.

I could be immolated in a fiery plane crash. Or I could be infected with a fatal flu, or flesh-eating bacteria. Suffer a massive coronary. Slip on an icy sidewalk and lie there for hours slowly freezing to death. Choke on a chicken bone. Fall down an elevator shaft. I could be robbed at gunpoint and stupidly resist and get shot. Get hit by a speeding beer truck while crossing the street. Get dragged out in a riptide and get consumed by sharks.

Fate has something to do with this. But there is no fate. There's just . . . happenstance versus my urge to control . . . my fate.

Still, I try not to smoke because lung disease, specifically lung cancer which is the most prevalent form of cancer, is primarily caused by smoking tobacco, which furthermore is a product that has no constructive use and is farmed and marketed by massive evil impersonal corporations. If for no other than political reasons, I should not smoke.

So I try not to smoke.

Plus, if I ever do get sick from smoking, I will hate myself. I will hate myself while I am racked in unbelievable pain, as I undergo chemotherapy and radiation and surgery. As my bank accounts are drained by massive uninsured health care expenses and as my wife and kids and everyone I know hate me for ruining their lives. Perhaps my last thought on earth will be, *I was so fucking stupid to smoke!*

But see the problem is, I like to smoke. It gives me pleasure. I like to smoke because it makes me feel . . . different. When I smoke, I stop worrying for a moment or two. I stop worrying about all the things that might happen that are bad. I lose my fear. I feel happy. Even a little giddy.

Deep down the truth is I enjoy smoking because I'm not supposed to do it. And sometimes I want to do things that I'm not supposed to do. It's just a deal I have with myself. An attempt at . . . freedom.

Anyway, I'm sure if this were a bad habit that I knew for certain would cause incredible grief to myself and other people, like for instance being a serial killer, then of course I would stop.

I think.

But stopping a habit simply because of a potential predicament in the future, well, that's asking a lot, isn't it? Of human nature. Of me.

And besides, the problem with completely eradicating this bad habit from my life is that a vacuum will be left behind, a kind of hole.

Something would be missing that was there before. Something that made my life complete.

The man on TV, the man who knows everything that's good for me, says: "Fill that vacuum! Fill that hole! Fill it right up. Now what are you going to fill that hole up with? How 'bout God? Have you thought about God? Just use Gaaawwwd like plaster. Spiritual plaster. And fill that hole up with Jesus or Buddha or Abraham or whoever you like. Higher power! Replace the bad thing with the new thing, the good thing!"

Just fill it right up. And then . . .

I'll be fixed. I won't need to do the bad thing anymore.

Because God will be there. Instead. Right? Godplaster.

It's logical, right? *God is love.* Replace that cigarette with love, with unselfish behavior, right? That's spirituality, right? But what if I don't have enough love?

See, it's all a matter of relative degree. Because sooner or later, no matter what I do, I will do something. Something. And if that new something that I do isn't absolutely perfect behavior, then that new something that I do will become the new bad thing. The thing to be cast out.

*If thine eye offend thee, cast it out!* Right?

Makes sense. Sort of.

Not really. Because if I never did anything bad, then I'd be a fucking saint. And even the major saints weren't good all the time. They went through all this trouble of being a saint, and *still*, they were bad sometimes. Imperfect. Augustine and Saint Francis of Assisi and Thomas Aquinas, all those guys. Major league saints. Bunch of nutjobs giving themselves a hard time. Because honestly, who wants to be like them? Those guys wore hair shirts and ate dirt and gave away all their worldly goods and all that, and I just think that's going too far. You know?

And by the way—I'm a human being! Humans are supposed to be bad.

I mean, all us self-improvement people who spend all day

obsessing about our own behavior, we're just this tiny little seg-
ment of the world's population. Not even a majority in the United
States. Just this thin, thin layer of humanity, this thin, thin, thin
layer, like a layer of scum floating on top of a very big pond, who
have either the time or the luxury to worry about whether we are
eating too much cholesterol or not getting enough fiber. Or aren't
recycling properly or aren't getting enough miles to the gallon in
our SUVs.

Whether we've booked our next Pilates session or yoga class
or tooth whitening or colonoscopy. Most of the people in the
world have no money.

None. Zero. No bank account. No pocket change. No jar of
pennies on the dresser. Nada. All they have are the flip-flops on
their feet and the chicken clucking in the yard. Spend all their
livelong day searching for clean water and firewood and hope
they don't trip over a land mine while they're doing it. These
people don't worry about sunblock. Or flossing after meals. Or
whether there's bacteria on the sponge. They don't. They don't
worry about any of it. And if they get a chance to smoke a cigarette, they smoke it. Whenever they can.

Claire Holt

**LAUREN SANDERS** is the author of the novels *Kamikaze Lust*, which won a Lambda Literary Award, *With or Without You*, a Lambda Literary Award finalist, and most recently *The Book of Love and Hate*. Her writing has appeared in numerous publications and journals, including *Book Forum*, the *American Book Review*, and *Time Out New York*. She lives in the great nation of Brooklyn.

# THE SUMMER YOU LIT UP
## BY LAUREN SANDERS

Gray clouds hang over the half-empty parking lot outside the A&P. It's cold for July but you're wearing shorts and buffalo sandals, toes painted sparkly Spirit-of-'76 red. Little bumps stitch up your arms and legs.

"That's gonna stunt your growth," Vye tsk-tsks, then asks for a drag of the cigarette you just started smoking. She's being kinda funny, so you hand it to her. She tries pathetically to blow smoke rings, and you both crack up. So hard you almost miss the station wagon turning into the entrance from the side street. It's your family's vomit-green car with wood paneling, Michael alone in the front seat wearing the shiny sunglasses the army gave him. He's flying down to Florida after the Fourth to start training. He doesn't care that the war is over, the draft as fossilized as the Boston Tea Party. He says we're still fighting the same war over and over again.

"We gotta go," you say to Vye, flicking the end of your Marlboro Light and leaning down low.

"Where?"

"Your house."

"Okay," Vye shrugs.

"Come on," you grab her by the arm. "Now."

She lifts her guitar from the curb and copies your hunched-over walk until you get to the alley between the drugstore and pizza place and run like hell the whole two blocks.

\* \* \*

Top forty songs float out of the kitchen, where Vye's mom stands over pots of boiling water and sauce for spaghetti. You sneak cigarettes on the porch and pretend to study triangles for tomorrow's quiz, before everyone clears out for the holiday. Vye and her mom are taking the train to the city on Sunday to see the big ships coming into New York from all over the world.

Whenever you look past the couch and color TV inside, you catch the back of her mom in faded jeans and gauzy pink shirt-dress melting into the music, her long brown hair sweetly ruffled. She turns and drags from an ultralong cigarette like in a magazine ad.

You scrunch your knees in, tugging the sweatshirt Vye lent you over them to keep warm. The air is dark and damp and smells like lavender.

"Vye, honey, you girls ready?" her mother calls, and Vye blows a final mouthful of smoke toward the street before adjusting the guitar on her back.

"You ever take that thing off?"

She shakes her head hard, like she's flinging bugs out of her scalp, then brushes past you in a way that says you're a moron for asking. Makes you want to bolt but you follow her inside. The house smells a little bit greasy, a little bit cinnamon-powder donut. You have never been so aware of scents. Candles of different shapes and sizes flicker in front of a picture window. You sit beneath them on a cushioned bench staring into the half-lit kitchen. Normal tiles and white cabinets, shelves bulging with appliances, plates, and bowls. The refrigerator is plastered with political stickers, flyers for rallies—women's lib and save the planet and Jimmy Carter for President—hours of the local health food store and public library. Vye's mom's schedule in the ER where she's a nurse, more bumper stickers. One with ballooning red letters says *LOVE CAREFULLY*. Focusing in you see it's for Planned Parenthood.

"I couldn't live without them," Vye's mom says, and your heart pops, caught. "Magnets."

"Oh, yeah," tripping back to yourself. "Our fridge is so boring."

"I'll bet your kitchen's not as sloppy."

"It's sorta cleaner but messier. Nobody washes dishes."

Vye's mom nods. "This one here can give you a lesson, maybe, she loves washing dishes."

"The hot water loosens my fingers."

"Loose fingers?" You look at her.

"For playing." She flips her guitar around and strums loudly, not really music so it battles the silky voices coming from the radio.

"Not while we're eating," her mom says, giving the steaming bowl in front of her a few final shakes of cheese from the green cardboard cylinder. Without a word Vye sets down the guitar, and you wonder what makes her listen. For all the screaming in your house nobody ever hears anything. Vye's mom scoops garlicky spaghetti with red sauce and vegetables, singing softly with the radio, shoulders rocking as she ladles.

*Skyrockets in flight*
*Afternoon delight . . .*

You imagine her down at the ocean on a rainbow towel.

She is divorced from Vye's dad, who moved back to Puerto Rico a few years ago. Vye said she sees him twice a year, more than you can say for yours, and she seems to like her mom no matter how much she calls her a Nazi for pushing her to graduate early, why she's taking summer classes with the rest of you just trying to catch up. Her mom knows the names of every teacher and volunteered to help with the Bicentennial celebration—a staged reading from the Declaration of Independence, exactly two hundred years after its first public reading. People are doing it all over the country next week. Earlier Vye's mom made her try on her outfit, a pair of loose black trousers cut to knickers, blowsy white shirt with a double-knotted bow tie. Those dumb triangle hats you've seen for months on TV. Vye keeps saying she's a pacifist and at dinner you mock, "The American Revolution didn't have pacifists, they're from the Vietnam War." You know because Michael called them sissies and hippies and un-American.

"That's not true," Vye's mom says, not unkindly. "There were many Quakers, especially in Pennsylvania, but some here too. They were for freedom but against fighting. They helped with the wounded soldiers."

She tells you about the different religions and cultures slapping up against each other here in the New World, offering seconds of spaghetti that's more watery now, a buttered roll with a few drops of honey on top. Paul McCartney's on the radio singing a song about songs on the radio. Vye twirls big forkfuls of spaghetti with both hands. You imitate her movements, rubbing your palms back and forth against the fork, and feel something you haven't felt in a while: like you can let the air out.

Before you leave you pocket the Planned Parenthood bumper sticker and two you've-come-a-long-way-baby cigs from her mom's pack on the counter.

He is not your real brother.

His father married your mother when you were little. Now you're old, with two younger brothers who don't seem as discarded. You hijack their ears from their father's perpetual barking (you never called him Dad, though you never knew your own), and he's been away a lot, working *offshore*. You have no idea what that means but your mother tells you he's a hard worker. He wears a suit, takes care of things.

Your mother is a drunk.

None of the doors in your house have locks.

You can't remember when Michael became *Michael*.

One day you're watching *Top Cat* and flicking Cheerios at each other, the next he's jammed up in your bed, reeking of beer and onions. He hugs you so tight from behind you can barely breathe, a poke against your back. Then rubbing.

When he says you can touch it, you do. It goes quicker that way. He puts your hand on his dick and shows you how to stroke it up and down, slow at first, then a fierce pump until it squirts. He never put it inside before he got kicked out of college and moved back home, each time telling you it's what you want. "No one'll ever know you like I do," he says.

You think, what if he's right? Then hold your breath.

After, you sit side by side on your bed, ten thousand pounds of air between. Sometimes he lights a Lucky and gives you a few drags. Flecks of tobacco stick to your lips. Before leaving he says, "Remember, this doesn't count, it's just me." You taste the Lucky in the back of your throat. He leans in so close you see the veins in his eyes, wayward freckles, feel his forefinger dig into your breastbone. "Don't you ever do this with anyone else."

July 4 you case the lot, lousy with groups of kids shooting Roman candles out of beer cans, others looking for rides down to the beach, sussing out who might surrender a real cigarette. The drugstore that'll sell you closed early, so no Marlboro Lights. All you've got is a half pack of pilfered Nows . . . *and who the fuck smokes Nows?* You know most everyone, at least by eye. Guy in gym shorts, no underwear, and hippie-blond waves kicking a Fibreflex. Girl in white skirt and tight American flag bandanna on top, she's that stupid skinny from drugs. The dirt bike crew careering in and out of cracked parking lines, stopping only when a black truck with two giant pieces of wood sticking out of the back rolls up under a streetlight. The kids pull out the planks, sand-bags and cinder blocks, setting up a jump in a grassy area across from the Fotomat. A seedy guy in faded jeans and matching jacket—burnout leisure suit—shouts tonight's the night, some Evel Knievel bullshit, as an audience forms. Kids pass around half-gallon bottles of vodka, tightly rolled joints. Two guys climb on top of the Fotomat to throw M-80s and cherry bombs. You are one of the few females, the only one by yourself. If Michael knew he'd say you're a slut.

When the bottle comes you drink, despite a rambling head-ache. Before the A&P closed, you'd emptied nitrous from ev-ery can of Cool Whip, knowing they'd stock up big-time for barbecues—the cans had stars and stripes shooting around the logo. Huffing surreptitiously under the creepy hum of fluores-cents, then carefully slotting each can back in place before tak-ing another, your entire body pulsed cloudy hits of glee. Coming down, you sat on a quiet sidewalk thinking what if you put the can up the other end? The gas might disintegrate whatever's in there, though it's the opposite of what the lady said when you called the number on the sticker. The word *suction* scraped your ears.

You're saving Vye a few cigarettes, not hard because they're fucking Nows, the pack stolen from Ms. Bonaventure who always says *it's not misses . . .it's mizzzzzzzz*, so you all call her *Mizzzzzzzz Bonaventure*, except when you sit on top of the pic-nic tables in the smoking area, you say *it's Mizzzzzzzz Goodtime* (because everyone knows just enough Latin) and the few kids out there laugh. You drink so much vodka the cars crawling up through the dim black night look like robots with raccoon eyes. You shuffle your hips next to the boom box and pick a favorite in the minibike jumps, putting down the few dollars you took from your mother's wallet while she slept, letting the taco meat burn dusty black. You cheer loudly with the crowd: HAPPY FUCK-ING BIRTHDAY, AMERICA!

When that song you love comes on you howl: *Ohhhh, wham bam thank you ma'am.*

You shake off your denim jacket and dance harder. Feel the cool air kiss your upper arms.

That cute guy who's been winning you money as they jack the ramps higher and wider to increase the canyon rumbles up and raises the stakes. What girl will jump with him? he shouts over the motors and gassy fumes. Everyone tosses in bills, sizing up the prospects who one by one back away, even the junkie girl who everyone says'll do anything.

You go, "I'll do it. What the fuck?"

They all chant a version of your name you don't recognize. Roman candles flit overhead in sparky orange explosions.

"Get on," he says, and you squeeze in.

First you circle the parking lot, your entire body rattling as he pumps his right hand in the air, then he brings it down to accelerate, left fist depressed on the clutch. You feel the air flatten your face, hair slapping across your nose and mouth as the crowd flies by, sulfur up your nose, red glare of the rockets. If you jump off now it won't work, so you grab tighter around the guy's stomach, the engine growling so loud you can't hear the kids or music or fireworks over the raging motor, gears roughly buckling, and a hotness on your calves as you circle once more even faster, dipping so low on the curves your knees almost hit the pavement. He screams a final time, gunning it straight to the ramp. You inch your hands back as the wheels clatter over the wood. A jolt up your entire body and you're weightless, flying. You reach your hands out—cover his eyes, you'll crash—but you can't—air flings your arms up, hang time—then the front wheel bangs down on the ramp so hard your head snaps forward and you grab him again. He pops a wheelie, circling onto the side street, shouting "FUCK YEAH!!!" You cruise back into the crowd a minor celebrity.

*She had her hands in the air!*

*What a pissah!*

Legs pure Jell-O, hands still trembling, and head awhirl, you make your way through the kids to your jacket, flipping the box of Nows when someone grabs your wrist.

You smell him before you see him, gut-soaked with booze.

He pulls you back into the alley and shoves you against the bricks. "Where the fuck have you been?"

You don't answer, hold his eyes with yours.

"WHERE???" He slaps his palm into the wall and winces, shaking back his wrist. "I'm heading out, ya know? You ever think about that? Anything but yourself?"

"I'll see you tomorrow, at dinner."

"What about . . . ? Tonight . . . it's a holiday . . ." He ducks his head and you realize he's hiccuping. Eyes shot red. "You're out here slutting around."

"I'm not—"

"Come with me! You're in real trouble!" he shouts, then pleads pathetically, grabbing at your arms, your face, your tits, trying to pull your face close and kiss you, saying how much you're gonna miss him, it's not like you have any friends. You want to scream, *yes I do!* and kick him off but you feel bad as he pokes at you, crying *why why why?* Maybe you could have stopped him early on. You wish someone would see and come over, one of the guys you'd just won big money for out there. He's crying, "You piece of shit! You little slut!"

Out of nowhere you say, "I think I'm pregnant, you asshole!"

The back of his hand smacks your nose, you hear it crack,

and for one second you are both stunned. Your face throbs, blood oozing down your upper lip, you taste pennies. He goes to grab you and you sink both sets of fingernails into his forearm like a cat and run toward the crowd. People tap you on the back, say awesome ride, shielding you to the first street of houses, your heart blowing cherry bombs. You zigzag through backyard sprinklers and fences, till you make it to Vye's.

Sitting on the toilet with the seat covered, you count rows of brown fish on wallpaper, head spins like you could puke. Vye's mom kneels in front of you cleaning the crusted blood out of your nostril with an ultralong Q-tip. She nudges your chin up, lightly touching the tip of your nose, and you flinch, *don't touch!* but the words won't come. Black spirals dance in front of you, a searing jab cracks between your eyes and you cry out . . .

"There we go," Vye's mom says.

"Is it broken?" Vye asks, balancing on the edge of the clawfoot tub next to you, zooming in and out with a flashlight to inspect your face.

"No," she says. Then looking at you as she grabs the first aid tape and scissors from the sink. "You're lucky."

When they pulled up and found you on the porch, you said you fell off a minibike. Now her mom dabs hydrogen peroxide around your nostrils and says she sees knuckle welts. Says it calmly as she sets the gauze square over your nose. Every ounce of blood drains out of you, stomach curdling like you might have diarrhea.

"Someone hit you . . . who?"

"Don't be a Nazi," Vye says. "She fell off a bike."

"This is assault," her mom says, and the walls pound. "You've been assaulted. Do you know what that means?"

"Mom, stop!"

"Okay," her mother says, standing up. "But you have to tell your parents."

She reaches over the sink to put away the supplies.

"I need to use the bathroom," you say, "it's an emergency."

Vye follows her mom out and you lock the door behind them, because it's there, like a normal fucking house. You sit back down on the toilet and empty the burning contents of your stomach. Everything in you stinks.

Outside, Vye's mom lays you down on the couch with pillows under your feet and head, a cold cloth over your face. She asks if you need anything else and you want to sink your head into her. But you bristle lightly, somehow muttering a no without crying or puking or giving anything away. She tells Vye to come get her if you look funny. Vye salutes her with two fingers, then swings her guitar around. She collapses into an overstuffed armchair next to you, her feet hanging off to one side, and starts picking out chords like the slow drip of a faucet, faintly singing . . . *C, E, G, C* . . . into warbled and familiar words . . . *nothing is real, nothing to get hung about* . . . you slip into mysterious strawberry fields and mountains, a seaside bungalow, tall ships and a guy in a sailor suit. When he smiles his teeth are made of coal.

You wake with a stir. Head throbbing.

Vye drags over a yellow phone on a long cord, scooches in next to you with a pack of Lights.

"Oh, thank god." You sit up slowly as she lights one and hands it over.

"Blow into the pillow," she says. "My mom says you can stay, but you need permission. Anyone around your house?"

You take a long, long drag and hold it, sip-speak, "No one who'll answer," then let everything out.

"Pretend," she says, so you pick up the receiver, keeping one of the plungers down with your thumb. You dial and the click-

click-click back of each number scorches. You say you're sleeping at Vye's, adding . . . *Yes, mom, I will . . . I love you too.* Vye's
forehead ruffles. You slam down the receiver so loud you both
lose it.

"Ow, ow, don't make me laugh," you say.

Vye puts the phone back and returns with her guitar, asks
what to play. You've each got a corner of the couch, staring
straight at each other.

"'Strawberry Fields,'" you say.

"I don't know all the words."

"We can make up some. Sing about poison strawberries."

"Dead cats."

"Broken noses."

"It's not broken. Remember?"

You look away.

"What's the matter?"

"I fucked up," you tell her. "Much worse than tonight."

"Yeah," she says, "my mom asked if you took that sticker off
the fridge."

"Fucking Nazi!" You laugh, softly at first. Vye too. "Ow!"

Michael misses his goodbye dinner. When the little guys ask
why, their father tells them he had to report early. Their brother
is a soldier, they can be proud.

Then he flips another burger on the charcoal grill and pulls
from a bottle of Michelob. Your mother fills a Donny Osmond
Slurpee cup with vodka and a splash of lemonade from the can.
No one says a word about the heavy makeup around your nostrils, the dark sunglasses despite the last gasps of daylight.

When you all finally sit down at the picnic table for dinner
your mother raises her glass. "Let's have a toast! What makes the
world go round? A good barbecue!"

Everyone raises their bottle or can and clinks. Sips.

"That wasn't my toast," she says sharply. You feel your appetite starting to slip. "To our missing soldier, may he find success . . . come on, keep 'em up."

You clink once more and your stepfather says, "Can we eat now?"

"I'm not finished!"

"Don't be a dimwit," he says.

Your little brothers repeat the word, pretending to toast each other a few final times. You feel the urge to rip off your glasses and show them who's the real dimwit. But they'd just blame you. Your mother takes a couple bites of her cheeseburger and returns inside. The rest of you finish eating without saying much as the stars blanket down.

The next day you look over your shoulder when you step outside. Every time you see a rusted station wagon a little bit of your heart falls out. Vye meets you early with a book of her mom's that talks about having an abortion. You look but can't focus on the words. Two days later you dress as a medic wounded in battle for the Bicentennial ceremony, Vye's idea since your nose is still swollen, purplish-yellow half moons under your eyes. Her mom lends you a long white apron and you scratch a red cross in front, fit your arm into a pretend sling.

She insists on driving you the couple blocks to school in her red Pacer, smoking a long skinny cigarette, looking like a *Cosmo* ad again. Vye says drop us just before the entrance, and her mom frowns, same as Vye but with added finger-wag.

"You're going to smoke, aren't you?"

Neither one of you says anything. She slams on the brakes and stubs her cigarette in the overflowing ashtray. The smell of charred tobacco turns your stomach. This morning you couldn't drink coffee.

"Look at my lips," she says, staring down Vye then turning to you in the back. "Look at all the little lines. Look at them. And the stains on my teeth." She opens her mouth wide and taps them. They don't look so bad. "If I can't appeal to your health, girls, please, can I appeal to your vanity?"

"See you inside," Vye says and opens her door. As you reach for your handle, she says, "Have you talked to your parents?" You've been wondering when she'd ask, afraid she might say something herself before you can pull together the 150 you need to get rid of the curse inside you.

"About what?" you play dumb.

"About who's hitting you."

"It was an accident!" You slam the door behind you, catching up to Vye near the picnic tables, and take a few deep breaths. She nods as you blend into the smokers dressed for battle, more blue uniforms than red, several in powdery wigs and tinfoil buckles on their black shoes. The few other girls wear prairie dresses and bonnets like on the butter tub. You laugh at each other's costumes, people paying slightly more attention to you since the minibike jump. One after another you suck your few last drags and head into the building to act out America's cry for freedom.

You grow boldly into your lies, the boyfriend from another town, that one closer to the beach with the perfect lawns and prettier name. Dress-up dates to the clam bar. You tell Vye's mom you stole the bumper sticker because you needed the number for birth control. Because you are smart, responsible. When you broke up he became a different person. "Any guy who'd hit you is not your boyfriend," Vye's mom says.

You nod soberly, begging her not to tell. You're not allowed to date boys, you say, thinking what a mother who gives a shit might prohibit.

Vye's mom buys it for a while, letting up on the questions when she's home on study nights. She cooks you steak sandwiches like at the deli, creamy chicken casserole topped with potato chips. You feel bad eating so well when every time you go home your mother's stacking bologna slices on crummy bread or pouring bowls of Frosted Flakes for your little brothers when they return from scouting camp. She lets the milk flow over the side, reads them stories from *National Geographic*. Everything's a bit easier without Michael. When she finally passes out you skim another twenty from her wallet. A few weeks into July you're almost at a hundred, you tell Vye, who looks worried.

"We have to move faster," she says, citing facts from the book that make you dizzy. By Vye's haphazard calculations you have only a few more weeks until things get risky. She says she'll pawn her guitar for the rest.

"That's like your third arm."

She flips her shoulders, "I'll get a new one."

Your throat swells, you don't know what to say.

"It's just a thing, you're a person," she tells you, and it somehow clicks why Michael wants to go off and fight in a war. Vye swears her mom won't notice when you leave the guitar at the music store and walk away with forty bucks, but one day after school her mom is sitting at the kitchen table, the instrument a blaring siren.

"You think I was born yesterday?" she says.

You drop to your knees and apologize. She says she's taking you home.

"No! No! Please!" You pull at her arms until she gives in and the three of you sit back down at the kitchen table. You tell her how your mother drinks, how she got pregnant at sixteen and had to live with her parents who hated her until she met your stepfather, who seemed to like her in the beginning. How she repeatedly curses at the women's-libbers she sees on TV—she calls them *women-fibbers*—saying just because something's legal doesn't mean it's moral. Several years ago when she caught you kissing Timothy Clark she sent you to a priest who put you over his knee and slapped your butt with a piece of plywood. All of this is true but sounds made up. You're terrified of what she'd do now.

As you speak Vye's mom twitches in her seat, an eyebrow up every so often. You map a clean line to the front door, then it's a straight shot across the street to the backyard trail without capture. She walks toward you and your throat clenches.

"I can't do it," you say, "I won't."

"You don't have to, there are other options," she says, and you blurt out, "No, I can't have it, I want it out of me!"

Tears ransack the three of you.

"Okay," she says. "I'll help."


The nurse hands you a couple of chalky white pills for pain, one for nerves. Vye peeks her head in, an Instamatic swinging around her neck, guitar strapped to her back where it belongs. She asks if she can take a picture.

"You're not even supposed to be in here," the nurse says, pointing to a black-and-white sign: no companions in exam rooms.

"Just one. *Pleeeease.*"

The nurse gives in, shuffling a few steps sideways to light a cigarette. You want a drag so bad. Vye snaps your craving face, your ghosted legs peeking out of the gown patterned with tiny gray squares, toenails frosted pink. The flashcube pops into what's already sickly bright space. Vye says move the gown up a little, but you raise your hand. "No way you're dropping pictures of my hairy legs at the Fotomat!"

"That's enough now." The nurse stubs out her half-smoked cigarette . . . if she leaves long enough you'll grab it. Vye shrugs, backing up toward the counter lined with cotton balls, metal canisters, syringes, and the half-full ashtray. "Can I have one?" she points to the slim pack. It's covered with flowers.

"No!" the nurse says, "Now come on, vamoose!" She jumps up past you and shoves Vye by the arm, clumsily escorting her out to the waiting room, where Vye's mom had dropped you earlier. You grab the butt from the ashtray and scramble unsuccessfully for matches, thinking how's Vye got the balls to ask? You're just a sneak.

The nurse returns and without a word removes a lighter from her smock. Lights you up.

"I'm sorry you have to do this," she says, her cheeks melting, dark rings under her eyes, probably more from managing a string of girls like you than a quick blow to the nose. You were the youngest in the waiting room, maybe the whitest. The clinic is in a black town, your first time there though you've heard about it all your life.

You smoke down to the filter, which also has flowers, though she seems more of a menthol type, a little spicy. When you finish she runs down the details again, like the counselor and doctor already told you . . . it's much safer now, they don't need to scrape. "It'll be over before you know it," she says, and you wonder if she's as nice to everyone else.

She leads you into another room, bright with lots of silver. In the middle is a table covered with white paper, lights hanging close, metal circles down at the end where another nurse gently places your feet, then a couple of sheets over your stomach. You vaguely register a flutter of voices, a guy in white saying you'll feel a pinch in your hip. The doctor you met earlier, his face both soft and hard, maybe the kind of father who talks to his kids, says relax and you take a deep breath, falling back against the thin pillow under your head. When a woman says hold my hand, you grab. A loud vacuum whirs . . . *you should feel pressure down there, if you feel pain squeeze.* Then a metallic crank pinches up your spine. You grab tightly without squeezing, just to feel her skin on yours, blocking out the noises, the galvanizing pressure, voices in your head saying you'll be sorry. The woman looks into your eyes and you see an angel. Sometime after that she lets go. The doctor glazes away, moving to the sink to wash, water running . . . so fast? A pang crushes in, like someone's kneading your insides with fire. The first nurse returns and helps you up, gliding you across the empty hallway to a third room with multiple beds, all occupied. She pulls a curtain halfway around. They bring you apple juice and sugar cookies.

You try but it's like eating chalk. The cramping's relentless, you see a lion tearing into a deer and you're the deer. You think you must be dripping blood and call for the nurse. Another woman moans from far off or right next to you, an elegant black lady in street clothes passes, staff muttering in low voices as they shuffle between pods. The nurse returns and checks down there, takes your temperature. She says you're doing great, and you feel proud.

At some point you catch Vye's head peeping around the curtain. She snaps a picture, and you give her the finger.

"For history," she says, before the nurse leads her off. You go for the juice again, cradling the paper cup between both hands like it's the first time you've ever seen one.

After, you stay at Vye's. It's Friday so you won't miss too many classes, and something's clicked recently. You can easily make equations out of squares and rectangles, apprehend the concept of volume, maybe you're not a total idiot. But those early days all you see is holes. You wonder if you're going to hell.

Vye's mom brings tomato soup and toast, even lets you smoke. The nicer she is the worse you feel. You read old copies of *Seventeen*, eat pasta with butter, swallowing a Tylenol with codeine every few hours. Vye strums her guitar with *Soul Train*, trying not to crack you up. You write down more lyrics to your "Strawberry Fields" song. Now it reminds you of the mall near the abortion place. *Let me take you down 'cause we're going to . . . Roosevelt Field . . .* You sleep twelve hours straight, the longest you can ever remember, and when you wake up you literally smell bacon. In the kitchen it's Vye standing at the stove looking like her mom from the back except looser, her hair a mess of jangly knots, jeans fringed.

She lifts the pieces of bacon with her fingers and drops them on plates already loaded with scrambled eggs. Four pieces of toast pop out of a toaster with wood paneling in front . . . like a station wagon.

"I have to go home," you say.

Vye drops the plate in front of you. "You need your vitamins."

"Who are you, your mother?"

"Just shut up and eat."

Vye walks you most of the way and before turning around says call her later, you can finish your song. You want to hug her or push her down to the ground. But you say okay, thanks. You hear the Instamatic snap as you head back toward your house and almost make it upstairs before your mother calls you into the living room. Everything's put away, the TV on low, lots of static. She's wearing a bathrobe with her hair wrapped in a towel, more makeup than usual. She takes a small sip from the green coffee mug that makes you shiver, lights a cigarette. Kool Milds—always turning the middle one upside down for good luck. Your stepfather sits on the couch aggressively turning the pages of *Newsday*.

"Nice of you to grace us," your mother says.

You tell her you've been studying. Say you're taking the Regents in a couple of weeks, you're going to pass this time.

She eyes you as if you said you're just back from killing a baby, dragging from her cigarette until the long ash curls off. "You need to watch the boys," she says. "We're going out. A celebration."

"What for?"

"What are you, stupid? It's your father's birthday. Well, yesterday . . ."

He has not looked up from the newspaper and he is not your fucking father. A familiar jingle escapes from the TV . . . *Who wears short shorts? We wear short shorts!* You slip back toward the staircase.

"By the way," your mother says, "you seen Michael?"

You turn back like she's crazy, fight of the century brewing in your stomach.

"Seems he never showed up for training," she says.

Your breathing stops. But you manage a shrug, pronounce words you forget immediately, and tear upstairs so fast the blood's dripping again. You're thankful for the pad in your underwear, everything's throbbing.

From Michael's room comes a brassy light, door wide open, and muffled sounds like someone's talking on a radio down low. You suck in your stomach to creep by when one of your little brothers calls out your name. Stepping back slightly, you spot the two of them sitting on the floor of Michael's room building pyramids out of packs of Luckies, eight, ten empty cartons scattered about. Deejay murmuring into a clash of guitar and drums . . . maybe the Stones.

It's just them. No Michael.

You walk in calmly at first, then blow. Kick down a pyramid.

Plow your foot into the crackling plastic, stepping on full packs as you swing your arms up and down. You're oozing blood but you don't care, dancing like a total spaz. One of the little guys laughs, and springs up with you. Then the other one. You grab both of their hands and the three of you stomp wildly, grinding down every last pack of Luckies into the dirty carpet, some cracking right open, others flattened to death. The whole room smells like tobacco.

Jake Hostetter

**ROBERT ARELLANO** is the author of five novels from Akashic Books, most recently the Cuban noir *Havana Libre*. He created the Internet's first hypertext novel, *Sunshine '69*, and wrote the story for a graphic-novel anthology from Soft Skull Press, *Dead in Desemboque*. He is a professor in the Oregon Center for the Arts at Southern Oregon University.

# CLIMAX, OREGON
## BY ROBERT ARELLANO

Ashland, deep summer. On the ragged edge of town, three Arabian palms stand sentry outside an oasis that's been open 1,001 nights, multiplied by twenty-five: Omar's Fresh Seafood and Steaks. That's the destination driving down 99 after work when someone throws a sack of rocks onto the hood of the car. Engine skips a thousand cycles but somehow the beater Buick keeps running. Through the passenger-side window I catch a glimpse of a white tail and what looks to be a twelve-point rack bouncing away in the trees of the college—not a sack of rocks at all.

The dining-room side is outfitted with leatherette booths and plush burgundy carpet, but I prefer the other end, under the three-letter neon sign, where it's cracked Naugahyde stools and linoleum tiles that still smell like the tar pits they pulled mastodon bones out of when the workers laid the foundation back in '46. I pull open the heavy wooden door and step inside. "Hullo, Robby." Bear tosses a coaster on the bar top to help me decide on a spot. "Here for dinner?"

"In a manner of speaking."

He shakes my usual and strains it into a lowball glass: Wild Turkey, straight up. The first sip is heaven to my lips; the second, a long draw, splits the fog in my head like a cold steel pick. It's still early and there's only one other customer in the corner, bent over his video poker machine under the red fingers-crossed sign. A television above the barback is muted on a B-list golf tournament. They say when it's real, real quiet beneath the bones of this old building, you can still hear the hum of the hot spring coursing underneath. After a big rain, Bear has to bail water that comes up through the subfloor six inches deep.

"What's goin' down, Robby?"

"Deer hit my beater Buick."

"Doe or buck?"

"Buck, a twelve-pointer."

"Out here we say six."

"Right."

"Did you at least get the venison?"

"He ran off into the trees."

"Next time, track him to the creek. A deer in danger will always go to water. If you hit 'em, you got to kill 'em."

"Like I said, he hit me."

"They all say that." Chided by Bear, I let that sink in.

I tell Bear about catching Dorris from forensics using me for target practice at work. Manny Dorris, old-growth cop, always at the station holding a cup of coffee but I've never seen him pick up a report, flashing the gleaming ivories like we've been pals since kindergarten. *Morning, Sergeant Relleno. Is it?* Not so sure myself. *Sure! Isn't every morning great to be sergeant?* He brushed past me and I kept my eyes locked on the double-plated glass of the dispatch window at the end of the hall. There in the reflection I saw Dorris stop, pivot, unholster his service weapon, and draw a bead on my shoulders, his expression one of undiluted hate. It made my spine freeze, but I kept on walking. Bear's only comment on my story is: "You ever need protection, Robby, just come to Omar's."

The front door swings open and silhouetted there against a blown-out column of Siskiyou sun stands a knockout figure in an evening gown. The way she sways inside reminds me of when my dad used to take me for rides on Sundays in his Oldsmobile, and I flash on a private nickname: Eighty-Eight. She sits two barstools from mine and Bear throws a coaster down to cement the spot. "The usual, Bear."

He starts fixing her drink and I do that thing guys at bars do like I'm just loosening up my shoulders, then look sideways nice and easy. Beautiful? You bet, but even more than her face it's that hair done up in great, piled-on tresses like peaks on Grandma's meringue pie. Bear puts the drink in front of her, something sparkly with a twist. I forgot to watch him mix it or to see whether he even went for the liquor. Could be a skinny bitch, or might just be club soda and lime. Eighty-Eight looks up at the pro golfer on TV silently hacking his way to the bottom of a sand trap. "Sure is hot," she says.

I oblige with a "Tomorrow's going to be hotter."

She slides down off her barstool to walk over to the jukebox, and she doesn't have to pull out any change to punch out familiar numbers with her pretty, painted fingernails. Over the opening riff to "Smoke on the Water," Video Poker calls out blandly like a guy who finally just won some money for a change: "Better call the fire department. This machine's on fire."

I swig the rest of my dinner and decide to hit the head. The men's room at Omar's is a tiny one-at-a-timer: six-by-six with a pedestal sink, porcelain throne, the cascading wall, and a latch on the door I don't bother to throw when the bar is this empty. Rumors of midnight trysts on these beehive tiles fly around the city like trash on I-5. The piney kiss of antiseptic is overpowering.

I am catching up on the fights in the *Trib* when I hear hinges squeak. Between door and jamb slips a delicate, feminine hand, pretty fingernails curling sinuously over the chipped paint. I'd hate to hurt whoever owns those digits—thousand-to-one odds it's Eighty-Eight—so instead of slamming shut I resist with my right hand, breathlessly chirping, "Wait! Wait!" but the pressure does not let up. It's a standoff until I can manage to arrange myself and zip.

She slips inside and throws the latch. "Man up, officer, we're both grown-ups."

"What makes you say 'officer'?"

"Everyone around here knows you're a cop. Bear buys you drinks because you're a cop."

"That's not exactly true."

"And because that lowlife car-stereo thief playing video poker out there is flapping his mouth about how you're a crooked cop, one that skims off the top."

I've heard enough. I reach past her and pull the latch.

The jukebox is turned up loud. In the corner where Video Poker sat there are two crumpled bills beside a sweat-beaded glass, but no lowlife, and a quick look out back shows the smokers porch is empty. I turn around and start to ask, "So where is this mystery . . ." but Eighty-Eight is already at the front of the bar, where the heavy wooden door swings open just for her. She turns and stands in the doorway a second and I can't be sure over Motörhead, but before she disappears her mouth seems to form the words, *It's coming.*

The void she leaves behind is filled by my old friends the farm boys, entering in a line: Sam holds the door, Jordy bellows something about breakfast, and John comes around from behind to throw an arm around my shoulder. "Robby Quizzical! We want to get drunk with you!" When I finally make it past them, Eighty-Eight is nowhere to be seen in either direction on 99.

Back in the men's room, the questions swell around my ears like a sink full of soap bubbles. Who was Eighty-Eight? Where did Video Poker go? *What*, if anything, is coming? I finish washing my hands and go back to the smokers porch to puzzle it over a cigarette.

*A crooked cop, skims off the top.* I suppose that rumor is my reward for the promotion I requested when they put me in charge of the contact station. *Community Policing,* we call it, with public outreaches and open houses and drop-ins during regular business hours. I spend the required hours at the firing range and keep up my gun license, but most days I don't even carry a service weapon. Worst of all, Community Policing is a success. The city council likes it and the retirees love it. I even have my own petty cash box so the contact station remains flush with donuts and coffee, and these are just a few reasons the old-growths on the force hate me. The tallest tree catches the most wind.

At the bar I ask Bear, "Who was the lady with the hands?"

"You mean gin fizz?" So that's what she was drinking. "No idea."

"But you knew her usual."

"I know everybody's usual."

"Seemed like she knew you."

"Everyone knows me."

"How about that guy playing video poker?"

"Left without cashing his winnings, if he even won."

"Did you get his name?"

"This is Omar's, Robby. Some people come in here, they don't even have names."

A miracle I make it to bed some nights. Wake up and can't remember how I got home. Shift to the edge of the bed, try to stand up. I don't have to hurl, not yet, but I postpone verticality until I can make it to the bathroom, get a grip up on the towel rack, let the window tell me the time. I lie there on the tiles smoking a cigarette, and gradually Grizzly Peak lurches back into the picture, enormous shoulders of a giant returned from wandering in the underworld.

I think about those two words, *crooked cop*. A phrase on the tongue. Repeat it often enough and it takes root in the ear, starts getting repeated inside people's heads. Pretty soon they start digging in the muck. Makes me wonder: what would that turn up? Go ahead, let them rake. Rafferty keeps the ledger itemized to the penny, right down to the petty cash—my community chest, or so goes the old-growth joke, to plunder.

Along with the contact station comes an assistant, another thing to piss off the other cops. Not commissioned, not even patrol, but quasi–law enforcement: Carl Rafferty, my right hand, with a full-time desk job, which is what lets me stay in plainclothes. The day the council is set to budget the new senior center, Rafferty reminds me, "City manager wants you to be there, Sarge."

"Right. What time do they vote?"

"Who knows. Public comments could go on forever, even though it's a nonissue—everybody agrees it's got to pass."

I check out his latest dashboard report and start to get dizzy. "I better head to city hall."

"Sign one thing for me first?"

I receive mountains of mail and public notices, but it's Rafferty who opens and actually reads each one. He prepares stacks of paperwork every week for me to autograph, little colored scraps of tape that read *sign here*: invoices for operating costs of the contact station; surveys the councilors want filled out; annual questionnaires from county, state, and federal agencies; and reams of responses to complaints and concerns sent in by community members, mostly retired. Carl always has the perfect touch in our replies: never ingratiating, but neither too condescending. Grateful I don't have to be buried in this crap, or how would I ever do my job? So many community touch points, so many so-called stakeholders, so much public entitlement! Feels like I'm always running late to another meeting.

At city hall I find Lehrers posted outside council chambers. Ed Lehrers: Dorris's partner, another old-growth but still just a corporal. Always wears his badge, even when off-duty.

"Nice of you to show, Sergeant Relleno."

"Afternoon, Lehrers. Here on duty?"

"Yep, in case the fogies get rowdy again, but so far it's endless testimony about paying taxes all those years and now they demand their damn senior center."

They were victims in the perfect crime, and the perp was never punished, even though everybody knows who it was: the US banking system. They didn't just rob a house, they robbed a hundred million houses of half or more their value, and the biggest loser was that citizen fifty-or-better, approaching retirement, who assumed their nest egg would be ostrich or at least goose, but after it got whittled down to hummingbird size, is looking ahead to living out their last decades in a drafty RV at a geriatric trailer park—excuse me: *Fifty-Five-and-Over Mobile Home Community*. I can't argue the seniors' point, but it's a shame they don't just get to the vote.

"If that's the case," I tell Lehrers, "I think I'll grab a quick cigarette."

"Remember to keep ten feet from the exits."

That funding is coming or trust me, heads will roll. Meanwhile, the public comments drag on; the retirees will be heard. Slipping back in to council chambers after my smoke break, I hear my name mispronounced on the PA followed by ". . . *is that okay?*" A hundred silvery heads spin my direction, and although I am not sure quite what the city manager is asking of me, it's clear from her enunciation that she desperately wants me to agree, and I can feel the room trembling with anticipation that an affirmative reply might finally bring the interminable meeting to a close, so I say, "Sure, okay with me." A motion, a second, a vote, all in favor, opposed, abstaining . . . it's unanimous: funds for construction of the new senior center shall be administered by Community Policing. The meeting is adjourned. "Wait a second . . ." I say to Lehrers, "wasn't this supposed to be Parks' job?"

"Was. But since the commissioner got shit-canned, Parks & Rec lost fiduciary authority, so the retirees requested that Community Policing act as interim treasurer." It's a long contract, with sizable payments every month, and a really big one at the end. Crap. Wait until Carl Rafferty hears about this.

When I get back to the contact station, it's the end of the day and Rafferty has already gone home. I am almost out of cigarettes, but Geppetto's up the road has one of the last great vending machines in the free world, or at least Ashland. Since I don't have any money on me, I borrow five bucks from the petty cash box, scribble an IOU with the date at the top, and leave it in place of the bill: *$5 plundered from community chest—RR.* That should be good for a laugh from Rafferty. He might even forgive me for getting us thrown under the senior-center bus.

I am on the smokers porch at Omar's when Bear comes out back to hose off the patio. On the horizon, past the freeway and Emigrant Lake, dark clouds are gathering over Grizzly Peak. Not the good kind: huge thunderheads, full of lightning but no water. The problem is when you get an afternoon of quick, violent cloudbursts and six or seven hundred strikes. All it takes is one of them moving fast in those dry forests. The city might get spared a scorching, but for thousands of square miles in every direction we're surrounded by fuel, and when it burns up there, there's one thing we can't escape down in the valley. I want the air to be filled with anything but the sizzle of city water on hot asphalt and the silence between Bear and me, so I say it: "It's coming."

Bear does not look up. This place was supposedly named for the tree, or maybe after someplace back east by an early pioneer, but anyone who spends more than one summer here will tell you it's really because of the smoke. The fire and soot and smoke: that's why it's called Ashland.

"Nothing anyone can do about it, Robby." He knows it's going to be miserable, but what's the use in whining? If it's coming, it's coming. You don't talk about it or weep. You keep doing what you do. Even if it feels pointless, you do it.

Over the next couple of days, the valley fills up with smoke. The deejay with the sexy voice on JPR starts saying, "Smoky air. Periods of smoke. Regions of smoke." Fires get their own family names: Illinois Valley Blaze, Wind River Inferno, Wagner Butte Complex. Your eyes burn all the time, and you always feel like you've been crying, because you have.

One morning I decide to take my hangover to the firing range. I'm cleaning my service weapon when Lehrers leans over and says, "You ever fire that thing in the field?"

"If you're asking have I ever had to shoot while on duty, then yeah."

"Nah, a warning shot don't count. You ever let the gun do its job and really shot someone?"

"Well . . ."

"Let me give you an example. A lot of people ask me why haven't I made sergeant yet. I tell them it's because I haven't gone up. Why not? Because there's something on the force called the clock. You get here as a corporal and your clock starts ticking. Don't try to speed up the clock. I mean, there's nothing wrong with asking for a small adjustment, but you don't just go to the chief and give yourself three years. That's bad for your brothers. A guy should wait his turn, especially a new guy."

New guy. I've been here almost five years, including four smoke-choked summers, and I'm still the new guy. The lead dog always gets his ass bitten. "What does this have to do with discharging a firearm?"

"If his buddies haven't gone up yet, a cop shouldn't try to speed up the clock. When I get a raise, it's got to come from somewhere. Some cop down the line, maybe my partner, gets shafted. But you wouldn't know about that, would you, Sergeant Relleno? You don't have a partner."

"I have Rafferty."

"Don't count. Not a cop. Have you thought of how that looks to the average guy on the force? Now maybe that stuff flies in Portland, but down here in this valley, with the gangbangers and the meth heads, you got a problem if you haven't got a partner." His words wash over me like verses of a prayer, one of those rambling catechisms that don't go anywhere. A long, sonorous incantation, a simple refrain: *Wait your turn*. When Lehrers is finished, he empties his clip in a scattershot pattern across the big paper outline of the perp.

Days on end, every forecast says *smoke* six or eight times. Smoke in the morning. Sunny with smoke. Rain and smoke. Tonight more smoke. Ash over everything: valley, mountains, and all the trees. Ash on the sidewalks, the shopping carts, the hood of the car. People start acting crazy. They want to be someplace they can see, they can breathe, but they can't, because there is no place like that, not for a thousand miles, and odds are it'll stay this way weeks upon weeks more. August, September, October: months of fire, days of smoke.

The Department of Environmental Quality's got a map full of gumballs. Some days the valley gets an orange; most days it's a red. Today cool air gives us an hour or two of yellow, but by midday the hot air will press down the ash and soot and the afternoon will be purple, like breathing hot tar through a wool blanket. The suffocating heat is squeezing sap from the roadside pines, ruining the finish on my beater Buick. Kids collect gobs of the stuff and make obscene designs I can't scrape off the windshield.

It's deserted on 99 and I'm driving past Omar's when all of a sudden there she is taking a *Trib* out of the newspaper machine, although I didn't see her put any coins in. I pull over right there. No way am I going to let her get away this time.

"Morning, officer."

Eighty-Eight is examining the top story when I say, "Who are you, anyway? What's with the prom dress?"

"The queen, and it's midnight. Seen the headline?"

"Never changes: all smoke, all the time."

"Except for when you make news."

"Oh yeah? Why?"

The possibilities flash through my mind. Maybe a mention at the end of an article about the senior center, how Community Policing got suckered into being lead contractor. If I'm naive enough to hope she's just teasing me, it all ends the moment she says, "The community chest."

"Let me see that." The adrenaline rushes to my brain and for a split second all that occurs to me is that I still owe the petty cash box a fiver. I flip over the front page and yes, there's a five in the headline: "Manhunt for Cop Who Stole 5"—I have to flip below the fold—"Million."

I say aloud, "What kind of . . ." but when I look up from the paper, I see that Eighty-Eight has gotten away again. Community Policing never has those kinds of funds, except for—and then I remember. *Except for the senior center*, when the council shifted the budget over to my department, to Rafferty. The perfect crime.

I don't have to read the article to know the rest of the story. I couldn't deal with all the paperwork until Rafferty and his arrows pointing to dotted lines, and rather than read them one by one, I just signed. Somewhere in there was a *pay to the order of* I should not have signed, an authorization to change a routing number, giving Rafferty power of attorney. Now it's all gone, the entire senior center construction fund: years' worth of monthly six-figure payments, right down to the really big one at the end, disbursed all at once. Five million missing overnight.

I've got to reach somebody, the city manager or the chief, but I can't go to the station, too many enemies there. It sounded like sarcasm at the time but it comes back to me now, what Bear said: *You ever need protection, just come to Omar's.* It's still hours before opening, but he just might be here. I go around back to the smokers patio and look through the window: a lucky break, he's there at the bar, watering down the day's booze. One look at me and he knows I'm in trouble. Or maybe he's already heard the news. Whatever the case, it's comforting when Bear unlocks the door and says, "Follow me, Robby." He leads me across the bar and through the short room.

I can't believe my eyes. The dining room doesn't serve breakfast, but here's Dorris and Lehrers already seated in the corner booth. I look to Bear but there's nothing he can do. "Sorry, Robby."

So quiet you could hear an olive drop on that plush carpet, the hum of the hot spring beneath the bones of that old building built in the tar pits. And it all makes perfect sense. Everything in Ashland—the leases, taxes, inspections, not to mention protection: it all goes through the city. Dorris and Lehrers are old-growths, dining room guys. What did I expect? I thought Omar's was my refuge, but this building has been here for the better part of a century, and I'm just a barfly, a new guy. *Was* the new guy. I try to explain. "I made a mistake. I didn't read the paperwork and Rafferty pulled a fast one."

Lehrers says, "I told you he'd end up here."

Dorris replies, "Saves us an actual manhunt."

"Listen," I say, "I don't have the money, but I know how to find it."

"Slow down, Relleno. Need a cigarette?" I have to admit I do, but I left mine in the car. Lehrers has my brand. He shakes one out and lets me pull it from the pack.

I look back at Bear and he says, "Just this once, Robby." Smoking inside Omar's: is this something dining room guys do? Bear puts out one of the Bakelite ashtrays they keep on the smokers porch, Dorris gives me a light, paper burns and tobacco crackles. Inhale and the relief fills my lungs, exhale and I know it can't last.

I've barely had three puffs when Lehrers says, "Put it out." Reluctantly I crush the cigarette into the ashtray. Lehrers reaches in and takes out the butt. When he places it inside a plastic evidence bag, I notice he's wearing gloves.

"Find Rafferty," I tell them, "and you'll find the money."

Dorris says, "The money's not lost, sergeant."

Another voice comes from the short room: "And neither am I." Emerging from the shadows like a sucker punch to the gut, Carl Rafferty.

"What the hell is going on?"

"Glad you asked," Lehrers says, showing me a leather sap. "Carl, why don't you start?"

"Sure. First, unbeknownst to anyone, you transferred that five mil through three different banks in as many days until it's virtually untraceable, and you were just about to leave the country . . ."

Dorris takes over: "But last night your assistant here discovered the theft. He's a hero, a whistle blower, and when you learned we put out an APB, you figured your best chance was to try getting out of the valley on forest roads."

"Which brings us to what happens next," says Lehrers. They're practicing, not for my benefit but their own, to have it all down to the letter, the story they'll tell from now until the day Omar's runs out of whiskey. "But first, give Carl your car keys."

"What for?"

"In a minute, you won't be fit to drive." I hand Rafferty the keys to the Buick, and Lehrers says, "Bear, mind putting the bottle on our tab?"

"Got it."

Rafferty exits, pursued by Bear. Lehrers resumes his turn: "On the back side of Grizzly Peak, you get lost in the dark and smoke. You stop and try to find your bearings."

Dorris continues, "You're drunk and tired and figure you'll wait until daylight to move on, so you decide to take a nap in the backseat. But first you smoke a cigarette, and like a dumbass you throw the butt out the window."

My arms and leg feel numb, like finally winding down to sleep after a long, sore march, when Bear comes back from the bar with a fifth of Wild Turkey and a glass. I look at the partners. "Aren't you joining me?"

"Nope. All for you." Dorris cracks open the cap on the bottle. "There is, however, a choice of how." He shows me a length of rubber tubing.

"Right." I grab the bottle by the neck. "No need to sully a glass." A cynical survival skill kicks in. Keep them talking. At best, it could yield some useful information, and it might even postpone my own onset of panic. "You couldn't spring for the good stuff?"

"Bear says this is your brand, and the extra proof should keep you knocked out for a while."

"If that's what you're after, why not just use the sap?"

Tired of my questions, Lehrers gives it to me cold: "Because a body will show evidence of blunt-force trauma. This, however . . ." He holds up the bag with the butt he plucked from the ashtray. "After the fire burns over, I'll be sure the Forest Service won't miss it."

We'd like to think that people have gotten smarter over the decades, but in fact we've gotten stupider. Not just government shutdowns, fiscal meltdowns, or other big ulterior-motive stuff, but regular, everyday stupidity: willful ignorance, sabotage for its own sake, secondhand smoke and mirrors, setting a wildfire just to see it set. A cigarette folded inside a burning matchbook, that's all it takes. Place it on a little pile of pine needles at the bottom of a steep, brush-covered hill and plan your exit in any direction, so long as it's upwind.

Dorris says, "Bottom's up, Relleno."

Lehrers says, "You never should have fucked with the clock."

They drag me out back through the smokers porch where the Buick is waiting with engine running. Dorris drives, my hands cuffed behind my back in the passenger seat, and Lehrers follows in an unmarked cruiser. We're winding up Indian Memorial Road in the direction of Grizzly Peak, and I'm almost done with my drink. Carsick and full of whiskey, I think about what happened to that hotshot crew. Hair catches fire. Lungs literally melt.

Dorris says, "I'll leave your service weapon, in case you wake up and want to finish it off quick."

The last thing I remember before my head spirals into the kind of vortex you don't recover from for a while, is standing in the smoky forest with Dorris uncuffing me and holding me by my wrists and belt, spinning me in a circle while Lehrers goes by, laughing contemptuously with every rotation. Who can blame them? It's a job like any other. Nobody gets into it for the public good. Don't be all high and mighty. Bide your time, take what's yours, but wait your turn.

\* \* \*

Struggling into consciousness, brain pounding to get out of my skull, Buick hotter than a sauna, thirstier than hell—for water, for once. Not so much hungover as still drunk, head spinning and lungs feel like I finished off an entire carton of smokes. Bailing water that comes up through the subfloor six inches deep. I need to throw some switch or something is going to explode. I have to pull some latch or something is going to collapse. Eyes stinging, throat half-closed with the thirst of a dehydrated drunk, coughing becomes gagging. I attenuate all my remaining focus on reaching for the door, burning my fingers in the second it takes to pull the handle, crawling down into the dirt, vomiting on hands and knees. They've taken off my shoes but not my socks, my belt but not my holster or gun. Vaguely remember someone saying *finish it quick*.

Ringed by a crown fire, flames leaping from treetop to treetop, branches ignite with a pop like dry kindling thrown into a scorching woodstove, because that's what the forest around me has become. Look at all the dry grasses and low, black oaks destined in minutes to be engulfed by the blaze. Forest roads are a labyrinth even for anyone sober and alert, even with a map. My only chance choosing a direction to make a mad dash; odds that I will choose right: 359 to one.

That's when I see the deer: a black tail this time, but six points on each antler all the same. How he got stuck out here is anyone's guess. Fell asleep, chased off, or ate too many fermented apples—drunk. Stagger after him in my socks, rocks and thorns cutting my feet. Surrounded by trees whose trunks burn down to the ground like birthday candles, all wick and no wax. Lose sight of him in the smoke, but follow the noise of crashing through brush, that not-the-same buck.

Make it to a shallow creek, buck long gone downstream.

Lie in the middle where it's deepest, eyes shut tight underwater, mouth sticking out on the surface. Ground fire is still two hundred yards away, but its breath is already in my face. The crackling and popping becomes a crazy flag flapping in a tornado, getting torn to shreds. A moment later it's louder than three F-16s, a wall of incredible heat hammering down on the creek. Short, quick breaths feel like sucking on the spout of a boiling tea kettle. Swallowing creek water, sputter and choke.

Noise dies to a roar. Lie still long enough to regain control of breathing. Be sure I'm alive. Stand, soaked shirt and pants, pistol an iron brand, blistered lips and chest pulsing pain. Keep to the middle of the creek and stumble downstream. The grass and shrubs to either side have burned off, and earth is scorched and smoking, but the wall of fire has moved downwind, uphill. Bump into a culvert and know I've hit a road. Climb out of the creek bed and follow the hot pavement, socks in tatters, feet bloody and numb, out of a wasteland of charred trees.

Below the fire line, a sign reads, *Antelope Road*, and another, *Welcome to Climax*. The General Store is open, a pickup truck parked out front. If it weren't for the shock, I might not hesitate before going inside, but good thing, because a glance through lead-paned window shows a face I almost don't recognize for want of a customary hate: Manny Dorris, fixing his coffee. I duck behind the pickup. It's got one of those bumper stickers that says *Proud OreGUNian*. Hidden from view around the other side of the truck, there's the unmarked car: Ed Lehrers with head tilted over the back of the driver's seat, catching a nap before the all-clear.

I walk right up to the window and unholster my service weapon: sure enough, they left me one in the chamber. The engine is running and Lehrers, big mouth wide open, drool on his chin, is blasting the AC because that's what you do even in the cool hours of morning when the air is this thick with smoke. *You ever fire that thing in the field?*

I am thinking about it, my hand on the still-hot metal, when a brick-red station wagon drives up. The driver rolls down her tinted window and I see those piled-on tresses. "Need a ride, officer?"

It's Eighty-Eight, and Bear is in the passenger seat. "Put that thing away, Robby, and get in."

I climb in back and gulp clean air. "How'd you find me?"

She pulls out onto Antelope Road and says, "Firefighters' channel." That's when I see the CB radio between the seats. "They're calling it the Shale City Conflagration. Need a cigarette, officer?"

"No thanks . . ."

"Ursula." She looks at me in the rearview, a nuked and half-naked zombie. "Papa knew you'd be all right."

"That so?"

Bear says, "You're smarter than those guys, Robby." We're winding down Valley View Road when he picks up the CB mic. "Now let's call in some crooked cops."

Boniface Mwangi

**PETER KIMANI** is a leading African author of his generation. He has published three novels, including *Dance of the Jakaranda*, a *New York Times* Notable Book of 2017. He has taught at Amherst College and the University of Houston, where he earned a PhD in creative writing and literature. He is a founding faculty member of the Aga Khan University's Graduate School of Media and Communications in Nairobi, where he teaches journalism and creative writing.

# FRESHLY CUT
## BY PETER KIMANI

There were loud whispers when my cousin Wacera left the village for the city; there were even louder whispers when she returned. Cousin, I should clarify here and now, does not connote blood relations—it's a generic term for distant relatives who defy easy codification. In that order of things, I readily admit Wacera—or Ceera, as everyone called her affectionately, before she fled school in a cloud of ignominy—was my first crush. There are many tales to tell, so let me start with the last one.

The Wacera of my childhood was the hair goddess. She kept her hair long, lush, and shiny and spent her entire Saturday plaiting it, when she wasn't straightening it with a hot comb, stroking every tuft until the hair touched her shoulders.

Wacera grew famous during the rainy seasons; she washed her feet every time she came across a stream to ensure she remained spotlessly clean, prompting other village girls to derisively call her Miss Munyu. Munyu was our village. Wacera's detractors had the last laugh as she routinely emerged the last in her class. This, too, was sneered by her peers as "leading from the other end."

My closest encounter with Wacera's hair was when I turned twelve—and I figure she was already eighteen, judging from the size of her breasts. The latter observation was Kaara's, not mine. Kaara was yet another cousin of ours. He said Wacera's breasts could feed the nation, an assertion that, ironically, proved prophetic.

Kaara was in my class, though he had tufts of beard and his voice had broken. He had an easy way with women, particularly Wacera, who often joked that he would be her husband when he grew up.

It was in that year when I turned twelve that Kaara broke his leg. Wacera and I were sent to visit him in the hospital ward where his leg was cast in what looked like a concrete slab tied to the ceiling. Kaara had to use a bedpan as his toilet and was restricted to his hospital bed. Still, I envied his position as he had bottles of Ribena and Tree Top orange juice at his disposal. These were luxuries that village boys only experienced at Christmas, if at all.

During the *matatu* ride to the hospital, seated next to Wacera in the driver's cabin, I could hardly breathe, caressed as I was by the gentle touches from her clutches of hair, or feeling her receding softness every time the driver swerved this way or that to escape a pothole.

It was a shame that I could not share this experience with Kaara, for such excitable news could not be delivered in a sterile, whitewashed hospital ward, where the walls probably had ears as well. It was the kind of story we reveled in as we—Kaara, the other village boys, and I—drove goats from the grazing fields at dusk, watching the naughty he-goats mount females one last time before being led to their pens.

I admit, goats provided our earliest lessons in sex and one particular boy called Mutwe, whose name meant head, let those escapades go to his head and one day tried to make out with a she-goat. The panicky bleating from the she-goat alerted Maitu, Wacera's mother, who quickly rushed to check on her flock. She took one look and understood everything. She wailed at the full volume of her lungs and within no time, the entire village descended on her homestead to witness the spectacle. Mutwe's pants were still around his ankles. He was saved from the irate mob by the village chief, who took him away. We later established that Mutwe was brought to a Borstal school where other goat-fucking boys were reportedly taken.

The next couple of days went by in a flicker, consumed as I was by my close encounter with Wacera. But before the week was over, Wacera's hair dominated the village talk, in ways none of us would have anticipated. Wacera's high school, which was located in the same complex as our primary school, had a new master who decreed that all students, within one week, have short, neatly cut hairdos. Many complied before the deadline, rushing to have their hair cut before D-day. Wacera ignored the edict altogether and went on with her hair-cooking routines.

A bubble of excitement was building as the deadline approached. All students in the entire school had had their hair cut—all but Wacera. Even the basic learning in the primary school was disrupted as all eyes were glued toward the high school wing, where the new master had vowed to teach a lesson to any student who did not comply. A duel was building between the village beauty and the stranger in town, so to speak.

On D-day, Wacera arrived at school with her hair looking shinier and bouncier than ever. With her fairly tall height and springy walk, there was no doubt Wacera was enjoying the extra attention that her hairy misadventure had brought.

The schoolmaster, on the other hand, short and diminutive, arrived at school almost incognito. All students had lined up for the regular assembly. The school's flag had been hoisted. The schoolmaster walked from one queue to the next, where individual classes were awaiting inspection, one hand in his pocket, the other clutching a plastic cane that he tapped on his thigh absentmindedly.

When the master reached Wacera, he paused and sized her

up. In that moment, the two resembled a cat and dog: the latter wagging its tail in fear, the former arching its back to inflate its small frame. The master's cane was the wagging tail; Wacera's hair had turned into a lioness's mane, her lips curled into a snarl, ready to pounce.

But it was the master who pounced first, a swift movement that saw him airborne, allowing him to reach Wacera's mane. He quickly fished a pair of scissors from his pocket and nipped a clutch of Wacera's hair in one stroke.

Wacera went wild. She grabbed the master's hand and wrenched him away, the effect sending the man tumbling down, scissors still in hand. In the commotion, the scissors dug into the rich, red soil and cast some earth into the master's eyes, momentarily immobilizing him. Wacera strutted to freedom, but not before enacting a gesture that would be discussed in every household for a long time. She hoisted her skirt to display her red underwear and mouthed: *Tikio thuruare!* It meant schooling wasn't as vital as underwear, so she could do without it.

Overnight, Wacera the village beauty became the village villain. In the aftermath of the school drama, she went into hiding. Older women said it was abominable for a young woman to fight a man older than her own father, and that Wacera would have to be exorcised before she would be admitted back to village life.

Maitu responded with stone silence. She had been widowed early and often said she had raised her children to walk in the light. Maitu doted on Wacera, her last born. She said that had she known about the schoolmaster's order, she'd personally have cut Wacera's hair as she slept. With the new scandal and Wacera's departure, Maitu seemed to descend into a fresh phase of mourning.

Yet, other villagers remarked that Wacera was old enough to

get married. In fact, her parting shot, *Tikio thuruare*, was misreported as *Ndire thuruare*, meaning she had no underwear.

I made a point of visiting Maitu once in a while, just to check if she had any errands to run. A couple of days after the felling of the schoolmaster, I bumped into Wacera. I recall the day vividly. Dusk was approaching. Wacera was still in hiding, so when I saw her in the waning light in her platform shoes and bell-bottom trousers, waist hoisted close to her bosom that sagged a little, just enough to excite the mind of a twelve-year-old boy, I was both horrified and excited.

"Kikimido," she called out. It was a childhood nickname for Dominic, my proper name that I couldn't pronounce in my younger days. Wacera was huddled with a young man smoking a cigarette in the shadows of the *mikambura* trees that ringed the village. The patch where the hair had been shorn off by the schoolmaster was visible, like a missing tooth. "Where are you going?" she asked.

I told her I was heading to Nana's to buy a liter of kerosene for the evening cooking.

"Let me fetch it for you," Wacera said, grabbing the bottle before I could respond, yanking the five-shilling note from my hand.

The young man with Wacera took the bottle and peed in it. "Take this to your mama, it should cook just fine," he laughed, his words echoed by peels of smoke. Within moments, the man and Wacera walked off and were soon swallowed by darkness. I headed to Maitu's home in tears, unsure whether to pour out the urine or deliver it to her as an exhibit. I chose the latter.

Maitu took the news of the incident with stoic silence, allowing only a shriek and: "Jehovah! What has become of my daughter?!"

That was where the matter ended and, Maitu being Maitu, she never uttered anything to anyone else. I, too, kept silent, partly because I would have been scandalized for having been mugged by Wacera and her rogue boyfriend.

With the passage of time, the episode grew fuzzy, the only details that I recalled with clarity being the fluid motions of Wacera's bosom that elicited vibrations all over my body. I even entertained the idea that once I became a man, I would grow a beard and smoke cigarettes—and look for Wacera.

The idea of coming of age seemed incomplete without smokes and Wacera, who had now gained notoriety as the epitome of waywardness, her name invoked as a cautionary tale to any teenage girl in the village.

"Hmmm. You want to become like Wacera? Just keep fooling around and we shall see how far that will take you," I recall Kaara's sister Neo being warned by her mother. Such talk reinforced our collective suspicion that there was something more sinister that Wacera had done, beyond felling the schoolmaster. Even so, she retained her attractiveness in my eyes.

At age eighteen, I faced the knife. Actually, it was a clipper, but no matter the tool, we still called it the knife. This was a ritual that every teenage boy in the village underwent to mark his transition from childhood to adulthood. About a dozen boys, including Kaara and myself, formed a line in that same hospital where Kaara had been treated for his fractured leg and had our foreskins shorn off with the muted wail of a well-oiled clipper.

After circumcision, we went into seclusion, where we were treated like kings, gobbling loaves of bread soaked in Blue Band spread, washed down by copious amounts of sweetened, milky tea and Tree Top orange juice. As we neared the end of the healing process, we were trained on how to seduce girls. The first test of our ability to adjust to adult life was to perform what we called "dusting off the soot." This was basically a test run to check if the organ was in good working order after the procedure.

The other unspoken marker of adulthood was smoking, although it was done in greater secrecy than having sex. It was Kaara, his voice now a booming baritone, who suggested that we try buying some sticks at the pub in the next village, instead of going to our own village's shops, whose keepers were likely to know our parents.

The stigma associated with smoking had everything to do with the founding of our village. It had started off as an outpost for Anglican missionaries who preached that the human body was the temple of God. Had God meant man to smoke, one famous preacher preached, He would have created an air vent in his head!

That's how we ended up at the pub in the village next door, Mutomo. The pub was named Moonshine and it was as unpretentious as village pubs can be: a few high seats around the main counter, which locals called *sina tabu*. The rest of the space was dotted with plastic seats and sturdy tables. One waitress served the entire pub, so any patron who finished his drink had to tap his table rather aggressively to get her attention.

Kaara and I walked quietly toward the main counter, our cigarette money at the ready, and waited patiently. Kaara placed the order with as much confidence as he could muster, his baritone succeeding in turning a few heads, one of which we instantly recognized. It was Wacera.

"*Ngai*," she gasped. "Kaara!?" She rose unsteadily and gave Kaara one of the longest hugs I had ever seen, then suddenly turned in my direction and reenacted the drama, though for a shorter duration.

"Kikimindo," she continued, before collapsing in her seat,

"you have grown into a beautiful young man!" It had been years since any of us in the village had seen Wacera; I was now taller than her and my Afro accentuated my height.

Wacera turned to Kaara. "It's only this husband of mine who hasn't grown taller all these years," she teased. Wacera looked like, as folks in the village put it, one who had received *dafrao* from the devil himself. She had aged considerably. Some teeth were missing; her curves were gone. Even her legendary hair had receded so that her forehead looked more pronounced. She gathered her bags from beneath her table and led us to the bar's patio; it almost seemed as if she'd been expecting us.

"*Ngai*, Kaara *na* Kikimindo, I didn't realize it was you guys. All grown up and looking so cool . . . Can I get you both some drinks?" she asked between billows of smoke from her SM cigarette.

Kaara and I looked at each other. We had never had alcohol.

"Come on, guys, what are you doing in a bar if you don't drink?" she said, then dropped her voice: "Aren't you guys old enough to impregnate a woman? And . . . wait a minute, wait a minute, this is the season that you guys got circumcised, right? Nothing escapes my attention! Now, tell me: have you dusted the soot?"

Wacera was speaking nonstop. Kaara and I couldn't tell if it was the drink doing the talking or her, or both. She placed her packet of cigarettes on the table. Kaara took one.

"Sure, go ahead," Wacera encouraged. "Help yourselves. Light? Never mind." She leaned forward to offer her lit cigarette to light Kaara's. He sucked in and his cigarette lit up, then he started coughing.

"*Kahora, kahora*," Wacera soothed.

After a few puffs, Kaara passed the cigarette to me. I repeated the ritual and coughed repeatedly.

"You guys are practicing smoking using my expensive SMs? You should have used maize stalks to practice before using the real thing. Too bad I can't teach you other things because I am your aunt!" Wacera laughed.

"Cousin!" Kaara challenged. "You are our cousin . . ."

"A cousin in Munyu could mean everything or nothing," Wacera countered. "It could mean a relation who is distant enough to fuck, but lives too close for comfort."

Kaara and I smiled. No one in the village spoke this way.

Our silence was filled by peals of smoke, as Wacera pulled on her cigarette and sipped her drink. My subsequent puffs of the cigarette were a little smoother and I was much more relaxed on the second stick.

"*Ngai*," Wacera swore for the umpteenth time. "I'm so happy to see you guys. I didn't expect to meet anyone from home, let alone my own family." She paused and smiled. "My own cousins." After another moment: "Actually, the reason I stopped here was to avoid meeting folks that I know . . ."

"Why?" Kaara asked.

Wacera was quiet. She pulled on her cigarette again, blew out the smoke, and looked out pensively. "Good question," she said. "I don't know."

"You haven't killed anyone," Kaara offered.

Wacera laughed, a bitter, short laugh. "How do you know?"

"We know," I added bravely.

"*Yaani*, you guys, who were infants just the other day, have now grown into men?" Wacera marveled. "What else do you know?"

"I know you robbed me of five shillings when I was sent to buy kerosene," I ventured.

Wacera doubled over in laughter, followed by a prolonged cough. "I have to pay my debts, Kikimindo," she said earnestly. "Yours and many others."

"I didn't mean it," I protested. "It wasn't my money, really."

"Kikimindo, were you sent by your mother when I mugged you?" Wacera asked, chortling. "I'm sure you reported I had robbed you, didn't you? Once I pay you back, you can go report that I have returned it . . ."

"Actually, it was Maitu's. She's the one who sent me."

"*Ngai baba!*" Wacera gasped.

There was an awkward silence. Wacera summoned the waitress and ordered a Kingfisher. "And give these *wazee* a drink of their choice," she said, pointing in our direction. We both asked for soda.

"*Braaare* fuckin'," Wacera cursed. "Aren't you men enough to handle alcohol?"

Kaara tapped the SM pack and retrieved another stick. "Light?" he asked Wacera.

"I'm not giving a light to freshly cut young men who are afraid of women and alcohol!" she blasted.

"We are not afraid of women!" Kaara countered.

"I asked a question," Wacera said calmly. "I asked if you have dusted off the soot since you emerged from seclusion. What did you tell me? I was met with silence. That means nothing. Nothing has happened."

"Don't jump to conclusions," Kaara replied.

"Fair enough," Wacera conceded.

"So, what really brings you here?" Kaara asked.

Wacera was quiet for a while, then: "You want the truth?"

Kaara nodded.

"Can you handle the truth?"

Kaara nodded.

Wacera's fresh drink was delivered. She poured herself a good measure, took a sip, and licked her lips. "I can see you two are *bure kabisa!*" she fumed. "You can't even pour a woman a drink." She pulled on her freshly lit cigarette.

Kaara and I looked at each other in embarrassment. When you learn about sex from goats, it's unlikely that such etiquette as pouring drinks will feature in your scheme of things. Our sodas were brought—a Coke for Kaara and a Sprite for me. We both drank from the bottle.

"I have lived my life without apology," Wacera started, dragging on her cigarette. "I have come home to die."

I had grown up in the village thinking Borstal school and hospital wards, where one's freedom is curtailed, were the worst things that could happen to anyone. Listening to Wacera's story, I understood—in that naive way of an eighteen-year-old—that there was a wider world out there that sounded like a bigger prison. Wacera narrated her story calmly to Kaara, who listened intently without interruption. I kept my head low and listened in, recording every word, without pausing to pass judgment or seek clarification. Every word was a revelation, every new sentence more surprising than the last. And throughout the narrative, Wacera smoked her SM cigarettes, the new stick clearing faster than the last.

"I was a fool to have fallen in love with Edu," Wacera chuckled. "That was the guy who peed in your kerosene bottle," she said, looking in my direction. "He promised me heaven in the city, and delivered nothing but hell."

Wacera explained that said boyfriend was a construction worker who lived in a Marigu-ini slum in the city. Quite often he did not have any work at all, so his day job became having sex.

"Sex is fine, as long as you have a full stomach," Wacera clarified, tapping ash off her cigarette. "But that bugger did not have that simple understanding of life. One day, he gave it to me so badly, I thought he would kill me."

Wacera was silent for a moment before continuing. "That's

when I knew I had to leave. To make matters worse, he'd gotten me pregnant. I had no doubt in my mind that I lived a better life in the village. I had been a student and I never had to worry about what I would eat or where I would sleep. But those were my constant worries in Marigu-ini.

"I could see that the life ahead of me was bleak, judging from my neighbors: one was a streetwalker who locked up her baby overnight as she scavenged the streets for men; another was a vegetable vendor who rose at dawn and returned at dusk, just to keep her children in school and put food on the table . . ."

Wacera paused to take a swig of her drink. "I admit I'm not the most industrious person in the world, but if I was going to undertake such backbreaking toils, then I needed to start right here in the village. So, I bathed in that makeshift communal bath held down by a flimsy clothing, put on my Sunday best, and took a *matatu* to town. I just wanted to walk away from Marigu-ini and be by myself. Just for once. Get some space to think about my future and my unborn baby."

Wacera lit another smoke and puffed furiously. "I walked around the city aimlessly, but from my pace, you'd have thought I had the most urgent appointment. Quite a few times, I heard catcalls when I turned a corner. By now, my body was taking the shape of a woman. My boobs had grown bigger and my skin had a glow that develops when one is pregnant."

"We used to say in Munyu that your breasts could feed the nation," Kaara smiled sheepishly.

"Foolish boy!" Wacera reprimanded playfully.

"That means they were sufficiently grown to feed the African continent!" Kaara said.

Wacera took a long puff of her SM and waved Kaara away. "*Kumbaf!* One time, a motorist screeched to a halt and propositioned me. I spat on him. Another stopped, and then another. All

drove flashy cars and dressed fancily. They were all middle-aged
men with balding heads and rotund bellies. Old enough to be
my grandfathers. One particularly persistent man pleaded with
me to join him for dinner. I didn't realize I was hungry until he
mentioned food. I realized then that I hadn't eaten all day. And
now I had two mouths to feed.

"I got into his car and he drove off to this private members'
club where he was received like a king. Someone took off his
jacket, another poured his drink, which they did without his
prompting, and his favorite meal was prepared without his or-
dering. The king—I didn't get his name—asked me if he was
having me for dessert. I just stared at him.

"*Ngai baba!* How in the world would I, a village girl from
Munyu, have known that dessert is what you have after a meal!!
Let me tell you, I was a proper village bumpkin!

"'One thousand bob?' King asked. I stared at him. I figured
he was now negotiating the price of pussy. See, I'm not too daft,
there are some things I get instantly, especially where money is
involved. In fact, the only math I understand is counting money.

"'Two thousand?' King asked. No response from me.

"'Three . . . ?' More stares from around the room.

"'Okay,' King sighed. And not being used to having to do
anything for himself, he turned the question to me: 'Okay, state
your price.'

"I said: 'Twenty.' I saw King lift an eyebrow, so I added
scornfully: 'I pay my housemaid more than ten thousand just for
washing my underwear!'

"'Deal,' King said, rising to go to the hotel room."

Wacera took another gulp of her drink. "Kaara *witu*, Kikimindo, do you know what twenty thousand shillings could do six
years ago? That was the kind of wage that Edu, that bugger of
mine, would have earned in one year doing construction."

She smiled. "I know you guys are still young and all that, and I possibly shouldn't be telling you some of these stories, but that was the easiest twenty grand I ever made in my life. I earned it without breaking a sweat. King was dead after one round of gentle lovemaking and I was gone before he woke up. I couldn't totally face up to the fact that I had now, by virtue of his payment, become a prostitute. He had placed the cash neatly on the table, like a teller does at the bank. The only missing document was the receipt acknowledging the transaction. I left his expensive watch, wedding rings, and other personal items untouched. I may be crooked and all that, but I'm not a thief. I took what was rightfully mine."

Wacera was quiet for a long time. Kaara and I were stunned into silence. She took the last stick from her pack and crumpled the packet.

"Another packet of Saidia Malaya!" she shouted at the waitress. "And get me the bill as well . . ."

Dusk was gathering. Kaara and I looked at each other; I was wondering how and when we would walk back to the village, especially if our new companion decided she would come with us.

"Okay, no more drunken stories, boys!" Wacera announced.

"You haven't told us anything yet," Kaara protested. "That was just the beginning . . ."

Wacera stared at him. "I should have married you, my good man, and never left the village. You sound older than your age."

"I am an old man," Kaara responded.

"You guys must have a drink!" Wacera ordered. "I'm not going to drown myself in liquor telling you tall tales as you sit here and stare . . ." Our sodas were finished.

"Let's smoke first," Kaara said. "I personally can't drink without smoking . . ."

Wacera looked at each of us suspiciously. The new SM pack

was delivered and she handed a stick to each of us, then repeated the ritual of lighting them with her own.

Our smoking was much smoother, without any coughing at all.

"So, what did you do with your twenty grand . . . ?" Kaara pursued. "That's a lot of money."

"Why do you want to know?" Wacera teased.

"I'm just curious."

After a moment, Wacera said thoughtfully, "I was only eighteen, just as old as you two. How would you have spent the money?" she asked Kaara, before turning to me.

Kaara said he would buy a music system and hold a big party. I said I would travel to Mombasa for holiday.

"Foolish boys," Wacera scoffed. "I had better sense than you both. I invested in my future. Rented a place for myself, bought lots of clothes and shoes and handbags and perfumes. My tools of the trade, you know. And I learned how to drink and smoke . . ."

"Really?" Kaara said.

Wacera pulled on her cigarette and knocked some ash into the overflowing ashtray. "There is a style to it," she answered. "It's a moment to show off your polished nails. Same with the holding of a glass," she added, illustrating as she took a swig. "As for you and your clan who drink from the bottle . . ."

Kaara and I laughed.

"What happened to the baby?" Kaara asked.

"What baby?"

"The one you were carrying?"

"Ooh, that was sorted immediately."

"Sorted?" Kaara said.

"When you are eighteen and living with an improvident man, how else do you sort it? I was about to say *you* try getting pregnant, but I realize you luckily cannot. Trust me, I sorted it,

204 CN THE NICOTINE CHRONICLES

once and for all. I never allowed myself to fall pregnant again."

Wacera took a few sips in quick succession, as though trying to drown the memories, then smoked even more rapidly, lighting one stick with another. "That first year in the streets was the most turbulent," she said wistfully. "I heard babies crying in the night. I could not stand the sight of a toddler, let alone hold one in my own hands. I turned to drinking for solace."

Wacera held her face in her hands. When she looked up, her eyes were moist. "Here's the thing: I was supposed to be a carefree, fun-loving girl, but I was falling apart inside. And men would line up waiting to be comforted by me. I drank even more. Strange as it might sound, accepting money was the hardest part of the bargain. I felt really humiliated that I, Wacera, daughter of Maitu, had ended up in the streets.

"The tragedy is that the streets can be addictive. It is empowering when a woman knows that a swing of her hip will have a man on his knees, literally begging for you." Wacera rose from her seat suddenly. She took one wobbly step and Kaara rushed to steady her. I hesitantly followed suit.

"I will be fine," she assured. "*Kuteleza si kuanguka*. I am happy to see that you will catch me if I fall. Please take me home." She was steady on her feet now, though she leaned lightly on both of us.

As we walked home, Wacera narrated her journey from one side of town to another. The western part of the city was peopled by the flashiest of prostitutes. They were the youngest and prettiest. Within a year or two, new arrivals with fresher and prettier face would dislodge the older women to the backstreets of the central business district. Pimps were there to ensure every prostitute stayed in her lane. By the time Wacera hit River Road, she said, she knew that was her endgame.

"I had done all there was to be done: blacks, whites, Indians, Arabs, Chinese—the United Nations of the world," she told us, adding that in her first two years, she had served as an escort to exotic destinations on the coast and Zanzibar.

"I grew up very quickly," she confessed. "I realized as soon as I landed in the city that a woman's beauty is like a flowering plant. Seasons come and go. Just like the hair that I cherished in my teens. I think that foolish master's cutting off my hair was the rite of passage that emboldened me to fend for myself. For no one defended me in the village when he scarred me before so many witnesses."

Wacera stopped in her tracks. "Boys, please walk ahead."

Kaara hesitated.

"I want to pass water, stupid cow!" she snapped.

We did as instructed. Pitch darkness had enveloped the land.

Wacera soon caught up with us. Kaara and I were carrying her luggage. She hoisted her arms around each of us.

"See, I have been places, from the so-called massage parlors of Kilimani, which is a sophisticated term for brothel, to the cars of penniless men. Pimps, who ensured I got paid by stingy men, got me out of police cells—by the way, even police will accept a little something to secure your release . . .

"But each year, I would be pushed to the backstreets by younger and fresher faces. Village girls with more juices for the city men to squeeze and draw from. When River Road beckoned, I knew it was time to leave the scene. From there, one knows the next destination is the village pub and, ultimately, the grave."

Wacera's turning point, she went on, was not triggered by her street life, but by a middle-aged man who had fallen on hard times. "His name was Zakayo. A short, quiet, old man who I thought was graying prematurely, but when I found his other bodily hairs had grayed, I knew I was dealing with the rock of ages. Zakayo was a retiree who chose to squander his pension in the city. Actually, squander is the wrong term. *Spent.*

"Because I spent part of it. Zakayo would order a meal and summon me to his table: 'Wacera wa Maitu,' he would call out, 'how can I eat alone as though I am a witch?' He never failed to invite me, and always addressed me as 'daughter of my mother.'

"That was the measure of Zakayo's generosity. I reciprocated in kind. He was among the few people who got laid for free—when I was in the mood.

"Then something happened and Zakayo's pension stopped flowing. Maybe the account ran dry, maybe his wife went to court or to his employer and ordered it stopped. I really don't know what happened and neither did Zakayo. All he mumbled was that his lawyer would deal with the matter promptly. One week grew into two weeks, one month, two months . . . In the fourth month, the landlord threw him out of his bedsit in Ngara. Soon Reke Mone, his regular haunt for thirty-five years, vowed that he would not be served any more meals before he cleared his debt. Before we knew it, Zakayo was scavenging in the streets."

Wacera stopped in her tracks again. "Where are we now?" she asked, out of breath.

"We're close to home," Kaara answered.

"Really? I can hardly see in the dark. Okay, let me finish this story here and now," Wacera said urgently. "One evening, the patrons at Reke Mone conducted a fundraiser. It was not to settle Zakayo's debts or to buy him food. It was to send him home. Somebody reported that Zakayo had told him he hailed from Murang'a. So, he was put in a Murang'a-bound *matatu.* The driver was instructed to dump Zakayo at a local market where some villagers were likely to identify him and deliver him home. He was sent off like a sack of potatoes, to be delivered to some address where someone was bound to identify the parcel. That's when I decided to come home, while I was still on my feet."

Wacera went quiet again.

Kaara and I looked at each other in the dark.

"I'm sure folks at home have lots of questions," Kaara said.

"I'm coming home, no questions asked," Wacera replied calmly. We had arrived at Maitu's.

Kaara knocked gently. *"Hoooodiiii?"*

*"Tonyai,"* somebody welcomed us in.

I could feel Wacera fumbling for her cigarettes. The door opened as she lit her stick; the blaze illuminated her face for a moment.

I don't know what alarmed Maitu the most—the face of her long-lost daughter or the sight of her smoking a cigarette. She unleashed a massive wail that soon brought her closest neighbors to her doorstep.

Wacera smoked furiously as more villagers arrived.

I reached for a cigarette and so did Kaara. Wacera obliged, leaning forward to light our sticks from her blazing one.

# PART IV

## INHALE TO YOUR HEART'S CONTENT

**DAVID L. ULIN** is the author or editor of ten books, including *Sidewalking: Coming to Terms with Los Angeles*, short-listed for the PEN/Diamonstein-Spielvogel Award for the Art of the Essay; the Library of America's *Writing Los Angeles: A Literary Anthology*, which won a California Book Award; and the Akashic anthology *Cape Cod Noir*. The former book editor and book critic of the *Los Angeles Times*, he has written for the *Atlantic*, the *Nation*, the *New York Times*, and other publications. He has received fellowships from the Guggenheim Foundation and the Lannan Foundation.

# SMOKE BREAK

## BY DAVID L. ULIN

I'm just starting to lay the PVC pipe into the ditch when Bugler comes around the side of the outhouse buttoning up his pants, that big belly popping out over his belt, a whiskery half sneer cut across his open wound of a face. The sun is hot, high in the sky and glaring, but across the plains I can see rain clouds gathering, picking up speed.

"You almost done yet?" Bugler whines, fitting a toothpick into the corner of his mouth. "Christ, you Northern boys are so damn slow. When I was your age, I'da had this thing dug and fitted and covered up again in all the time it's taken you . . ."

I don't look up, just keep fitting lengths of tubing together and laying them into the ground. Bugler is the boss, but he's never got anything to say, just the same shit spilling out of his mouth like the spare tire spilling over the top of his pants. He's a man of excess, is Bugler, and he doesn't like me. He doesn't even expect me to listen, just prattles to get on my nerves, and mostly I ignore him. Although every now and then I nod or make some small response, to keep him off his guard.

"You don't seem to have the knack for laying pipe," he's saying now. "'Course, it's a man's job. Only reason I give it to you is I thought you was a man."

He takes a step toward me and sticks his full-moon face into mine, leer cracked wide. "You know what I mean by laying pipe, don't you?" he asks now, breath hot, an assault, smelling of stale coffee and Winston cigarettes, lips stretched nasty and thin.

"Yes," I say.

"Didn't know if they still did that stuff up north. Thought they might have some kind of machine for it by now . . ."

*It'd be nice if they had some kind of machine for* this, I think, screwing another piece of plastic pipe together and laying it into the ground. I've been out here all day, and my back is coated with sweat that runs in rivulets down my pants and plasters them to the skin of my legs. There used to be a work crew to do this stuff, me and four other people, but, one by one, Bugler has transferred the others during the last few weeks, until now there is only me. And, of course, him, standing around and picking at me while I do whatever dirty work he can think up. Yesterday, I dug out the foundation for a concrete platform—twelve feet square and two feet deep—and today . . .

Well, today, I'm hoping, it's going to rain before I get done putting this pipe together, before I have to cover up this ditch. Even in the couple of minutes that Bugler's been standing here, the horizon has moved several miles closer, and I can see the first long lashes of water lacing the ground in the distance. I slow up on the pipe just a fraction, working the weather like a tired baseball pitcher who's lost his best stuff, trying to weasel a delay.

The rain is the only thing I like about Texas, the way it looks as it moves across the brown, scrubbed plains. Out here, you really get a sense of the force of nature, the way the sky can change so suddenly, the way a storm will come on out of nowhere and sweep past you in a matter of minutes, with a strength that can sometimes level houses. It's because there's nothing to stop it, no points of resistance. The plains are so wide, so empty, and anything that gets thrown up in their way is so damn small . . .

No wonder Bugler's who he is. Me, I'm from Manhattan, where nature has ceased to be a factor anymore.

Bugler keeps chattering, toothpick bouncing in his mouth

like a taxi dancer, face a shifting storm of moods. The only constant is the beady black pinpricks of his piggish eyes, like buttons encased in dough then baked beneath the heat of the Texas sun. He's about forty, his skin lined like old leather, and although I've never touched him, my guess is that it feels that way too.

"You know what?" he says. "Let me give you some advice. You know what I was doing last night?"

This time, I don't nod, just thread some more of the pipe through my hands and slide it along the length of the ditch. A wind picks up and blows against my back, drying it in spots. The air is heavy now, smells like water, but the sun is still high and undeterred.

Bugler stops for a second, as if he is waiting for a response. He spits the toothpick at my feet, fishes a Winston from the soft pack in his breast pocket, and lights it. I watch him, calculating, before pulling out a Marlboro.

Smoke break. Most days, this is just about the only rest I get. When I first started, we would smoke together, all of us on the crew. Once an hour, once every forty-five minutes, whenever we could work it in. It's not that we were friends, or had anything to say to one another. But the work is mindless and relentless, almost as mindless and relentless as Bugler's voice. And smoking, it breaks the tedium, it divvies up the day. Those times, they are as close as I have felt here to fitting in.

For a moment, we stand in silence, pulling on our cigarettes. I feel the aching in my muscles, the tension in my lower back. Then it's like Bugler gets tired of waiting. He's a man who needs to hear the sound of his own voice.

"I was with a woman," he says, and takes another drag. I can see him leer, the hot stench of his breath filling the air like he's an animal stalking prey. Every week or so, he tells me about some new sexual conquest, dressing it up like a story from *Penthouse* when you can tell just from looking at him that it was probably a frantic little fuck at best, him huffing and puffing like a rabbit, scared to lose his hard-on before it came time to jam.

"She was fine," he goes on. "Couldn't have been much more than nineteen. One of them little girls, real pretty—looked like she'd hardly know how to do it. But she did." His cowboy-style snap-button shirt fits him kind of tight, and it's come untucked at the bottom so that a patch of hairy belly peeks out like a kid playing hide-and-seek. "She was married too," he says, grinning though the smoke.

A lot of people marry young in Texas. Not like in New York. Here, everyone I meet seems to be nineteen and matched for life, with a kid and a late-model car, and a twenty-eight-year mortgage on a brand-new tract house with a view of the setting sun. Even Bugler, ugly as he is, has a wife somewhere, although no one I know has ever seen her, and he isn't exactly what you'd call young.

Bugler exhales a cloud and scratches the ground with the toe of his boot. As he does, his smile starts to fade. I watch him while I finish my cigarette, squash it underneath the sole of my boot. In the ditch, the PVC pipe is almost all in place, and pretty soon I'll have to get to work connecting it, unless the rain arrives before then. I check the horizon, slow my work to a crawl. Bugler'll never notice anyway.

Now the wind picks up again, a pushing wind that whistles all around us. It's not a friendly sound. Underneath it, Bugler coughs, starts to talk again. His voice is soft, and although I don't want to, there's something in his tone—an edge, an insistence—that makes me strain to hear him through the rushing air.

"I got a lot more than I bargained for with this one," he says. "You want to know what happened?"

No.

"I got shot at last night." He takes a last drag on his Winston and flicks the butt. For a moment, we just stand there, while the wind takes hold of the cigarette and rips it apart, casting shards of glowing ember everywhere. Then he continues.

"We were at her place. It was just as cozy as you please. But when we get down to it, right in the middle, I hear this screeching sound, like a door on rusty hinges. I stop for a second, ask her where's her husband. She tells me not to worry, he's working the night shift, won't be home for hours, and I say unh-hunh, and then the bedroom door slams open and what do I see but the barrel of a gun . . ."

Bugler's got me interested now, I hate to admit it, but I'm looking at him pretty hard, waiting for the next part of the story. The rain keeps advancing, and now I'm hoping it'll hold off for a while so he can get to the end. He's not even noticing me, those hard eyes gone all dreamy now, as if he's trying to see something that's not really there, something that if he could just concentrate hard enough he might be able to conjure, but which he'll never be able to reach out and touch.

"The gun goes off," he goes on, "and the whole side wall of the room explodes. And I'm moving—I ain't never moved that fast, not even when I was a boy. I'm reaching down to the floor for my pants, gathering up my boots, my shirt, whatever I can get ahold of, 'cause there's no time to be choosy, and meantime, this guy's standing in the door yelling what the hell is going on here, and the girl is in the bed, hiding under the covers, and screaming. The funniest part, too, is I'm still thinking about that girl . . .

"But her husband is blocking the door. He raises the gun again, and I know this is it. Then I see that his first shot has really taken out that wall—I mean, you can see moonlight through the holes, all it is is Sheetrock and plywood, one of these home-construction jobs—so I put my shoulder down and plow right into it, and the gun goes off . . .

"I hear that shell whistle by my ear, except I'm already out-side. Then another shot when I'm getting in my truck. As I drive away, I can see him in the rear-view, waving that gun like he knew how to use it. But look"—and his eyes return to focus, his lips twisting back into their cynical sneer—"not a mark on me." He turns a slow, ponderous pirouette, arms extended and belly jiggling beneath the taut fabric of his shirt. "What a hero, huh? Shoots his own house to kingdom come, and I get away without a scratch."

Bugler laughs: a short, yapping bark like that of a lapdog. He reaches for another Winston, and I wonder how that hulk of a body managed to evade the shots.

"Gotcha interested that time, huh?" he says. "Betcha that kind of shit don't happen much up in New York."

"Not to me," I say.

"Yeah, well," he drawls, "you ain't even heard the kicker yet."

The dust starts to swirl now, all around the construction site, and in the distance I can see the first work crew heading in to-ward the makeshift lean-to structure of the tool shop. It's a huge space, supported by an array of tree trunk braces. On the side nearest the impending storm, a carpenter is unfurling a canvas tarp and securing the corners, tying everything down.

And on Bugler's face, the leer is back, all traces of his former reticence brushed clear by the wind. It's as if, now that he's told someone, the bullets are really gone, no more a threat to him than a dream. Now it can be just a story to tell, now he can laugh . . .

Which is exactly what he does, laughs again and exhales a burst of smoke that gets caught in the tangle of the wind. It moves like a ghost, not quite shapeless but not quite formed ei-ther, swept back over Bugler's shoulder toward the lean-to in a pattern of movements like an underwater dance. I'm starting to feel submerged too, not from the water in the air but because I can't escape, because he's got me now, I gave him an opening, and he knows I'm his, and he can draw his moment out.

At the same time, work has stopped, suspended not by weather but by this strange and loaded dance that we are doing, as if there were anything between us, as if we weren't adversaries. I light another Marlboro, not asking, just trying to take hold of my own small piece of the moment, the way the wind is taking hold of the smoke.

"See," Bugler tells me, "it was early, and I didn't have nowhere to go. So I drive around for a while, and then I go home. But when I get there, the house is dark. There's no one around. I come inside—nothing. No noise, nothing. And now I'm starting to get a little angry, you know what I mean?"

Bugler peers in close again, and I get another whiff of his deadly breath. I want to pull away, but he's speaking so softly that his words flee across the angry air.

"I don't say anything. I don't make a sound. Then I see a sliver of light coming out under the bedroom door."

The rain is close enough now that I can hear it, like the patter of hooves, of the cavalry.

"And low voices," Bugler adds. "Coming from inside."

A little smile starts to twitch around the edges of my lips. Bugler waits, and the moment expands between us like the coming storm.

"So I creep up to the door. There's a man's voice, and I can hear my wife laughing, and . . ."

Now *I* start to laugh. It's not a good thing to do, I know that: Bugler's opening up here, and this is serious business. But with the storm brewing and all, there's little else to do. The situation is so absurd. Bugler looks at me funny, his cheeks balled like dough and his eyes almost obscured behind the massive roiling of his cheeks. And as he does, I get a flash, as if lightning had lit up the sky.

"The husband, right?" I ask, and strike a casual pose over my shovel, cigarette in my mouth like I belong here, like we're just two good old boys shooting the shit.

What that question does is it takes the space between us and bursts it, just as the first stripes of rain begin to cut the earth at our feet. I can almost hear the bang, can see it in the way Bugler's face blows from confusion to rage in the time it takes for the words to come out of my mouth.

"What?" he asks. "What'd you just say?"

I don't utter a word.

"You think you're being smart? Well, let me tell you something, boy, you're one dumb piece of shit."

Bugler's right hand shoots out, the hand with the Winston in it. It's a thick, meaty hand, scarred and stubby, and it grabs me by the collar of my T-shirt and pulls me in until my face is no more than two inches from his. My cigarette falls to the dirt between us as the tip of his darts dangerously close to my left eye. Water sweeps across the work site, falling in thin, sharp drops. Already, the lean-to is getting hard to see.

"You don't never want to talk back to a man about his wife," Bugler growls. "You take my meaning?"

I hold my ground. The deluge blots out both our cigarettes; his disintegrates in his hand. Water streams down our faces. In the distance, a roll of thunder explodes like timpani.

"Hey," someone yells from somewhere, "y'all better get under cover!"

All around the site, people are running for shelter. Bugler looks once at the horizon, then back at me.

"I don't know what it is with you, boy," he hisses, releasing me. "You came down *here*, not the other way around." He spits into the wet ground, steps back.

The thunder sounds again, closer, and the air fills with the smell of ozone. And Bugler turns away.

"I'll tell you something, though," he says, looking back over his shoulder. The rain is falling so hard that he has to yell to be heard. "You're just trying to rile me up, but you're too damn dumb to do it right. 'Cause you know what? That wasn't no man in the room with my wife." He snorts, cracks a thin, venal little smile. "It was the TV. And let me tell you, she was glad to see me."

It takes a moment for his meaning to come clear through the tumult. Then I understand. Bugler must see it on my face, because he spits that harsh yap of a laugh and curls his lip even more, belly jiggling like he's some out-of-work Santa Claus waiting for the rain to turn to snow.

He waits a second, to see if I have anything to say. When I don't, he chuckles to himself, then steps away from me and through the storm. I stand there and let the rain fall, washing off the ditch-digger's sweat. It's cold, but not too bad, and it's such a relief to be alone. In the ditch, the PVC pipe lies half-submerged in rising water, and I know I'm going to have to do the whole thing again tomorrow, but for now, it's okay. I just want to stand here, feel the weather blow by.

I don't move until the storm has passed.

*Makeda Miller*

**BERNICE L. McFADDEN** is the author of ten critically acclaimed novels, including *Sugar, Gathering of Waters* (a *New York Times* Editors' Choice and a Notable Book of 2012), *Glorious, Praise Song for the Butterflies,* and *The Book of Harlan* (winner of a 2017 American Book Award and an NAACP Image Award). She is a four-time Hurston/Wright Legacy Award finalist, as well as the recipient of four awards from the BCALA.

# GOD'S WORK
## BY BERNICE L. MCFADDEN

When Officer Fox dug into his trouser pocket for the soiled handkerchief he'd been swabbing his nose with since the start of his shift, his wilted pack of L&M Filters fell to the floor.

He'd only had two cigarettes since breakfast. Well, that wasn't entirely true. He'd had six or seven *puffs* of two cigarettes since breakfast.

He was currently fighting a cold, or maybe it was the flu because every time he lit up, his lungs exploded.

Fox stooped over, retrieved the pack, and stuffed it back into his empty pocket. "'Scuse me," he muttered, turning away from the grieving woman to blow his nose. After that, he carefully folded the handkerchief into quarters and shoved it back into his pocket. Clearing his throat, he touched the back of his hand to his forehead to check for fever.

When he turned back to meet the tearing eyes of Gigi and the bowed head of her daughter, his lips were curled into a reassuring smile.

Her youngest daughter was the fifth child to go missing in a year.

Runaway?

Abducted?

Dead?

Nightly, the local news reported on the missing Kilduff and Mihalko girls.

*Have you seen these girls?*

They resembled each other so much they could have been sisters. Both were fair-complexioned with hair the color of corn silk, except the Kilduff girl had brown eyes and the Mihalko girl had eyes the color of wet sapphires.

Little girls with those particular features were highly desired and well sought-after on the black market.

*Black market.*

He didn't like that term. He only used it because that's the expression Father Mann used. But when the priest said it, it didn't sound dirty.

The first girl who went missing was seven-year-old Maria Lopez. Three and a half months later, ten-year-old Chantrelle Washington vanished. Their disappearances hadn't raised too much of a fuss among the residents of Annunciation. The families were upset of course, and to be fair, the local news had reported on it, although it was less of a report and more of a mention, a blip that was severed by a True Filter cigarette commercial. You know, the commercial with the male and female singing duo?

*Ain't it the truth when you smoke True, you get all of the flavor and the filter too . . .*

Fox's wife smoked those True cigarettes. She didn't break out into song, but she seemed to like them just fine.

Anyway, it's not that the people of Annunciation didn't care about those first two little girls, it was just that they didn't care about those first two little girls as much as they did the ones who followed. You see, the Mihalko and Kilduff girls were real, true blood members of the Annunciation community, a community of European immigrants stretching back two hundred years.

That said, the business owners did agree to post flyers of the missing Maria and Chantrelle in their storefront windows:

\* \* \*

*Have you seen Maria Lopez?*
*Have you seen Chantrelle Washington?*

After seven days the flyers were replaced with what the proprietors felt was more relevant information.

When the families of Chantrelle and Maria saw that their flyers had been replaced with announcements about the church bake sale and the official crowning of the Spring Flower Queen—well, they felt as if their already missing daughters had gone missing for a second time.

But then Rose Mihalko didn't come home after school, and, three days later, Laura Ann Kilduff's mother walked into her daughter's bedroom and found Laura Ann's teddy bear in her bed, but not Laura Ann.

Flyers bearing photos of both Laura Ann and Rose were posted in windows of every business between Annunciation and Devonville. That covered a good eighty-seven miles.

Later, when the photos on those flyers faded and the edges curled, they were quickly replaced with crisp, bright new ones.

Initially, a search party had been dispatched. Residents scoured the surrounding woods, shouting the girls' names. They kicked through piles of dead leaves, turned over logs; Josh McNamare even sent his twin hound dogs, Jake and Judd, into the cave at the base of Abbey Mountain.

The hunt went on for several days, often stretching into the night. Frightened children watched from porches and bedroom windows as long yellow cylinders from the flashlights sliced through the darkness like Luke Skywalker's lightsaber.

They hadn't done any of that for Chantrelle and Maria.

In the midst of searching for Laura Ann and Rose, a mysterious fire consumed Ike's Ice Cream Shoppe. Some people thought it might be arson, some sort of retaliation from the parents of those "other" missing girls, because Ike had been the only business owner in Annunciation to flat out refuse to post a flyer of them.

No one was really surprised. I mean, Ike never tried to hide his thoughts and beliefs where the Negroes were concerned. Hell, he didn't even sell chocolate ice cream! Ike said he didn't believe in it, said it was an unnatural and inferior flavor.

That's just how Ike was.

But then there was some talk that maybe Ike himself had burned down his business for the insurance money because he was flat broke on account of his wife having cleaned out his bank account.

Seems as though she'd met some man through the "Lonely Hearts Club" column in the local paper. Some Frenchman. At least that was the talk. People said that she'd emptied Ike's bank account, bought a first-class ticket to Paris, and that was that.

Figures.

Fox never did like her. He thought she was a sidity type of woman—conceited. Stuck-up. Fox believed he could tell a person's character by the type of cigarette they smoked. Ike's wife smoked Djarum Black. Clove cigarettes?

Who in the world smoked cloves? Stuck-up sidity people smoked cloves, that's who.

Anyway, with those flyers all around like they were, people seemed to see the missing girls everywhere. Someone thought they saw the Mihalko girl at the pizza parlor in Henderson, another claimed they'd spotted Laura Ann dressed like a boy in the back of a pickup truck cuddling a puppy in her lap. Fox followed up on each and every so-called sighting, but always came up empty.

A few weeks after Laura Ann disappeared, federal agents descended on Annunciation in a fleet of dark sedans. Outfitted in neat blue suits and shiny black shoes, the agents swarmed Annunciation like locusts. They questioned the parents of the missing girls as well as the residents, and then demanded from Fox every piece of evidence he had. Every piece. Abduction was a federal crime, one agent told Fox, as if Fox didn't know the law. "And anyway," the federal agent had added with a smirk, "you yahoos would probably just screw everything up."

That comment had hurt Fox's feelings.

The federal agent's name was Donald L. Smiley. Funny thing was, the man was as stone-faced as a wall. Not once did Fox catch him smiling, not that missing girls were anything to grin about. But still, imagine having a last name like Smiley and not ever smiling? It's weird, don't you think? Now, that Agent Smiley rolled his own cigarettes. He kept his tobacco in a pricey-looking brown leather pouch with his initials embossed in gold on the hide.

Fox didn't know what he thought about people who rolled and smoked their own cigarettes. Maybe they didn't trust folk. Maybe they themselves were untrustworthy. It was one or both of those things.

Anyway, the feds dragged the lake; divers clad in scuba suits sank themselves into the water towers and long-abandoned wells.

They'd found some things—a rusted tricycle covered in moss, headless dolls, plenty of beer cans, and several onion sacks containing whole litters of kittens—well, the skeletal remains of kittens. They found all of those things but not those little girls.

Fox wondered about the heart and soul of a person who could drown one innocent animal, let alone six or seven at a time. He wondered what type of cigarettes the murderer of innocent animals smoked.

Father Mann had said that the world was full of monsters, and Annunciation was in the world, wasn't it?

Not too long after the feds left town, a correspondent and crew from CNN arrived and set up cameras on the courthouse lawn and in front of McDougal's Diner on Main Street. They ran down residents coming out of the hair salon and the hoagie shop, shoving microphones into their startled faces.

*Did you know the girls?*

*Are you afraid for your own children?*

Even when CNN reported on the disappearances, they didn't mention Maria and Chantrelle.

So, if CNN didn't mention Maria and Chantrelle and the feds didn't come running when they went missing, then it was clear to Fox and anyone else paying attention that Maria and Chantrelle didn't matter enough to count, right?

Anyway, the last time CNN had come to Annunciation was back in '84 when Vera Singer picked up a jar of fruit preserves and saw the face of Christ etched into the fleshy half of a peach. Of course, you had to hold it to the light just the right way to see it. After that, people traveled to Annunciation from all over the country just so they could witness the miracle with their very own eyes.

Yes, they'd called it a miracle, and Fox didn't doubt it. Annunciation was blessed and especially favored by God. Father Mann had always claimed it was, and that peach half was proof.

Fox glanced out the window. He could see the blue and yellow lights whirling silently in the glass cone atop his cruiser. Beyond that, Eddie Larson, his towhead deputy, was puffing on a cigarette as he shot the shit with the flip-flop-wearing, graphic-T-shirt-clad trailer-park trash.

Some of the people gawked and pointed at the trailer, while others stood a safe distance away as if the trailer itself were diseased or dangerous.

Now, that Eddie Larson was a Marlboro man. But he smoked Marlboro Lights, which in Fox's opinion wasn't as manly a cigarette as the full-flavored Marlboros in the red-and-white box. Fox believed Marlboro Lights were what women smoked, manly women, like Eileen Shepard who drove a tractor trailer and had three children, but no husband. Eileen Shepard wore her hair cut short like a military man.

And no one had ever seen her in a dress or heels. She never wore lipstick, but she did sport a pair of diamond stud earrings.

Fox thought that women acting like men smoked Marlboro Lights, but couldn't figure out why a man would smoke Marlboro Lights, unless of course he was a man who liked men.

It was still bright outside, but already evening mist was gathering over the pine trees that dotted the mountains like pushpins.

Autumn was just around the corner. In a few more weeks, Abbey Mountain would start to sing.

Abbey Mountain was the second piece of evidence that Annunciation was blessed and favored.

A scientist had published an article in the *Scientific American* claiming that the elevation, the mineral content of the soil, and the spacing of the trees and power lines on Abbey Mountain all contributed to the chorus that sailed off of it when the seasonal winds came through.

Fox thought the scientist had gone to great lengths to disprove God's existence. Sometime back, he'd watched a PBS special with yet another scientist who claimed to have disproved Moses's burning bush. Apparently, the scientist had stated, there was a species of bush that could self-combust if the sun was hot enough. They showed a bush bursting into flames as evidence of their claim, but Fox seriously doubted it was real. Hollywood, after all, was known for creating magic. Movie magic.

For instance, Godzilla was just a man in a Godzilla suit. Just an average-sized man in a Godzilla suit, but on the screen that prehistoric terror looked taller than the Sears Tower in Chicago, and everyone knew that the Sears Tower was the tallest building in the world.

If Hollywood could do that, then creating a bush that erupted into flames all on its own couldn't have been too difficult a hoax to pull off. Fox supposed he could rig a bush to do the same if he had the time and the know-how. Those Hollywood folks were not to be trusted, they were charlatans the lot of 'em.

They probably smoked cloves like Ike's cheating, thieving wife.

Anyway, Father Mann said that there were angels living in the Abbey Mountains. Singing angels.

"Why do you think they're called the Abbey Mountains? There was once a community of monks who lived up in those mountains. Monks live in an abbey.

"It's still up there," Father Mann had added. "I imagine it's in ruins, of course. The monks are all gone, gone off to heaven, but they visit every autumn as angels, and they sing the Lord's praises loud enough for all of Annunciation to hear."

Father Mann smoked a pipe. Wise men smoked pipes. Good, wise men smoked pipes. Fox's grandfather had smoked a pipe and he was the nicest, kindest, and wisest man Fox had ever known. Fox remembered that Abraham Lincoln had smoked a pipe. He believed Lincoln had been a wise and kind man, too kind for his own good, so kind he'd ripped the country apart by ending slavery. Fox supposed no man was perfect.

He pulled the pack of L&M cigarettes from his pocket and stared at it. He really needed to have a smoke. Fuck this cold or this flu or whatever it was.

He had been a lifelong Lucky Strikes man before he switched to L&M Filters. He'd made the change at the behest of his doctor, who had claimed that L&M Filters were better for him. Healthier.

Days later, when he was in the body shop waiting for Jeffrey Maddox to buff scratches off the hood of his pickup truck, Fox had picked up a battered copy of *Reader's Digest* and right there on the fifth page was an advertisement for L&M Filters. The ad had a photo of the Academy Award–winning actor Fredric March. Beneath the photo was March's very own testimony about the health benefits of smoking L&M Filters.

Well, Fox couldn't say why exactly, but it made him feel special that he and an Academy Award–winning actor both smoked the same brand.

He looked at GiGi. "Do you mind?" he asked.

GiGi shook her head. "No, go 'head." And then she whispered, "Can I bum one?"

"Sure." Fox handed her the near-empty pack.

He lit his own cigarette and sucked on the filter until the smoke clogged in his throat. "'Scuse me," he gagged, turning and stumbling through the door. After a few racking coughs, Fox spat a glob of phlegm onto the ground. Cussing under his breath, he dropped the lit cigarette into the rheumy pool.

Yeah, he thought as he cleared his throat, it was the flu for sure.

Fox stepped back into the trailer just as GiGi pulled her stringy blond hair atop her head and wrangled it into a loose knot. With her face thoroughly exposed, her cheekbones stuck out more severely.

He gazed upon her used-to-be-pretty face and imagined that before life sunk its teeth into GiGi Stamford, single mother of two, she was probably as beautiful as her missing daughter.

What a shame, he thought, what a downright shame.

GiGi Stamford took one last pull on the filter and stubbed the cigarette out in a gold tin ashtray. When she did so, the glass nesting table wobbled on its uneven legs.

Fox figured she was saving the rest of the cigarette for later when he wouldn't be there to give her another. He might just leave the rest of the pack with her, seeing as he was the one who had taken her daughter in the first place. Plus, his flu-like symptoms weren't going to allow him to enjoy a decent smoke.

Fox sighed.

His eyes traveled around the trailer. It was untidy. The carpet on the floor was stained and bald in places. The walls needed a fresh coat of paint and perhaps some new screens on the windows. The ones that hung haphazardly in the metal frames had holes and gashes large enough for a child's hand to push through. With openings that big, he couldn't imagine why the trailer wasn't filled with flies, especially with the pile of dirty dishes in the sink.

Fox looked back at his notes. The remaining daughter was . . . Fox flipped through the pages of his notepad . . . twelve years old. "What's your name again, sweetheart?"

"Elvia," the young girl sitting alongside her mother mumbled down to the filthy carpet. She hadn't raised her head the entire time he'd been there.

Fox scribbled: *L-via*.

GiGi patted the girl's back.

"Mrs. Stamford—"

"Ms.," GiGi corrected him. "I'm not married," she whispered.

Fox already knew this, but it was important to pretend he didn't.

She had two children by two different men, townies who cycled in and out of jail on minor offenses. They weren't bad guys, just men who didn't want to leave their childhoods behind.

Fox supposed if he hadn't gone into the military for four years, he too might have ended up just like them. The military and Jesus Christ had saved his life, no doubt in his mind.

Now, those boys smoked Newport 100s. He was surprised by that because Newports were mostly smoked by Negroes, both the Negro men and the Negro women. In fact, the father of the Chantrelle girl smoked Newports. He remembered seeing the pack on the kitchen table when he went to talk to them about their missing daughter. Fox supposed that white boys smoked Newports because they thought it made them seem cool. Like soul-brother cool. Fox didn't know why any white man would want to emulate a black man, but he also didn't know why people put peanuts in their Coca-Cola. He supposed to each his own.

Elvia excused herself and disappeared into the back of the trailer.

Fox wrote: *Single mother.*

And then: *Meth-head??*

From what Fox had observed, GiGi had at least three missing teeth. The ones that remained were stained a shade of brown that suggested she was doing more than smoking cigarettes and drinking coffee.

Meth was a problem in Annunciation.

"Amanda, she's, uhm . . . she's special, you know?" GiGi sputtered.

Most mothers believed their children were special.

"Of course she is," Fox said, his smile brightening a bit.

"No, no, not like that. She's special to me, of course, but I mean she's . . . she's retarded."

He raised an eyebrow. "Oh?"

In the back of the trailer Elvia flushed the toilet.

He wrote on his pad: *Retarded.*

He hadn't thought Amanda Stamford was retarded—maybe a little simple, very agreeable, trusting to a fault, but not retarded. Retarded, he decided, was too harsh a label. He struck two lines through the word.

Amanda had been an easy catch. No, correction—Amanda Stamford had been an easy *lure.* Fox had pulled up alongside her early that morning just as she rounded the bend in the road that was as blind as a blind spot in a trucker's side-view mirror. He'd rolled down his window and said, "Hop in, Amanda, I'll take you all the way to school."

Amanda had climbed into his cruiser without hesitation because everyone in town knew Officer Fox.

*Friendly Officer Fox. That very nice and helpful Officer Fox. That Officer Fox is such a nice policeman. What a good husband that Officer Fox is, and a fine Christian to boot!*

"Can you turn on the siren?" she'd asked, blinking her pretty green eyes.

"Of course," he'd said.

No one could accuse Fox of being a small man. He liked his strawberry pie, cheeseburgers, and beer, and it showed. Fox might not have been the tallest man in Annunciation, but he was a respectable five feet seven inches. So, he was caught off guard by the amount of fight the ten-year-old Amanda Stamford had in her when he brought the chloroform-soaked cloth over her face.

His eyes glided over the thin red scratches on the back of his hand. These acts of mercy were necessary; Father Mann had said so. He had assured Fox that they were sending the little girls to loving homes, to loving people who could not have children of their own. "Like you, Fox, like you and Janine."

Fox blinked, and then wrote: *Barren.*

He and Janine had been married for eight years, and to tell

the truth, they were happy; but a space had developed between them and it grew bigger each month when Janine's period made an appearance.

The doctors had said they were both fine, both healthy. It was just going to take a little longer for them.

"How long?"

The doctor couldn't predict that.

With what the priest was paying him for snatching the children, Fox would have enough money to grease the palms of those people who could bypass the bureaucratic crimson tape and deliver unto him, unto him and Janine, the baby they so desperately wanted. Or, maybe they could pay someone to carry a child for them. People were doing that too, he'd read.

The idea of having a child of his own was nice, but this wasn't just about what he wanted. He wasn't a selfish man, after all. He was saving lives. He was doing God's work.

A year before Fox snatched the first child, Father Mann had invited him to the rectory for a Cuban cigar and a snifter of fine cognac.

Up until that day Fox had smoked only two cigars in his life, the first one at his wedding reception and the second in celebration of the birth of his brother's first child.

Those cigars had been cheap White Owls that could be purchased at any convenience store. The Cuban, however, was as smooth as the cognac.

Fox remembered that it had felt spooky in the room because the rectory walls were covered in shadows. Father Mann preferred candlelight or lamplight. That night the room was awash in both.

"We would be saving them from themselves, you know," said Father Mann in between sips of cognac and puffs on his

cigar. "This is a fine town; not the best town, it has its problems, as you well know." Father Mann had paused, his hazel eyes
searching Fox's face before he leaned in and lowered his voice to
a whisper. "There's no perfect place, Fox, but there are plenty
of places better than here. Look at it like this: we're giving these
little girls a chance at a better life, with a better family."

Fox had nodded in agreement before draining his glass.

"There are so many desperate people in this country, good,
God-fearing desperate people who are able and willing to donate
exorbitant amounts of money to make their dream of having a
family a reality."

Father Mann called them donations. Not payments, *donations*.

Fox was perspiring. In the far corner of the trailer, the standing
fan was silent and still.

It was August, for Chrissakes, he raged in his mind, swiping
at the sweat beading across his forehead. Who in the world just
resigns themselves to this type of heat? It was torture.

He thought to ask GiGi Stamford to turn the fan on, but then
he spied the clumps of gray dust clinging to the plastic grill and
knew that as soon as the blades began to spin, the entire trailer
would fill with flying bits of filth.

Elvia was back at her mother's side. She seemed to be studying him. Well, not him, but the scratches on the back of his hand.
When Fox saw her staring, the sympathetic look on his face
cooled and Elvia quickly lowered her eyes.

Fox wrote on his pad: *Nosy, busybody. Careful or you'll be
next . . .*

**JERRY STAHL** is an award-winning author, journalist, and screenwriter who has published nine books, including the best-selling memoir *Permanent Midnight*, along with the novels *I, Fatty* and *Happy Mutant Baby Pills*. His work has appeared in *Esquire*, the *New York Times*, and the *Believer*, among other places, and he edited *The Heroin Chronicles* for Akashic Books. Stahl's screen credits include *Hemingway & Gellhorn*, *Maron*, and, most recently, *Escape at Dannemora*, for which he received an Emmy nomination.

# MENTHOL
## BY JERRY STAHL

started smoking at six and a half months. *Negative* six and a half. More or less.

My mother, Floss, used to call herself a "working girl." And she liked to smoke when she worked. At the time of my conception, Mom was, as she liked to say, "a three-pack-a-day gal." Strictly menthol.

So Kool.

So Salems.

So Marlboro Green.

What she breathed, *we* breathed. Me. And by me, I mean me the fetus, cured for months in her menthol cloud. I like to think, when they yanked me out of the womb and spanked me, I didn't cry, I coughed, a puff of minty-fresh smoke wafting from between my baby-blue lips. Blue because I arrived so ahead of schedule. Three and three-quarters pounds. Sweet as a sick Chihuahua in a cup.

Not that I'm mad about it. *Cough, cough.* It's not like I was born with a harelip. I mean I *was,* but still . . . Nicotine does that sometimes. One of the side effects, along with that teensy birthweight, and tendency to be born premature. (Did I mention the six and a half months?) Since the beginning, I've been early for everything. But things work out. One of Mom's regulars was a cosmetic surgeon. Dr. Ono. So he fixed me up when I was five. Not that he wanted to. He had to. He knew we had pictures. And *I* knew. Because I took them. That was my job. Mom called it insurance. But I just liked holding the Polaroid.

Peek through the viewfinder. Press the magic button. Pull out and hold under armpit—it's always warm—for a few fun seconds while Mom beams at me over the client's pillowed behind, bound hands, whatever's going on, between us. Without saying a word, my mother taught me my first lesson: *Never get done, always do.*

I watched, and learned, from my perch at the foot of the Murphy bed.

The Spank and Burn, the Filter Tip, the Brown on Top, and my personal favorite, the move that Mom invented, the one Dr. Ono loved: the Bottle Rocket.

Floss talked as she worked.

"You see the pee-hole, doctor?"

"Mmmf . . . Yes, mistress."

"I'm going to take this match . . ."

"Uh-huh, uh-huh . . ."

Floss produces the wooden match, clutches the doctor's *thing* like a roll of Play-Doh, squeezes—just at the tip, where it's got the army helmet—and his purple snake mouth just kind of *gawps*, like it's hungry. Like it's eager. Like—

"*Now!*" Mom's voice goes low. "Are you ready?"

She tells the doctor what she's going to do. But she's also, this comes to me later, also telling me how to do it. "We put the stick in the wee-wee. We twist. No squirming!"

And all the while, Dr. Ono, Dr. Ono, lashed to the iron bars at the head and foot of the bed with bright-red rope so that he reminds me of Gulliver, in the story, if Gulliver were gift wrapped, Dr. Ono on whose hairless chest Mom has written words in lipstick I can't read, Dr. Ono's mouth twists in an expression I only recall—nothing fancy here—as happy. He even purrs. He mewls. Wet-lipped, eyes crinkled to slits. The weird thing, through it all, the doctor wears a hat, a goofy sailor's cap, like Gilligan, which somehow stays on his head while my mother, this tiny lady, holds his rancid dumbness (that's what she calls it) now stiff and at, as they say, attention, in her two doll-hands.

"Oh, my *haha*, my *haha!*" Dr. Ono's eyes roll back, shoulders hunching.

Floss barks, "*Shush!*" Looks my way. Whispers: "Japanese for mommy." Continues, very calmly, "Okay, like we practiced, count to ten, and shoot." And I do! I do! Aiming straight at eight, finger on the button at nine. At ten, pressing down, then—*whoosh*—like a magic trick, the matchstick's lit, Dr. Ono's rancid dumbness spitting flame.

Even now, I can't figure how she did it. The mechanics.

I just watch. Keep snapping. Pull Polaroids.

Shoot Dr. Ono, blubbering. Shoot happy Dr. Ono, who swings his fiery unit side to side. Who singes his silky seagrass pubes. Shrieks, "Haroo! Haroo! Sooo happyyyy!" Then stares straight at me, so white-eyed I forget the camera.

I think, *He can see me!* though I know he can't. Because I'm inside the cabinet, with the built-in hiding space, and the missing panel. Just big enough for little girl me.

"Please, lady, now!" The doctor's voice all squealy, "*Now, now, now!*"

And Mom, I don't know how she does it, goes from tiny to tall, like that, in front of my five-year-old eyes.

A woman engorged, like Dr. Ono himself. Because she is not having it.

"What's this?" Mom asks, icy soft. "Did someone forget who gives the orders?"

The doctor only quivers. "Please! Please! *Please*, pleasey, please!"

"Begging? That's what we're doing?"

"No, no, no! No begging. I want—"

"You *what?* You *want?*"

Doctor Ono burbles. Mommy Floss says nothing. Silent now. She snaps her wrist. Another trick! Cigarettes materialize. Newport shorts. In a box. Mom snaps again, the top pops open, and out—just an inch, no more than a filter tip—slides one cigarette. Like that, it's in her mouth.

"Watch and learn," my mother says, "watch and learn!"

And Dr. Ono, who by now beams, whose eyeballs would probably glow in the dark, stares at her with something like love, something like happy terror, as she reaches for that red rope, and pulls. It was never a real knot; just there for show, and the doctor wriggles out.

Another life lesson: If you really want control, you don't need ropes. Don't need cuffs and chains. All you need is obedience.

O-be-di-ence.

It's obedience that has Dr. Ono still flaming as he begins to move. (Mom gets her matches from magic shops, so even if you blow them they won't go out. Fun at birthdays!) Dr. Ono gets up and kind of waddle-walks. He's not fat. Not *fat-fat*. But he's fleshy, and soft. And he shivers. Staring down at the fire between his thighs. Because he believes, from prior waddles, in prior sessions, that his waddle will keep the flame from going out. Even if we know—Mommy and me—that he could kneel down in front of an electric fan and the flame would only flutter.

"Get over here and light me!"

"Yes, yes, yes! I will light you, mistress."

The doc waddle-walks straight to Mom.

Ever breathed burning pubic hairs? They don't smell like roses. The menthol helps. When Dr. Ono shimmy-shammied his way to Mom's throne, I thought he might combust. But wait—have I mentioned her throne? It's a love seat really, beside the bed. Paisley quilt, on which Mom sits, in the lotus position, lipping her Newport so the doctor has to bend forward to get the flame just right, tip of her cigarette touching tip of him.

Mom lights up, inhales, blows out a billowing cloud. "Get that thing out of here." Now she licks her fingers, wets them good, and tamps out the penile match.

When Dr. Ono, deflamed—but still at eye level—tries to move closer, Floss swats at his member as if it were an errant bat, or a fly, trying to land on her face.

*Ah, memories!*

There were many versions of Dr. Ono. I can reach in the photo box right now. Pull out—oh my God!—another Polaroid. Reich Marshal Malcolm. Who came to the door dressed in uniform, complete with epaulettes and Iron Cross on his chest, and worked at City National Bank. He helped Mom with the mortgage, though I'm not sure how. Reich Marshal (he insisted Mom call him that, and paid extra) liked the Roman Candle. So Mom kept a box of fat wax candles in the kitchen drawer. Reich Marshal, in my mind, seemed like a giant. He always brought Salems, by the carton. Mom would tell him to assume the position the second he entered.

"Excuse me?" he'd say.

"You heard me."

I remember how Mom took her time opening the long box, removing that first pack, slowly pulling off the cellophane, folding back a corner, doing her wrist snap and flipping the cigarette directly into her mouth without touching it.

The whole time, of course, the enormous Reich Marshal Malcolm knelt at her feet, crisp green uniform yanked down to blue-veined, shiny ankles, face pressed to the carpet

"*El gape-o*," Mom snaps, talking around that Salem angled out of her mouth.

Reich Marshal salutes. Obliges. Proceeds to clamp his hands

on his nether-cheeks, with great theater, as if gathering the strength to pry himself open. While he works, Mom positions the dinner candle, I go back to my coloring book. Use the green for Jiminy Cricket's face. Orange for his eyes. But how to color the little cigarette I put in his mouth? You can't color white, so I go with yellow, with red for the tip. Same with Tinker Bell. Peter Pan, Captain Hook, I give them all cigarettes, all twirling plumes of smoke. Tinker Bell's Kool almost looks like another wand.

"Ready?" Mom calls, after she works in the long fat candle, giving me a wink over the prone wannabe-Nazi.

Reich Marshal thinks she's talking to him. He replies, all aquiver, in a strange fake accent. British but not, like he'd watched an old Sherlock Holmes movie and wanted to sound like Watson. "No ma'am. I am most certainly not ready. I will never be ready. *This* Reich Marshal has been to the veld, let me remind you. Captured by natives. Who had their savage way with him. Unspeakable duress! Unspeakable . . ."

He was the only person I've ever seen who actually harrumphed. It went with his mustache, what Mom called his pregnant caterpillar, the same ginger as the brush cut under his military hat, but faded under his nose, which he was always wiping with a folded handkerchief the same martial green as his outfit. For a man buns up, hosting a candle in his sphincter—the Reich Marshal had enormous dignity.

"Why, if I told you I was put in a pot and boiled with rodents, I'd be painting too pretty a picture. You can't do anything these primitives have not done already. Done worse. Done repeatedly. The nightmares!"

His speech was part of the event.

"You know Hitler hated tobacco," he might rail another day. "The Führer was the first man in the world to ban smoking. For Jews! You see the irony. He would kill them by the millions but he wanted them healthy! No tobacco before the gas. Eventually he banned smoking for the whole nation. Such a visionary!"

Floss might indulge him for a moment, before lashing out. "Stop talking, scum bucket!" He was a regular. Sometimes Mom would switch out the Polaroid and give me the little Super 8. The Kodak Instamatic M2 movie camera. If he heard the whirring, Reich Marshal did not let on. Of course—do I have to say it?— the sight of a man on the floor, doing the kinds of things Mom did to men, the kinds of things men did in font of her, was hardly shocking. It was normal. It was *my* normal.

The movies were strictly for Mom. Her idea of fun. But not great for blackmail. Not that she ever used the word. She sometimes called these transactions "arrangements." Plus, she explained, it was harder to get money from people for Super 8s. They'd need to have a projector, a screen, enough know-how to wind the film in the sprockets to actually see the thing. But a Polaroid is a Polaroid. Portable, effective, and so easy that a child— me!—could shoot them.

Sometimes I heard her on the phone to one client or another. "If your wife doesn't believe me, darling, we'll take the polygraph." While she talks, I get the wink, and some Johnny Facecream, whichever human ashtray she's plopped her feet on, squirms and eeks under a bun-stubbed Newport.

"Mama likes her pollies, right, Johnny?" All the mouches— half men, half couches—were "Johnny Facecream" to my mother. Beefy furniture who paid.

Dr. Ono, Reich Marshal Malcolm, Johnny, Johnny, and Johnny—to me they were zoo animals. The cabinet gave me distance. "Pretend you're at the movies, honey."

And I did. I did. I became a voyeur, and a professional, almost before I could read.

Mom had a credo: "I believe children should have jobs."

\* \* \*

But listen, I hear you wondering—if you've read this far—what is the *story* here?

What is any story? One Smoking Bottom, then another Smoking Bottom? There was this, there was this, and then there was *that*. Do you read to find out what happens next? Or do you read to flee what's happening now, while you are reading?

Mom was once premed. She knew things. Like how, drug-wise, nicotine is peculiar; how it changes from stimulant to sedative, the more you do. The phenomenon—how *up* turns to *down*—is called "Nesbitt's Paradox," after the doctor who discovered it in 1969. Mom claimed to have dated the actual Nesbitt, as a very, very young woman. He got her into tobacco action. Her eventual specialty. Mom owed some of her style, her technique that is, to Dr. Nesbitt. Beyond his paradox, Nesbitt also had a theory about sex and cigarettes: that, counterintuitive as it sounds, cigarettes were not, inherently, oral items. In fact, as he laid out in a keynote paper delivered at the Airport Hilton in Queens in 1971, to the National Society of Nicotine Studies, suppressed ethnographic research suggests that early tobacco users did not restrict themselves to breathing in the burning leaves. Rather, there is significant evidence that the first tobacco aficionados—in still not wholly understood rituals—would carve elaborate pipes, some long as flutes, and decorated with intricate filigree—then fill their bowls with cured leaf, set them aflame, and, after a few puffs, insert the pipes in the shaman's anus, what Nesbitt's treatise labeled "the Shamanus." The upshot: rather than the lungs, that nicotine's chemicals were delivered into the bloodstream via the porous, nerve-dense rectal portal. Special tabs were cut to slide over the burning leaf, forcing the smoke through the pipe and out of the opening.

I've seen the Polaroids the doctor himself took of the pipe extended between his own ample nether-globes. In a sense, these were early selfies. But this is not the point. Leave that aspect to panicked doctoral candidates looking for an angle. The point is that for half a minute, a minute tops, what smoke was trapped in the pipe's interior escaped and entered the client's alimentary canal, an even more effective nicotine-to-bloodstream delivery system.

Dr. Nesbitt himself—at least in my mother's telling—liked to "wear" his native pipe extended from his rear and do a kind of Pan-inspired goat-dance around his living room. (Back then, my mother did outcalls. This was before the big bed and secret cabinet setup, before Mom had her headquarters. Before me.)

But still . . . just marching out a sample butt-sub does not a story make. Did I mention—my memory again!—that it wasn't till two years ago that I came upon the book of Polaroids, the ones I took, and under that, an older box, taken by who knows? Rifling through them, I made two (to me) shocking discoveries.

One: that what Floss had written on the chests of her most flamboyant customers, like Dr. Ono—what I'd seen her write before I could read—were two words, *CIG PIG*, vividly rendered in Mom's trademark shade: Scarlet Desire.

Two: that one of the gentlemen she'd scrawled on was a man of note. In this case a jowly, big-haired, orange-tinted real estate heir and lout-about-town. His special fancy involved two women and one lit cigarette; specifically, lit and inserted in the vagina of Woman One, who stood astride the head of Mr. Orange Tint, eye-to-eye and belly-to-belly with Woman Two, who also straddled him, perfectly positioned to pull herself open, tilt her pelvis toward the ceiling, and urinate, so that a small fountain arched onto that smoldering cigarette clamped in the labia of the woman before her, ashy pee-drops falling directly onto the face, and lips, of the big soft orange man below.

And yes, the man liked to talk the whole time, mostly about how "filthy" the two women were. Mister Orange, possessed of some weird, or weirdly predictable, shame, would not even remove his own tighty-whities. Would not expose himself. But he was always eager for the ladies to expose *them*selves, to put on their brazen display, poised (as mentioned) nipple-to-nipple over his own prone loaf of a body. He liked to get wet, then explode in shock that "these whores" would spray him.

"Men," one of Mom's favorite quotes, "are not mysterious."

All they want is to be listened to, Mom explained one morning. They don't even want what they say they want. Not really. What they want, what they really want, more than anything else, is to be listened to. Especially powerful men. All power is cosplay, really. They all want to tell their secrets.

"Because they're lonely, Mommy?"

"Not exactly."

"They're not lonely?"

"Not just, honey. They have people around them. And everybody sort of listens to them. They want to be important men. Some of them, they *are* important men. But deep down, deep deep deep deepity down, they want Mommy to tell them they're not really powerful. Deep deepity down, they're worms. And they want Mommy to know. They want Mommy to see, and to hear what they can't tell anybody else."

"And that's what you do?"

"That's what Mommy pretends to do."

"You pretend to listen?"

"Yes."

We had our talks, in the morning, while she drove me to school, her eyes meeting mine in the rearview. At red lights, we would both stare out the window, at the faces of the men walking by with briefcases on their way to work. I knew, even then, that the way Mommy saw people was different from how other people saw them. What she did in our apartment—the men, the menthols, the smoke and flames—what she did was our secret. Not a bad secret. Just something we didn't talk about. Except to each other. I was Mommy's special helper. If I talked about it, then other kids would want to know why they couldn't help their mommies. They'd want to be special too.

"I understand," I said. "It's just, I don't know why . . ."

"Why what, honey?"

When I couldn't figure something out, I'd chew the inside of my cheeks, and if Mom noticed she'd ask me, gently, to stop. Nobody else but her could even tell I was doing it. But if she didn't stop me I'd keep at it until I spat blood.

"Why what, honey?"

"Why it's important? To the men, I mean."

"Why is *what* important?"

"Why the men, you know, want you to listen. I mean, why you?"

Here she stopped, and thought. Which is one of the things (one of many) that I loved about my mother, the way she never patronized, the way she always took great pains to let me know she was thinking about my questions. (Later, people would say Mom was a monster—especially therapists, early on, when I'd make the mistake of telling them what my mother did, and how she'd let me help her do it.)

"Because," she finally told me, smiling that funny smile she had when she was happy/sad, sad and happy at the same time, "because they know I don't matter, honey. Because Mommy does . . . what Mommy does. And they like it. And they hate what they like."

She never said, *Someday you'll understand.* Never said, *Wait till you're older . . .*

Instead, she told me everything. The way it was. So later on, nothing ever surprised me.

Outside of our house, out in "the world," my mother's tininess always came as a shock. In our apartment, doing what it is she did, my mother towered. Even large guys, in her presence, seemed less large. Seemed small. Seemed cowed. Like the puffy orange man. A man with strange, specific needs.

Like most men. From what I've seen.

It's all so obvious now. But then, what did I know? What does anybody?

But forget all that. Those Polaroids are still in a box. In a safe. (Inside another safe.) Sometimes it's nice (if nice is the word) to just have a look, to remember. When I do, I get excited. And then I get very, very tired. That's the paradox.

We are none of us young more than once.

And never again.

Just thinking about it, I need a cigarette.

*Charles Gross*

**JOYCE CAROL OATES** is the author of a number of works of fiction, poetry, and nonfiction. She is the 2019 recipient of the Jerusalem Prize, and became a member of the American Philosophical Society in 2018. She is currently a visiting distinguished writer in the graduate writing program at New York University. She is the editor of the anthologies *Prison Noir, New Jersey Noir,* and *Cutting Edge: New Stories of Mystery and Crime by Women Writers.*

# VAPING: A USER'S MANUAL
## BY JOYCE CAROL OATES

S ix forty a.m., first vape of the day.
Jesus!—your heart just *skids*.

S-L-O-W helping your mom down the brick steps.

Hate the way her fingers clutch—*Don't let me go, Jacey . . .*

Vaping makes it okay. Brain rush! (Though not as good as that brain rush the first time you ever vaped.)

*It's okay, Mom. I've got you.*

Weird how it's still dark. Six fifty-five a.m. Like, you'd been awake all night. Mom in her room and you in yours. Eyeballs like sea anemones floating in the dark.

Mom coughing, choking, gasping for air, could hear through the walls.

Four a.m. brought her the asthma inhaler. Got her sitting up, pillows behind her back so she could sleep/try to sleep that way.

Attacks are getting worse. Since last April.

In the morning, helping Mom put on clothes. Stumbling one slender leg into the black suede trousers, then the other leg, Mom teetering, panicked, grabbing your arm. (Jesus!)

Even going to the oncology center, your mother has got to look good. Has got to *try*. Closetful of clothes, some of them never worn, expensive. Also, high-heeled shoes.

But not today. Flat-heeled shoes today.

Next, the (hateful) walker. Foot of the stairs. Have to position it for Mom. She's scared as hell trying to use it. Hey, look, Mom, you can't hang onto *me*. We're both gonna fall.

Doesn't trust the fucking walker since the time she fell. Fell hard. Looked away from her for one minute out in the driveway, fuck, she fell.

Okay, Mom, it's steady.

Okay, Mom, you can *let go* of me.

Wouldn't know that Mom used to be a beautiful woman. Just a few years ago.

Used to be chic, blond-streaked hair. Now white-streaked, and thinning.

White of her eyes showing over the iris like a thin crescent moon.

(How old is Mom? Fuck, not *old*. Forty-three?)

Appointment is seven forty-five a.m. but we're leaving early. In case something fucks up. As Dad says, *Always keep in mind the fuck-up factor.*

Last time you took Mom for her infusion there was an accident on the turnpike—traffic backed up for miles. Oil in skid-streaks across the highway gleaming like fresh blood.

The sky is lightening, like cracks in a black-rubble wall. Sun at the horizon like the damn city is on fire!

S-L-O-W driving to the oncology clinic. Three point seven miles to the Mercer Street Exit. Already seven ten a.m. traffic backing up like a shit-blocked gut.

Mom sitting stiff beside me. Staring ahead. (Seeing—what? And what is she thinking?)

Before last April, Mom would be talking. You're not even in the room, your mom is talking to you, casting her voice out like a spider's thread—making sure you are there, you are *connected*. Kind of exasperating, expecting you to be listening and to reply, but now she's silent like her mouth has been sewn shut, you miss it.

And if you look at her, she won't be smiling at you like she used to—might not even look at you at all. Panicky, staring inside herself.

*Does divorce cause cancer?—or, does the (undiagnosed) cancerous condition cause the divorce?*

Clickbait on the Internet. Crappy article in one of Mom's magazines.

Okay, I'm gonna take a chance. Passing on the right to get to the exit. Assholes gaping at me humping along the turnpike shoulder, must be passing ten, twelve vehicles. Fuck, it's an *emergency situation*. Gotta get my mom to the clinic.

Running over debris, part of a rusted fender, broken glass. Mom gives a scream like a little killed mouse. Me, I just laugh.

*Juuling is cool-ing. You just laugh.*

Each Thursday first week of the month early a.m. my mother has a three-hour infusion—gamma globulin. Have to laugh thinking—*Gamma goblin?*

Because something is wrong with Mom's white blood cells: immune system.

Best fucking thing vaping does for you, makes you *immune*. Best damn infusion.

Special permission for me to come to school late on those days. Primary caretaker of my mother. *I need you, Jacey, please. Don't abandon me.*

Christ! Embarrassing as hell. Mom pleading for me not to abandon her like her damn husband did. Somebody should shoot *him*.

That first hit of the day, best hit. Press your hand against your chest feeling the heart pound pound pounding inside the ribs like a fist.

Feeling good in the car. Terrific sensation, behind the wheel. The Lexus Dad left for Mom, I'm driving.

Asshole'd have a meltdown, he knew who's driving.

Mom has the driver's license, I've got a learner's permit, it's cool. Nothing illegal. Good, I remembered to grab Mom's purse on the way out. Wallet, driver's license. Credit cards. Cash.

(Loose bills, in Mom's wallet. Last time I looked, twenties, two fifties. Tens, fives. Helped myself to one twenty and one fifty and guess what?—on painkillers Mom never had a clue.)

Brain buzzing, hive of bees. All good.

*Okay, Mom. You can open your eyes, we're here.*

When the high wears off, feeling like shit. Air leaking out of a balloon. Seems like the high wears off faster and faster these days.

*My* size balloon: five feet eight, 123 pounds, shoulder muscles, arm muscles okay. Swim team, track team, JV football, but like the other guys vaping, kind of short of breath these days.

Like, *fucking panting.*

Coach stares at us, disgusted. Steve, Carlie, Leonard, Jacey. Coach hears us panting. Maybe Coach can smell us. (But you can't smell e-cigs like you smell fucking cigarettes—right?) Like, Coach isn't going to accuse anybody of anything. Even if he guesses what we're doing behind his back. Knows he could get his ass sued by *irate parents.*

Defamation laws. Slander, libel. Lawyers for the school district.

So fuck Coach, who gives a fuck? Mom is in no condition to come to our meets anymore, Dad stopped coming years ago. And when Dad came, and I set a county record for the 400-meter sprint, he was on his fucking cell phone most of the time.

*Hey, kid. I'm proud of you.*

*Yeah, okay, Dad.*

*I am! I goddamn am.*

*Okay, Dad. Cool.*

Like I gave a shit. Like I'm panting and wagging my tail like some sorry-ass little mutt for Dad to pet.

That sprint was my best time. Still the county record.

Why vaping feels so good. Turn them all *mute*.

Why e-cigs are the greatest invention. Nothing like fucking tobacco cigarettes that stink and stain your teeth and you can see the damn smoke.

Only (old) assholes *smoke*. Dad boasts how he'd quit but he's such a fucking liar, who can believe him?

Have to laugh seeing teachers' mouths move so seriously, but you can't follow what the fuck they are saying. Fun-ny!

*Jacey, what's so funny? Would you like to tell us?*

Trying to keep a straight face. Sputtering, hot. Friends in the class turning to grin at me behind their hands.

*Nah. I'm okay.*

*You're—"okay"? Are you?*

Let adults get the last word, that sarcastic tone, that's cool. Like anybody gives a fuck what they think.

Joke's on them—teachers. Don't know shit.

Every few years they vote to strike. But then, some shit happens, they don't strike. Chump change they make for salaries, they deserve it.

In the beginning, last year, there were just a few kids vaping. And not in class.

Now it's right in class, and half the kids doing it. (Including girls.) Teacher turns his back, you take a quick hit.

Inhale. Exhale. Cloud: chill. Laugh. Cough. Almond nicotine. Good shit!

Whatever it costs, it's worth it. Clears the sad sick crap in your head like a power wash.

Vaping alert.

Soon as you step into a building. Quick-scope where you can Juul without being detected.

Any medical facility, *NO SMOKING* signs everywhere.

Like, at the oncology clinic.

Nothing about e-cigs. Nothing about Juuls, vaping.

Number one: restroom in the corridor (single occupant).

Number two: men's restroom, stall.

(Yeah, I brought the Juul with me. Not intending to use but, like, to test my willpower.)

Goddamn: the infusion nurse can't find a vein in Mom's arm. Tightening a tough rubber band around her upper arm, searching her forearm for a vein. A sight I hate to see. Makes me feel queasy. Shivery. Shaky. So fucking sorry for Mom but disgusted with her too. You end up blaming them—*victims.*

Girls at school, who guys have treated like shit. Should feel sorry for them but fuck it, you do not.

Mom's trying not to whimper. Trying not to cry. Arms bruised, they're looking for a vein in the wrong damn place. *Try the left arm, Jesus. By the elbow.* Young nurse keeps poking her, apologizes, which only makes things worse.

*In vain, seeking a vein.*

*They sought a vein, in vain.*

Yeah, I should exit the infusion room. Right. Should get out, there's nothing for me to do but watch. I'm getting upset, telling the nurse to get somebody who knows fucking what she's doing, which doesn't help. My voice is loud, everyone is looking at me. Other patients in their chairs, having their infusions. Other nurses. If I say fuck you, goddamn fucking fuck all of you, the security guard will peer in the window glaring like he did last time. If I don't calm down, they will eject me from the oncology clinic. Then, what will happen to Mom?

Okay, it isn't Mom's fault. None of it is Mom's fault.

Still, I resent Mom. Leaning so heavy on me. Wanting to protest, I'm only fifteen!

Three fucking years before I can leave home. If I'm lucky. If I can get into college, and if Dad will pay for it. Fucking *if*.

Then it sweeps over me like dirty water in my mouth—*What if Mom gets really sick, what if Mom dies?*

Luckily, here comes another infusion nurse, to the rescue. A guy, big soft-bellied Andy, his badge says. Weird, male nurses! But some of them are pretty good.

Clumsy-seeming Andy, but he's guiding the needle slant-wise into Mom's arm at the elbow. Just a pinch, ma'am. Sor-ry. But Andy gets a vein on the first try which is pretty damn impressive.

By this time my heart is beating so hard, it's an adrenaline rush without vaping.

When I return to the infusion room two hours later the oncology doctor is waiting for me. Seems that Mom is *in discomfort*. Face white, wizened.

It's explained to you, your mother's blood pressure is *dangerously low*. Her blood work is showing *abnormally high white blood cells*.

Oxygen intake abnormally low—eighty-three.

Christ!—eighty-three out of one hundred?

Also, Mom has been complaining of *lower right abdominal pain*. So the oncology doctor is saying he is going to call the ER, prepare for Mom being brought to the ER which he recommends immediately. Don't go home first, go to the ER and the office here will fax over the blood work, vitals, infusion record, etc., but Mom is pleading no, please no, she *does not want* to go to the ER. She is just agitated, she says. Gets high blood pressure in the infusion room, she says. Her pulse is high, she doesn't breathe correctly in the infusion room. Once she gets outside in the fresh air, she'll be okay, Mom pleads.

Yes, but there're markers in the blood work. Renal failure? Creatinine level high.

How high?—I'm asking.

Three point something. Shit—that is *high*.

Mom refuses an ambulance. She walks leaning on me, then on the walker, swerving and skidding through the plate-glass automatic doors like a drunk woman.

Just take me home, Mom says. No ER!

So I'm saying okay, Mom, but first you need to get checked out at the ER, then if it's okay we can go home. So I'm able to get her over to the medical center, checked in at the ER, start the process going. Turns out, Mom's blood work is pretty bad. Anemia, plus other shit. *Chronic abdominal pain*—the oncology doc has recommended a scan.

While Mom is being examined by a (young, Asian-looking) doctor in one of the cubicles, I'm starting to feel really anxious. Maybe it's withdrawal—(already?)

What I'd resolved was not to Juul for, like, twelve hours.

Problem is, you made that decision just after your morning vape, forgetting what it would feel like when the buzz wore off.

When you're *high*, no thought in the world for dickheads that *crash*.

Don't ever smoke, Jacey. Promise me.

Yeah, okay, Mom. I promise.

. . . the things it does to your lungs, your heart, makes you short of breath plus your breath smells, teeth stain. Plus it's expensive. Plus it's disgusting, sucking smoke into your actual body, exhaling it to pollute the air for others.

Okay, Mom. I get it.

Last week at school. Decided to test my willpower leaving the Juul at home hidden in my bureau.

Like, I am no *addict*. (I just like how e-juices taste.)

First hit of the day, early morning in the bathroom. Fantastic!

It's the chill cloud, the *chemical fruit* smell. Like, some kind of sci-fi.

Actual fruit—strawberry, pineapple, melon—has a sickish smell, like rot. Like, you can smell the rot to come.

But vapor, fruit vapor, that's pure. No rot, ever.

But then by noon fucked up and feeling like shit. Staring at the classroom clock. Fuck fuck fuck *fuck*. Instead of going to lunch had to bicycle home from school, sneak into the house so Mom didn't know, take a hit, one two three, savor the sensation, return on my bicycle to school at top speed, Spider-Man-fast, but fuck it, ran out of breath on the Cedar Street hill, vision blotched and reeling but made it, walked into geometry class while the fucking bell was ringing because of course I was going to get back in time, flying high.

All that week I left the Juul at home. Goddamn determined not to bring it with me to school. Goddamn determined to exercise *willpower*. And all that week, middle of the day feeling so fucked had to bicycle back home two point six fucking miles and having a hard time pulling uphill.

By Friday I was too fucked, tired. Just borrowed Carlie's Juul.

*Hey, okay. I owe you—okay?*

*That's cool, Jacey. No problem.*

The guys are, like, *bemused* with me. Everybody knows e-cigs are not addictive so what's the big deal?

Not like we're *junkies*. Pathetic loser *addicts*.

First, kids at school who vaped were creeps. Losers. Then later, kids I knew, and some of the guys I hang with. Then, guys on the team.

How I was turned on, last summer. At the pool with the other lifeguards. Observed them taking hits, e-cigarettes, weird concoctions—nicotine and fruit flavors—Christ! Sucking strawberry mist, not smoke, then exhaling—evaporating.

That's so cool like magic, the way the smoke evaporates before your eyes.

And Ben Marder says hey, Jacey, want to try?—and I kind of sneered, *Nah. Why'd I want to do that shit?*

You'd tried cigarettes, your dad's butts he'd left in ashtrays. Never got any *nicotine rush* but choked and coughed and felt like puking. Nasty-tasting tobacco shit.

But then later, Carlie offered me, saying how cool it was, so I said okay, by that time I'd been smelling the chemical cloud a lot and was kind of envious, I guess. Figuring just one time.

Carlie showed me how the e-cig works. You don't "light" it—it's battery-operated. Like, cutting-edge technology. Not crude shit like tobacco.

Very simple, actually. One two *three.*

Jesus! What a brain-fuck . . .

Guys laughing at me. Must've been a weird look in my face. *Je-sus!* (I'll never forget that first brain rush.)

How I discovered, there's nothing like vaping. Nothing so cool, by far.

Better than sex. (Everybody says. Not like I'd know.) Way easier than sex. And way cooler than sex, you don't need another damn person.

Whenever you can eliminate the *other person*, anyone you depend upon, anyone you need, that's a bonus.

Why vaping is so cool: makes you strong like Spider-Man.

Why vaping is so cool: undetectable.

Not like sloppy-ass cigarettes. Adults can smell the smoke on you across the room—breath, hair, clothes. Can't keep cigarettes secret like you can vaping.

And Juuling is best. Way cool.

How much?—you don't even think to ask.

Because whatever it is, it's worth it.

Because whatever it is, if you can afford it or not, there's ways of acquiring the means to afford it like (for instance) your mom's credit card she isn't going to be using (much) anyway, sick as she is in the hospital now. Seventh floor.

Notified me on my cell phone, your mother is being admitted to the hospital. Brought by gurney to the seventh floor, room 7731.

So at reception I'm like, hey, why's there an extra *seven?*—and the receptionist looks at me like I am the weirdest white boy she's seen.

Tried to explain, see, there's an extra *seven* in the room number, shouldn't it be just *seven hundred* not *seven thousand?* So finally she got the joke, sort of, and laughed, like women laugh when they see you're trying to be funny in some dumbass way. Because (maybe) (they can sense) you are a little nervous, anxious, and a woman or a girl will feel sorry and play along with you.

Especially nurses, nurses' aides. Jesus!—they have got to see *everything there is to see.*

*Who is the patient to you, are you a relative?* (Eyeing me like there could be anyone else my age and looking like me who'd be visiting my mom except a relative.)

*Yes. She is my mother.*

(Weird that you would never naturally say, *Yes. I am her son.*)

(Because you only have one mom. While a mom could have more than one son. Is that it?)

Handing me the ID badge saying, *Have a good day.* Like, if I didn't know better, I'd think the receptionist was laughing at me.

How I discovered that with an ID visitor badge you can wander through the hospital. As long as they see you have an ID, nobody looks at it closely or questions you. A hospital is a crazy-busy place, especially in the morning.

Depressing as hell in Mom's room. Though it's a single room, with a view from the window of the city skyline. Also the sky—clouds to watch. Poor Mom with IVs in both her arms scheduled for a kidney biopsy in the morning.

Didn't leave the Juul home today, figuring the stress would be so bad in this place. Knew I'd need to score a hit—probably more like three or four. Seems like it takes more and more to get my brain buzzing. There's a lavatory in the room I can use, slide the door shut. No smoking in the hospital, but—no vaping? Would they kick me out, if they knew?

Lucky, no smell that lasts beyond a few seconds. No ashes!

Nurse enters my mom's room pushing a little cart to check her vital signs—(oxygen intake, blood pressure, pulse)—but I'm in the bathroom grinning at my face in the mirror and the smoke has evaporated, and when I come out I am ultranormal seeming, I am sure.

My brain is still buzzing and I don't hear what the nurse is saying. Is the oxygen intake improved, or worse? Is the pulse fast? Blood pressure low? High? Mom's hurt scared eyes looking at me but I don't even see.

On some doorframes, white sheets of paper with autumn leaves printed on them.

Meaning?

Hanging out in the visitors' lounge, far end of the corridor by the elevators. Three, four people in the lounge and one of them crying, two of them crying, someone with a deep gravelly voice trying to console a child, none of it makes the slightest impression on me, like, could be TV. Admiring the fantastic view of the city, late-afternoon sun like a broken egg yolk. My head is feeling dry like bone but the taste in my mouth is good.

Staring out the window toward the turnpike. S-L-O-W rush hour traffic moving out of the city like zombies. Land of the dead. Jesus!—it's good not to be one of those zombies but Spider-Man flying high above.

Vaping dreams.

Long-term plan is: buy an assault rifle, online. Mom's Visa Explorer.

Scope out where Dad is living. Google Maps: 54 Roslyn Circle, Bay Ridge, NJ. Follow Dad to, like, the Bay Ridge Mall. Asshole has got to drive to the mall sometime.

Well—if he saw me in the Lexus. That'd end it.

(If he saw, like, the license plate, he'd recognize it. I'd be wearing a hoodie, dark glasses.)

If the kid is with him, the new wife's kid with the asshole name Tyler, eight years old, or so Mom says, too fucking bad— *collateral damage.*

Telling Mom, who told me, your father feels he has failed you, honey. He feels he cannot *reach you.* But with the new son, he's gonna start over again.

Mistakes he'd made when you were young, because *he* was young, a young father, didn't have the perspective he has now.

*Fuck him!* The look in Mom's face, I stomped out of the room.

(Yeah, Mom liked to hear it. Sure she did.)

(Any bad-mouthing my dad, in Mom's presence, if it's her relatives, some friends, or me—Mom won't seem to agree, but for sure, Mom is cool with it.)

Plan is: no fucking camouflage gear. Hoodie, backpack. No

black trench coats, etc., like those Columbine assholes. Baseball cap pulled down low over your eyes. Red joke cap—*Make
America Fake Again.*

Plan is: Deep inhale, slow exhale. Brain buzz. Feel the
strength surge through you like every pore in your body is on fire.

Get into position. Sight your target. Quick then, before your
dad sights *you*.

One-two-*three* spray the crowd with bullets. What's it you
have in your hands—AK-47? Kalashnikov rifle—cool! No one
will figure out that one person in the crowd was the designated target. If you can mow down, like, thirty people—*Benjamin Fowler,
forty-seven, Roslyn Park CPA* is just one of the fatalities.

Assuming you don't get caught, identified. No connection
between *mass shooter* and *victims*. Quick-spray the scene with a
"fusillade of bullets," rapid retreat, follow your designated escape
route, discard incriminating evidence, disappear.

Perfect high: *disappear.*

No more *you*. Just—fruity chemical smell, moist cloud
e-vap-or-at-ing
before your eyes.

Where can I buy a gun (legally)?

Internet guns for sale. *ArmsList, Craig's List, GunsAmerica,
Cheaper Than Dirt.* Got to figure that undercover cops are trolling these sites like they do looking for pedophiles. So, maybe not
a great idea.

Asking the guys, did they know where I could get a gun?—*I
mean, like, legally.*

And the guys kind of shaking their heads not looking at me.
Like, they know about my dad leaving my mom and me and
(maybe) they've been hearing me say things I'd like to do to that as-

shole. So they kind of say they don't know—*Unless online? eBay?*

Like hell. Easy way to get caught. State requirement is you're eighteen years old or more. If you have no record. Type in *AK-47* and you're fucked. Like typing in *kiddie porn.* Which is why I've given up asking. If I'm buzzing I feel like tearing out their fucking teeth, laughing in their faces, but if I'm not, if I'm crashing, feel so shitty-low strung-out, the wish is, somebody would tear out my throat with his teeth and put me out of my misery.

*Would you live with your dad, then?*—the guys ask. Meaning, if something happens to your mom.

*Yeah. Guess so.*

*Where's he living now?*

Shrug your shoulders, like fuck if you want to talk about it. Fuck!

Why vaping is cool. Assholes ask you questions you don't give a shit, just roll with it like, *Sure, okay, any kind of shit you say. Sure.*

Problem is, like I already said, the highs don't last like they did. Just a few weeks ago. Slow deflating like a balloon, you can almost hear the fucking *hissing.*

Yeah, it's kind of expensive. E-cigs and apparatus, not cheap.

One pod is equal to one pack of cigarettes. Or is it one hundred cigarettes? But how long would it take you to smoke one hundred cigarettes? Like, e-cigs go much faster.

Nicotine is much more concentrated. Fantastic!

One of the guys, his dad also moved out of their house so you can talk to him, kind of. Saying, *My father doesn't give fuck-all about me. Got to face it. He's married again, he has a young kid, my stepbrother, his wife has two kids of her own. I'm out.*

He says, *Yeah. I guess.*

*What I'd like is, to kill him. Just—wipe him away.*

*Yeah. Me too.*

But he doesn't sound interested. Like, he'd like to *wipe away* his old man if it wasn't too much fucking effort.

The single time I visited them in Bay Ridge, the hot new wife complained that I "smelled"—my underarms, crotch. Didn't like the way I dressed, including my running shoes, which she said were "rotted."

Just that I was trolling her. (Joke!)

Didn't get all the soap out of my hair in the shower (I guess) so I looked like a "banshee."

(Fuck, the bitch knows what a *banshee* looks like.)

(Maybe kill all of them including piss-pot Tyler. *Collateral damage.*)

Hid in the fucking bathroom getting buzzed on spearmint e-juice. Like, my eyes were crossed by the time I was finished and fuck eating with them, no appetite for anything to be shared with them, and anyway, too excited to sit still.

Well—maybe some things got broken. Maybe precious little a-hole Tyler got scared and started crying. By the time I got home (via Dad's Uber account) my mouth was so dry, couldn't swallow. Chest weird-feeling like something was inside clawing its way out.

*Next time, you will know what to do. Bring the AK-47 with you, asshole.*


One morning returning to Mom's room to discover autumn leaves posted outside the door.

Ask a nurse what's it mean and she tells you—*Patient is in danger of falling.*

Meaning, patient cannot be trusted to get out of bed unassisted. Patient *should not try* to get out of bed unassisted.

So, Mom is getting weaker? Fuck them.

* * *

Anything I can do for you, Jacey, let me know.

*Please! Your mother is such a lovely person.*

Their mouths are sad. Their eyes are pitying.

First you just thank them—*Yeah. Okay.* Like, you're embarrassed they know about your mom and (you think) they care about her, and you.

*Anything I can do for Lilian, Jacey, let me know.*

Then one day outside school where she's come to pick Billy up after practice you ask Billy's mother could she drive you to the hospital tomorrow morning?—and she hesitates and says she will summon an Uber for you, because she has an appointment in the morning, on the other side of town.

*Let me know what I can do, Jacey*—Len's mother says, so you tell her that your mother would appreciate a visit from her sometime, and Len's mother says quickly yes, she would love to visit Lilian, she will try to get to the hospital tomorrow, or the following day, but so much is happening in her life right now—*It's kind of crazy. Frankly.*

Still, your mom receives cards, flowers. Potted wax begonias from the ex-husband.

On the card—*Hope you will have a speedy recovery. Yours, Ben.*

*Speedy recovery!*—like, is this a joke?

*Yours.* That is a joke.

So furious, pulses are strumming in my head. Dying for a hit!

But shit, I'm short of cash. Like somebody is turning me upside down by my ankles, shaking out money from my fucking pockets.

Bad dream, a vampire bat is sucking my throat. Carotid artery.

Except suck-suck-sucking my blood, the bat is also regurgitating into my blood a sweet fruity-chemical taste and releasing a chill cloud to conceal us.

Funny sensation in my chest. Lungs? (Bubble-lung? Sounds like a scare tactic/fake news spread by the tobacco industry.)

(Whatever I spend on vaping isn't as much as you'd spend on cigarettes. And there's no tobacco. *No cancer.*)

Dad would be furious with me if he knew about the vaping. If he knew my track performance isn't so great. Fuck Dad, what does he know?

Calling and asking, *How's it going, Jacey?*—in this guilty-sounding voice, and I say kind of mumbling, *Okay.* (Not calling him Dad. Not calling him anything.) And there's silence so he says in the fake-Dad voice, *You okay, Jacey?* And I say, *Yeah, sure.* And he says, *How is your mother, Jacey?*—which is a trick question, so all I say is, *Mom's okay.* Like rolling my eyes, the asshole hasn't got a clue what he sounds like, but this time I'm still buzzed, still feeling good and not like shit, which is what Dad makes you feel like, except not now, now I am inside the Spider-Man costume laughing in his face—*What the fuck do you care?* And Dad's so shocked, he can't even answer at first, then finally sputtering—*Don't talk to me like that. Goddamn you. Who the hell do you think you are! I am serious, I care about your mother and I care about you.*

Laughing at him, saying, *Fuck all we care about you. And Mom too says—Fuck him.*

So Dad is shocked. Like he could believe that his wife/my mother would say such words aloud is ridiculous, but he will talk himself into it, and the new wife will believe him. Sure.

Turn it all inside out, to justify his behavior.

Sure. I know.

Why you are gonna die, asshole? Spider-Man is closing in on you!

* * *

Prowling the hospital. Gliding like Spider-Man on invisible threads. No one does more than glance at the ID on your shirt front. Not a glance at your bloodshot eyes, your zombie grin like a crack in concrete.

Running out of cash. Restless sensation like you're hungry—but not for food.

Floor below, take the stairs. Easy access. Carrying a tray, like from the cafeteria downstairs. Bustling hallways, staff change, seven p.m. Mingle with visitors, enter a room, and if there're people inside back out, honest mistake, easy to make in the hospital—("Hey, sorry—I guess I'm on the wrong floor!")—but if there's nobody in the room except a sleeping/comatose patient, go to the bedside table, see if there's a wallet in a drawer, glasses, hearing aid, quick remove the wallet, quick remove the cash, replace the wallet, nobody knows.

Heart pounding like an e-shot to the chest: cool.

Scored seventy-three dollars, first time.

Vaping gives me the courage. Brain rush. (Weaker and weaker each time.) Running up the stairs two, three at a time—then flying. *Spider-Man!*

To be able to afford *vaping*, you need to prowl and scavenge. But to be able to prowl and scavenge, you need to *vape*.

Second time, 110. Plus some old guy's fancy wristwatch in the bedside drawer along with dentures, hearing aids. (The patient's in the bed sprawled with his mouth open, skin like yellow leather, IV fluids dripping into his bruised arms.)

(Trying not to look at him. Turn your eyes away, quick.)

Another time, on the fourth floor, no money in the drawer. (No wallet.) But a rosary you snatch up and stuff into the backpack.

(Glance at the figure in the bed, Jesus!—a pixilated face you can't tell is female or male.)

No fear. Cool. Quick escape like Spider-Man.

The trick is looking like you know where the hell you're going. Nobody gives a shit about visitors.

Except: *Excuse me. Who are you, and where are you going?*

Female in dark-blue uniform, must be a nurse. Middle-aged, hatchet-faced, no smile and no bullshit. Staring at you suspiciously like with X-ray eyes penetrating your backpack seeing exactly what you've scavenged tonight.

Trying not to stammer. Saying, you are visiting your mother in room 7771.

*Well, this isn't the seventh floor. This is the eighth floor.*

Express surprise: eighth floor! You'd thought it was the seventh . . .

Got off at the wrong floor, you guess.

Smiling, not sweating. E-juice cool: tincture of lemon.

But the nurse isn't persuaded. Husky arms, taller than you. Looks like she could hoist you over her shoulder. No-bullshit kind of (dark almond–skinned) female squinting at your ID. Pretending she is memorizing your name, face. You are sure she's bullshitting. If she wasn't she'd ask you what's in the backpack, what's in your pockets. Could summon security guards. But maybe, since it's late, past eleven p.m., she doesn't want to get involved. Might be she'd have to report you to the police, file an actual complaint, show up at a court hearing. Might be, it isn't worth it for her. If you have stolen cash, cash isn't traceable. A wristwatch, could be yours. There'd have to be a search of the hospital room by room to determine if the watch was missing, plus isolated bills. Fuck, she's thinking, just fuck, it isn't worth it to burn this white boy's privileged ass.

So the suspicious nurse glares at you disgusted, in a snotty voice saying she will have to escort you to your mother's room.

So you say okay, affable and unguilty. And the two of you

take the elevator one flight down and she escorts you to your mother's room (with the fucking autumn leaves posted outside the door), which is dim-lit at this hour as a wake. And there's your mother in her bed, IV fluids dripping into her battered arms. By chance an attendant is checking your mother's vital functions, heart, blood pressure, oxygen intake, so she's awake if slightly dazed, but a smile lights up her tired face when she sees you—*Jacey! You didn't go home, you're here . . .*

First time since the infusion room, your mother has smiled at you.

In this way you escape detection. The suspicious nurse melts seeing how Mom reaches for you like a sleepwalker. Seeing how you take her hand, you don't shrink away as another kid might do, embarrassed and scared.

Yeah, okay. Though you'd been ready to strangle her, the nurse, not your mom. Stuff her lumpy body in the utility room with the sign *Soiled Linen*.

Alone in the room. With your mom. Blank black windows reflecting only the room as in a concave lens, subtly distorted. But safe!

Clutching your mom's (chilly, limp, thin) hand, though your mom (still smiling, wanly) seems to have drifted off to sleep. Jesus!—the wild plan comes to you: you will activate the Juul in your pocket, bring the e-cig to your mom's mouth, give the patient a jolt to the brain like an electric shock.

*Wake up, Mom! You're too young to die and I am the one to save you.*